Spectre of El Dorado

Brian Leon Lee

Copyright © 2018 Brian Leon Lee
Cover Copyright © 2018 Brian Leon Lee

The moral right of the author has been asserted. All rights reserved. No part of this publication may be reproduced, stored in a retrieval system, or transmitted in any form or by any means, electronic, mechanical, photocopy, recording or otherwise, without prior written permission of the copyright owner. Nor can it be circulated in any form of binding or cover other than that in which it is published and without similar condition including this condition being imposed on a subsequent purchaser.

ISBN-13: 978-1987407037

ISBN-10: 1987407032

By Brian Leo Lee
(Children's stories)
Just Bouncey
Bouncey the Elf and Friends Meet Again
Bouncey the Elf and Friends Together Again

Mr Tripsy's Trip
Mr Tripsy's Boat Trip

Four Tales from Sty-Pen

By Brian Leon Lee;
Trimefirst
Domain of the Netherworld
The Club

All available as eBooks

www.bounceytheelf.co.uk

**Check for Free selected
eBooks
Brian Leo / Leon Lee
@ smashwords.com**

The Author

The author was born in Manchester. On leaving school, a period in accountancy was followed by a teaching career in Primary Education.

He has published, as Brian Leo Lee, several children's short stories including the popular Bouncey the Elf series.

Trimefirst, a science fiction novella, the fantasy, Domain of the Netherworld and The Club, a short story; are published under the name of Brian Leon Lee.

Now retired and living in South Yorkshire.

For Rita

Rita Clements Lee
1948 - 2020

1

The piercing whine and the incessant muffled chatter of the whirring rotors of the sky-taxi penetrated the headset-cum-ear protectors that Chaz Lorimore (a red-headed Brit) was wearing as though he hadn't put them on.

That last bottle was a killer. I bet some swine gave me a drink spiked with Casquito, the local rotgut. Everything was fine until then. He grimaced at the thought and looked over at Esha Leung sitting on the other side of the cabin and winced.

Jeez! I can't even bloody remember going back to the hostel last night. She wasn't there when he woke thank God, half frozen to death on the stone tiled floor of his room, his jeans wrapped round his knees and his stinking vomit soaked shirt stuck to his hair.

Painfully, he turned his throbbing head back to look out of the helicopter's side window. He couldn't help but be impressed. A range of snow-covered mountains towered high above them. Below the snow line, some sort of vegetation was colonizing the rocky outcrops. Lower still, far below them, the rainforest was beginning to thicken in the valley bottom.

Now that's what I call a view. What can beat flying through the Andes!

A couple of days ago he had arrived at Cocha. The centre of paragliding in Bolivia he had been told and they were right. A diversion on his Pan-American road trip he had begun at Valparaiso two weeks ago, his reward for graduating from Uni.

The first morning was beautiful; warm bright sunshine, blue skies and incredible views across the mountains. The flight was absolutely sensational; of course it was tandem flying - I'm not that stupid! The second flight even better, swooping much closer to the mountain then soaring up to around three thousand metres, well - ok then, the town is already some two thousand five hundred metres above sea level before you start.

'I say everyone. This is your pilot, Brody 'Chuck' Nielsen. Sorry to butt in. I can see you all need a bit of space in order to aid your recovery from last night's festivities but I have just spotted something unusual.'

Chaz jerked his head round to look at the pilot. Then wished he hadn't.

Esha Leung (A dark haired, slim Aussie from Cairns, Queensland, where her parents, who were originally from Hong Kong had settled) closed her iPad mini reluctantly. The guide she was reading was full of interesting stuff about La Paz. Then she turned, smiled at Chaz, thinking it was just as well she had gone back with her roommate Lela last night and looked at the pilot, wondering what all the fuss was about.

Makhassé Aguilera slowly opened his eyes at the sound of the pilot's voice. Around the same age as Chaz and Esha, he actually came from this area.

He was a Quechuan and a trainee eco-agri consultant on his way back to La Paz with a report that might, just might, earn him a promotion. He hoped it wasn't bad news, like a storm ahead, which meant they had to turn back.

'If you look left at about eleven o'clock,' continued Chuck somewhat excitedly. 'See the highest peak covered in snow? It's called Chaypanquo and it has just started to emit a plume of smoke. It's a volcano that hasn't erupted for hundreds of years.'

'My God!' Chaz gasped and he leant forward hoping to see more. 'Is it dangerous?'

'Naw,' Chuck replied knowingly. 'As you can see, it's only a small plume. If you guys don't mind we'll go and check it out. The authorities will be glad for any info.'

Makhassé opened his mouth to say he thought it was the wrong thing to do, when Esha said that she didn't mind. In fact, she would like to take a few photos.

Before Makhassé could say anything, the helicopter rolled into a turn and began to climb towards the volcano, so he leaned back into his seat with a big frown. He was worried but didn't know why.

It took about half an hour to reach it and Chuck began to pull the collective control (it changes the angle of the main rotor blades) and twist the throttle for more speed with his left hand. At the same time he used his right hand to gently push the cyclic control (similar to a plane's joystick) forward. To stop the helicopter from swinging round because of the push from the tail rotor, he pressed down with his feet, on a pair of rudder pedals left or right, depending on which direction he wanted to go.

As he gained more height they could see that the plume of white smoke, (steam) was coming from a vent just below the peak. A river of melted snow was already flowing down the upper slope, gouging deep runnels in the pristine snow and ice.

Esha had her iPad mini pressed against the side window taking shot after shot, shaking with excitement.

'Wow!' she kept saying.

'These pictures will be worth a fortune.'

Chuck's hands tightened on the controls. He was

beginning to have second thoughts about this.

The helicopter had just passed through 5000m when the volcano ejected a strange yellowish mist, which quickly coalesced into a cloud. It seemed to hover for a few seconds and then began to descend at an accelerating rate.

Before Chuck could react it had enveloped the helicopter. A yellow layer, presumably dust, completely obscured the windows. In a panic reaction, he flicked a switch and a jet of water squirted onto the windscreen and actuated the wipers. A smear of yellow gunge made things worse, if that was possible. He was blind to the outside world.

'Keep calm guys,' he called through his mike. 'We have a small problem. Give me a minute to work out our options. Okay.'

'Jeez! Have we got a bloody minute,' shouted Chaz, a tremor of fear in his voice.'

'What choices do we have?' asked a quiet voice.

Makhassé was leaning forward in the glow of a set of cabin lights Chuck had just switched on.

'Well, we have a proximity warning system that tells me when we're 50m above the ground and its not gone off yet. I have taken the precaution to do a 180-degree turn and reduced speed to the minimum safety level. I'm also now going into hover mode to give us time to discuss our predicament. Any questions?'

'Are we ...'

Esha was interrupted by Chuck's voice.

'What the hell... we're still moving but I'm hovering. I can't believe it,' he cried out in amazement.

'Hang on a sec guys, while I increase the throttle.'

The turbo-engine's whine increased in intensity.

'God! Nothing's happening. I've never come across anything like this before,' he yelled anxiously. Then the engine coughed and then stalled.

'Jesus! Were going down. Hold on! Hold on!'

2

The abrupt loss of noise and the lack of a juddering, shaking cabin, made the new sound of whispering air passing over the fuselage all the more terrifying.

Esha, eyes wide-open in terror, grabbed Chaz by the arm; her gaping mouth was ready to scream as she felt her stomach churn over when the helicopter began to drop.

Unbelievably, before she uttered a sound, the fall began to ease.

'The rotor is freewheeling. It's gone into autorotation mode. Give me a sec while I change the pitch,' shouted a relieved Chuck. 'I should be able to … sod it. I still can't see a bloody thing. This yellow stuff is still blocking my view.'

'We're still going to crash though, aren't we?'

The calm voice of Makhassé somehow eased the tension.

'Well yeah but in a more controlled way,' replied Chuck with as much confidence as he could muster. 'I mean this sort of thing does happen, err, I mean not like this just now. Engine failure is allowed for in the design of helicopters you know.'

'Excuse me,' Chaz interrupted in a taut voice. 'Isn't this rather academic. Are we not seconds away from being a squashed pancake and we're debating the finer points of helicopter designs?'

Esha finally cracked, her grip tightening on Chaz's arm as she screamed out, 'For God's sake do something Chuck. I don't want to die.'

'Easy! Esha! Easy! I'm with you all the way. Sorry, no pun intended,' Chuck answered reassuringly.

'Can't you feel the difference in the way we're going down. It's much slower and with a bit of luck we'll get down in one piece. I guarantee it.'

'What do we have to do?' asked Makhassé, going straight to the point. 'We must be near the ground by now.'

'Yeah! Right man,' said Chuck, 'But the altimeter is stuck. The way I see it is that we were sort of pushed outwards, by what I don't know, away from the volcano's slope. Otherwise we would have hit the ground by now. I guess we are more or less over the rainforest. So make sure that your seat belts are really tight and bend forward, head between your knees, legs back and grab hold of your ankles. Okay. You guys done that …'

The blare of the proximity warning klaxon jerked Chuck into emergency mode. He pulled the cyclic right back and flared the helicopter into a nose-high attitude, hoping to use the densest growth of the trees (if it was solid rock, well…) to absorb the energy of the fall as well as providing a protective shield for them.

A moment later, a massive jolt shook the cabin. The shriek of metal sliding down something solid was ear splitting mixed in with the terrified screams of Esha.

The cabin was tipped over as a branch smashed through a side window piercing the roof before snapping off, leaving a broken piece some 2m long and a tangled mess of leaves and a host of creepy-crawlies over the floor.

Bumping and sliding through an assortment of different sized trees the mangled 'copter tumbled to the forest floor.

'Is everyone okay,' shouted Chuck as the 'copter cabin rolled over onto its side, snapping the remaining rotor blade as it did so, before bouncing back onto its skids. 'We have to get out, the fuel could ignite anytime.'

Chaz gave a loud groan. The broken branch pinned him to his seat and he couldn't straighten up to release his safety belt. He managed to twist his head round and called out to Makhassé.

'Can you give me a hand? I'm stuck.'

Across the cabin, Makhassé rubbed a painful bump on his forehead. 'Just a minute,' he said as he tried to get his bearings. He could see outside.

The yellow stuff covering the cabin windows had gone.

In the gloom of the forest floor he was able to make out Chaz, trapped in his seat by a broken branch. Next to him Esha stirred, and fumbled with her safety belt buckle. It sprung open and she sat up and stared blankly about her.

'Are we down?' she whispered.

'You bet we are,' said a much-relieved Chuck, as he forced his way into the main cabin. 'Come on Makhassé, we need to get Chaz free as quickly as possible. Esha, can you make your own way down if I can get to the door?'

She nodded in reply as he pushed it open.

With Esha out of the way there was enough room for Chuck and Makhassé to pull the broken branch off Chaz and help him down to the ground.

The falling 'copter had crushed the undergrowth into a small clearing. Esha was crouched down, shivering in shock by the edge of it as Chaz was helped over to her.

'I'm fine now thanks,' he said to Makhassé, rubbing a sore back as he bent down to see if Esha was all right.

Then Chuck cried out in an urgent voice.

'Get well back, just in case the fuel goes up. Though with modern self-sealing fuel tanks we use today, I think we should be okay,' he added ruefully, realizing that it was a little bit late to worry about that now.

He looked at Makhassé. 'Would you mind helping me get our stuff from the 'copter as well as anything useful we can find. We won't be coming back here for sure.'

Fortunately they each had a backpack, (even Chuck, who had made arrangements to meet up with friends in La Paz) filled with the necessities for travelling up-country, including tents.

A couple of machetes that all 'copters carried were well received by Makhassé who said that they would prove to be invaluable in the rainforest.

After a few moments thought, Chuck brought the 'copter's flare gun along with its five cartridges.

As they each gave their backpacks a last check-over, Chaz and Chuck began to curse the local insects as they both slapped their faces and necks.

'Jeez,' Chaz cried out, 'Why are we being picked on?' He looked over at Esha who was calmly adjusting her backpack straps.

'Well, I suppose in my case it's because I put on some insect protection. Back in Queensland I work in one of the state national parks as a veterinary assistant and developed a Deet based repellent of my own. It works quite well. Would you like some?'

Chuck beat Chaz by a fraction of a second.

'You bet, Esha. I was thinking of having to plaster myself in mud or something.'

'I wouldn't do that,' said Makhassé. 'The parasites in the mud are worse than insect bites. A minute boring lava can penetrate the skin in seconds and I...'

'Don't say another word. I believe you,' said Chuck with a shudder.

'Anyway, what do you use? I don't see you flapping at these damn bugs.'

Makhassé smiled. 'This is my country. The insects don't bother me.' He let it be known that he was of the Quechuan people and that he knew the area quite well.

Once Chaz and Chuck had smeared themselves with Esha's repellent and complimented her on its immediate effectiveness, they set off.

Makhassé believed that he could make out the sound of a river. (However he did it impressed Esha, who was both enthralled and deafened by all the different birdcalls she could hear. They seemed to be everywhere).

Leading the way, he cut a path downhill through the thick undergrowth. It was slow work. The ground fell away quite steeply, so just to keep from slipping or tripping over hidden roots or rocks was bad enough. To slash and cut at the same time took a lot of skill with the machete.

Plus the fact that every second bush seemed to be covered in wicked thorns that kept hooking into their clothes or pricking the legs or a badly placed hand or arm. Razor sharp leaves shaped like narrow swords were particularly nasty.

Chuck for one was glad he wasn't the one doing it. He was sure he would have cut a hand or foot off by now.

Sweat was dripping off his face in torrents when Makhassé stumbled onto a stone paved path about one and a half metres wide. He stopped in astonishment. 'This can't be true,' he said, looking at the others. 'This is an Inca road but it looks like new.'

'Who cares,' said Chaz cheerfully.

'We can press on now. You won't have to cut your way through half of Bolivia, will you old sport.'

Makhassé gave a sort of grin but said nothing and took the lead again, slashing at hanging vines and low branches blocking their way with renewed vigour.

The Inca path followed the bank of a river but soon began to climb up the side of the valley. They were thirty or forty metres or so above it when a break in the trees enabled them see the other side. A similar Inca path was just visible to them and as they watched, a flicker of movement attracted their attention so Makhassé raised a hand. The stop signal.

More than a little puffed with the climb, Esha was glad of the rest and sitting on her backpack lifted the small but powerful binoculars hanging from her neck to her eyes, focusing them for a closer look.

'My God!' she exclaimed, 'I don't believe it. It must be a party of fancy dress people. Makhassé, is there a pageant or something going on in this area? I can see a group of what I would call Conquistadors riding horses. They look great, so real looking.'

'Can I have look Esha?' asked a worried looking Makhassé.

'Sure, go ahead,' she said, handing over her binoculars. 'Be quick though, they're almost all through that gap in the trees.'

Holding them up to his eyes, he gave a loud gasp as he focused and saw one of the riders. Sure enough, a head covered by a metal helmet, the upper-body protected by steel plates, the arms and legs with metal greaves and a sword fixed to the belt. As he watched the rider disappeared behind the wall of trees.

3

'What did I tell you,' Esha said excitedly, 'What do you think?'

Before Makhassé could say anything he heard a loud scream from the other side of the river and a metal clad body fell through the undergrowth by the path and careered down the steep sides of the valley, bouncing off shrubs and rocky outcrops before plummeting into the rock strewn river but not before the horrified group had seen a long arrow sticking from his throat. Then the sound of men yelling in a Spanish dialect Makhassé found difficult to understand.

'My God! What the hell's happening over there?' shouted Chuck, pointing to the path opposite them.

In the tree branches hanging over the spot where the horse riders were passing, several half-naked men could just be made out firing arrows.

More shouts in that strange Spanish dialect and then the noise of horses galloping away.

The sound of retching jerked Makhassé back to reality. Esha was bent over by the side of the path. Chaz, hand on her shoulder was trying to comfort her.

'They must be a gang of nutters,' he was saying. 'Makhassé, can we call the police or something?'

'Yeah and what about that poor devil in the river, shouldn't we try and see if he needs help?' added Chuck. 'Bloody hell, what a situation.'

'Well, Chuck, first thing. Have you looked at the river? It's about thirty metres below us and it's practically a raging torrent. Anyway, the body will be kilometres downstream by now.'

Esha stood up, pale faced and said in a shaky voice, 'What about us? Are we safe on this side of the river? Can they shoot their arrows at us over here?'

She glanced furtively across the river as she spoke.

Makhassé, still holding the binoculars had a quick look. 'I think they've gone. Anyway I don't think they knew we were here. They were too preoccupied with their ambush. Just thank your Gods we are on this side of the river.'

'Amen to that,' said Chuck.

'I think we should push on. Time marches on and we need a place for the night. Any ideas Makhassé?'

'Well, I have a rough idea where we are. I think this Inca road leads to a village down the valley, if we can reach it by nightfall.'

He looked at his watch, 'Which will be in about six hour……'

'Hang on,' interrupted Chaz.

'Do you mean to say that we might not reach this place before dark. Why the hell not?'

Makhassé sighed.

'Look at this path or roadway if you prefer, Chaz. Stone cobbles are not ideal for fast walking. Then, if you haven't noticed, it's fairly level here but I can assure you there will plenty of places where you will be on your hands and knees because it is so steep. Finally, we are at a height of some two thousand five hundred metres, is that right Chuck?'

Chuck gave a start. His mind had been wandering. He was still thinking about that poor devil in the river.

'Oh! Yeah, two thousand five hundred metres to around three thousand metres.'

'Just think about that Chaz, walking for several hours at this altitude and don't forget that the oxygen level is lower up here. You will need to breathe faster to get the same amount that your body gets at lower altitudes.'

Makhassé stopped for a moment, then smiled at the three worried looking faces staring intently at him.

'Hey! Why the long faces? It's not as bad as it sounds. From what you have been saying, you have been up here in the Andes for a couple of weeks, Chuck even longer.'

Chuck nodded.

'Well then, you are quite acclimatized and as long as you act sensibly, you will be all right.'

The sense of tension eased and Esha delved into one of her backpack pockets and passed pieces of half-melted chocolate to each of them.

'We will take it slowly. If anyone feels the slightest bit dizzy tell me. No false heroics. Your life could be in danger, okay.'

With that Makhassé turned and led the way along the stony path.

Half an hour later, Chaz sagged to his knees. The last climb had taken its toll.

'I say!' he called out in a wheezy voice to the others, walking in front of him.

They stopped and turned round.

'I just need a few minutes....'

Makhassé dropped his backpack to the ground and went back to Chaz.

'Sit on your pack and take five. Better to get your breath back now rather than collapse with exhaustion a bit later. Oh! Have a drink. I forgot to remind you about dehydration. At altitude you need to drink often, so plenty of fluid from now on. Okay.'

On cue, Chuck and Esha pulled their hip water bottles off their belts and took a swig. Although Makhassé didn't need to, (as a high altitude Bolivian, he was quite adapted to this environment) he took a sip from his own water bottle.

A bit more than five minutes later, they set off again, this time Chaz making use of a trimmed branch that Chuck had made for him as a walking aid.

The terrain levelled out for a while and they were making fairly good progress when Makhassé held up a hand.

Chuck eased past Esha and Chaz, who had immediately taken off their backpacks and sat down on them, breathing heavily.

'Something wrong Makhassé?' he asked.

'I'm not sure. You have a look.'

A few metres ahead, the path entered a cleared section of the forest. To the left were several stone huts with thatched roofs. On the right, a series of terraced fields dropped down towards the river. There were crops growing in the tiny fields and as they looked further, not one person could be seen.

Makhassé looked worried.

'This can't be,' he said in a puzzled voice.

'This is a small Ayllu village, as it was hundreds of years ago.'

'Well I reckon they've done a fantastic job,' said Chuck. 'Your tourist people seem to have it right down to the last button. It looks just great. Yes sir, just great.'

'Chuck! Chuck! This isn't a tourist attraction. It's the real thing.'

'Now come on Makhassé. Stop pulling my leg. How the hell can it be real?'

'Before I answer that, lets go up to the village but don't say anything yet to those two.'

Makhassé pointed over to Esha and Chaz.

Baffled but curious, Chuck nodded his head in agreement.

'We're going to the huts,' shouted Makhassé as he led Chuck through the gap in the forest and then he abruptly stopped. 'Don't come any nearer.' His voice was pitched unnaturally high.

'What the … Hey, I nearly knocked you over. Why have you stopped? …… Oh my God!' Chuck's face went absolutely white and he turned and yelled out. 'For Gods sake, you two stay back.'

Chaz and Esha stood still. 'What's the matter with you,' cried Chaz anxiously. He had picked up that something was seriously wrong.

Chuck looked over Makhasse's shoulder and saw again a vision of hell. A deep pit was strewn with men, women and children impaled on sharp stakes.

'Who the hell is mad enough to do this?' he tried to say and as he looked away, his stomach turned over and he vomited his guts out.

'It can only be the Conquistadors,' whispered Makhassé.

4

Waving at Esha and Chaz to stay where they were, Makhassé began to cut down large fronds of tree fern and other large leaved plants.

Chuck realizing what he intended to do, wiped his mouth with back of his hand and pulled the other machete he had been carrying free from his belt and joined him. They soon had a pile of leaves and branches big enough to cover the gruesome sight of the dead bodies in the pit. Only then did Makhassé call the other two over.

'Let's go over to one of the huts. I need to get away from this,' he said, his voice breaking with emotion.

He led the way to the nearest hut and went inside through a trapezium shaped doorway. An oven made of stones cemented to the floor with mud was in the middle of the one room.

It was still smouldering and since there was no vent, the smoke was filtering through the thatching of the roof.

'Ugh! I can hardly see,' said Esha, glancing round the gloomy room.

'It's a bit iffy too,' Chaz said sniffing the stuffy air. 'Where can we sit? I can't see any chairs.'

Makhassé pointed to a couple of animal skins (probably alpaca or llama), arranged on the mud floor by the oven. 'The Inca sat or squatted on their heels, there was no need for chairs.'

'Well! After what I've just seen, I'm having a shot of something strong,' Chuck said as he pulled out a small bottle of bourbon from his backpack and offered it to Makhassé.

'Would you like a pull?'

Makhassé shook his head.

'I say you two, why all the mystery?' asked Chaz curiously.

'I know Esha wants to know as much as me. What was in the pit that's so bad we couldn't see it?'

Chuck's hand holding the bottle froze on the way to his mouth as he recalled the sight of the impaled bodies and he looked over towards Makhassé, who had now put his backpack by his side and was crouching down in front of the oven, poking the fire with a small stick.

His back to them, hardly visible in the dark room and in a voice so quiet Esha and Chaz could only just make out his words, Makhassé told them that the whole village had been massacred in a brutal and savage way. He had not wanted them to see the grisly sight.

The shock of hearing such an unexpected and horrific account left Chaz and Esha speechless.

The silence lingered, interrupted by the crackle of a branch burning. The smoke thickened and Chaz sat down on one of the animal skins. The air down there was a lot easier to breathe. His urge to cough eased and he said in a shaky voice, 'What have we walked into? People killed by arrows, others butchered. Are we in a war or something?'

Esha came over and knelt by him.

'Yes, I agree with Chaz. What do you know Makhassé? We have a right to know what's happening don't we?'

A loud slurp and a small belch came from across the small room as Chuck took the bottle of bourbon from his lips and after fixing the cap, stuffed it back into his backpack.

'I reckon that you have some idea of what's going on, don't you Makhassé. Ever since that funny yellow cloud surrounded us, you have acted as if you knew something was going to happen. Am I right?'

Makhassé rocked on his heels. It looked as if he was praying but he just poked the fire again before turning his head and with large sorrowful eyes so wide open that Esha held a hand to her mouth to stop a gasp of alarm escaping, said, 'Yes Chuck.'

He spoke barely above a whisper. 'I have an idea but only an idea. Of what's happening here.'

He poked the fire again and a shower of sparks floated around in the gloom like a swarm of fireflies.

'My forebears believed in many Gods, one called Ngen-Xanapu was the God of volcanoes. He was not a very nice God and he had to be kept happy by people giving him living sacrifices. It was said that when he was angry, a young virgin had to be left tied to a stake on the edge of the crater. A yellow mist is said to flow up from inside the volcano and swallow up the sacrifice.'

Makhassé paused and poked the fire again. 'When the helicopter was enveloped by that yellow cloud, I knew that it could only be Ngen-Xanapu.'

Chaz nearly fell over. 'You've got to be joking,' he said in astonishment.

'Tell me, it's a joke!'

'Think Chaz, think about the things you have seen and witnessed since the crash.'

Makhassé looked at him and continued in a quiet voice, as though he didn't want anyone outside to hear.

'Remember the state of the Inca road when we first saw it. I said it looked new. Then the horse riders, dressed as Conquistadors, being fired on with arrows by Inca in the trees. You wouldn't know but the strange Spanish voices we heard were in a dialect hundreds of years old and they were fluent accents too.'

Makhassé poked the fire again with his stick; the half burnt embers flickered brightly for a few seconds before settling back to a warm glow.

Before anyone could speak, he went on, 'Then there's this place, a working Ayllu village. This hut is genuine Inca. The bodies in the pit are wearing the simple tunics of the farmer. They were killed by the Conquistadors because they didn't know where the gold was. That's all they want - gold. The pit is their, what do you say, trademark.'

Chuck, now sprawled on the animal skin next to Esha, nodded his head.

'Well! That sure takes the biscuit but how the hell did we get here Makhassé; it's incredible. If what you say is true, we're back in the time of the Incas but I ask you again. How in Gods name did we get here?'

Makhassé stood and stretched his arms and legs a few times and then looked down at them. Before he answered Chuck's question, he asked for a drink of his whiskey.

'Why the hell not, anyone else for one?' Chuck asked as he held out the bottle.

Chaz and Esha shook their heads, so taking a quick pull, he gave it to Makhassé who had a quick swallow before handing it back.

Squatting down again after his drink, Makhassé paused and looked uncomfortable.

'What I have to say might be embarrassing,' he began, 'But there is no other way.' He licked his lips nervously and began to speak.

'I believe that the Ngen-Xanapu came out of the volcano looking for a sacrifice victim. It was angry for some reason we can't understand. That's why the volcano was showing signs of erupting. The yellow mist came out expecting to ensnare a victim. It hovered as we saw, before it turned into a cloud and dropped down and engulfed the helicopter. It had found one.'

'Hey! Hey!' interrupted Chaz.

'I thought you said that this Bogeyman only collected virgins and....'

His jaw dropped.

'I.... Err....' He felt his face flush and he looked at the mud floor.

'Yes!' said Makhassé quietly.

'He did find a virgin but couldn't get to her. Our helicopter's fuselage prevented it, so he made us crash but to the time of the Inca.'

Three pairs of eyes locked onto Esha and she buried her head in her hands not knowing what to say.

Chuck broke the silence.

'Well Makhassé, that is sure interesting. You had me worried for a while, yes siree, you sure did. Now why don't you tell us about the local bandits holding tourist as hostages, instead of making this young lady shit scared about some mumbo-jumbo spirit God out to get her....'

The sound of some kind of horn interrupted him and Makhassé jumped up and ran outside.

Wondering what was happening, the rest got up and followed him.

They didn't get very far. Chuck, being the first of them to pass through the doorway, bumped into Makhassé and nearly sent him flying.

The contrast of the gloomy room and the outside had temporarily blinded him.

Steadying himself, Makhassé, in a whisper said, 'Nobody move and don't make a sound.'

Huddled behind him, the other three could now make out a figure standing not too far from the path looking at them as though he had just seen a ghost.

He actually looked a bit like Makhassé in build, though a lot more fit looking but there the resemblance ended.

A headband kept his long black hair in place. He was wearing a short tunic and a sort of blanket was wrapped over the shoulders and tied to his waist and he wore a pair of sandals. A large conch shell was in one hand the other held a strange-looking bunch of knotted strings.

The figure shouted something and Makhassé stood transfixed for a moment and replied in a language similar to the strangers tongue.

Then without any warning the stranger turned and running like an antelope disappeared along the path. A blast of a horn suddenly echoed along the valley, the only evidence that he had been there.

'I need a drink,' said a bemused Chuck.

'Let's go inside. I think Makhassé has something to tell us.'

Stooping to avoid banging his head on the door lintel, Chaz led the way in and went over to the fire and poked it with a stick after placing a small branch on it, whilst at the same time pondering over the latest turn of events as it burst into flames.

As the others sat or crouched down on the animal skins around the oven, Chaz leaned over and took the bottle of bourbon from Chuck.

This time, he and Esha had a pull. The recent episode was unnerving as well as unsettling.

Makhassé coughed. He was nervous too. 'He spoke to me in Quechuan, well, a sort of Quechuan, the old kind and said that he was a Chasqui runner and asked where were the farmers that usually gave him a drink. Then he said that you looked like the devils riders and took off.'

He went on. 'A Chasqui runner is a messenger of the Inca government and carries a conch shell horn called a Pututu to signal he is near. There are regular rest stations for them, Tampu's, (a bit like inns) dotted along the Inca roads. The knotted strings are called Quipus, (the knots carry information). That blanket thing on his back is a Qipi, a sort of backpack. The Chasqui run at a fast rate and can cover over 200k a day. That, Chuck, was a Chasqui runner. An Inca runner.'

'Give me that bottle Chaz; I believe I might be ready for the funny farm. I'm beginning to believe you, Makhassé. So what the hell do we do now?'

And Chuck took a pull and then, another, a much longer one.

5

The Tampu resting house was busy with corvée (unpaid) servants bringing in clay bowls and wooden plates of food from one of the adjoining rooms and placing them onto a reed mat by the central oven. Smoke from the oven fire drifted slowly upwards to the roof, where it filtered away through the thick thatch.

Princess Inkasisa, squatting by the back wall, her long tunic hitched up, idly watched as her younger brother Prince Maichu crouching in the inner courtyard by the open doorway, played with a small green lizard, trying to make it eat a leaf held between his fingers.

She gave a big sigh. He would soon turn fourteen. There was a coming of age ceremony that allowed all boys of his age to demonstrate their physical and military skill. Afterwards, in a special ceremony, they would have their ears pierced and a golden disk would be inserted in their earlobes. Then, they would be presented to the sun god, and only then could they take their place as adults among the people.

The sudden wail of a conch shell made her jump. *A Chasqui runner,* she thought, scrambling to her feet and made her way to join her brother in the doorway.

'Beware! The devil riders are near,' the runner shouted, before he turned and fled. Then a scream of fear, 'They're here! They're...' his voice was drowned out by a thunderous bang and a cloud of smoke drifted over the Tampu buildings.

Princess Inkasisa grabbed hold of her brother by the arm and dragged him inside.

'Quick,' she cried, 'Close the door,' realizing as she said it that it would do them no good.

A figure in shining armour emerged through the quickly dispersing smoke of a discharged arquebus, sword in hand, accompanied by a Cañari peasant who spoke a little Quechuan.

Standing in front of the door, the peasant shouted through a mouthful of rotting teeth.

'Where's the gold?'

Before he could hear any kind of answer, four more armour rattling Conquistadors, one carrying an arquebus, rushed into the courtyard.

Hearing the noise, Capitán Mendoza turned and ordered two of them to break in.

It only took two hefty kicks to smash open the flimsy woven reed door and the conquistadors ran screaming into the room, swords ready for any resistance.

Princess Inkasisa was standing by the oven in the middle of the room. She had placed herself in front of her brother who had at first protested that he had a knife and would protect her. The three servants cowered in the far corner whimpering in fear.

The Capitán entered the dark hut and stood to one side of the door waiting for his eyes to adjust to the gloom. A few moments later, one glance at the clothes of the two young people who were looking at him with faces of abject terror, especially the gold ornaments of the girl, told him that they were nobles.

'Seize the servants,' he commanded.

A conquistador walked over to the corner, casually

kicking aside any bowl or platter of food in his way. Jabbing his sword at the crouching servants, he made them stand and form a quaking line in front of the smoking oven.

Waving his sword at Inkasisa and Maichu, Capitán Mendoza indicated that they move back to the rear wall. He then shouted for the peasant.

The Cañari sidled into the room, a nasty green-toothed smirk on his face. He stood in front of the line of servants and asked again in his rough Quechuan dialect.

'Where's the gold?'

The terrified servants were too scared to talk and as one dropped to their knees begging for mercy.

Cursing, the Capitán slapped his thigh and went over to the oven and began to kick the top layer of stones.

Inkasisa and Maichu watched in amazement, wondering if the conquistador had gone mad.

When several stones had been knocked off, the exposed fire flared up.

'Enough of this,' he snarled.

'String them up.'

A conquistador grinning with anticipation unwrapped a coil of rope from his shoulders and using his sword, poked about in the thatch until he found three wooden roof supports over the fire.

It only took him a few moments to check how much rope he would need.

After cutting three appropriate lengths, he beckoned to the Cañari who, obviously well practiced at this, climbed onto the conquistador's back and reached up looping the ropes through the roof supports.

Before the servants knew what was going to happen,

they were trussed up, hands and feet and a rope tied around each of their chests. Screaming with fear, they were hauled up, one at a time until they were all dangling over the oven fire.

In moments the heat began to reach the writhing bodies. Bent knees lifted bound feet. The respite lasted just a few seconds.

The Cañari, a sworn enemy of the Quechan, snickered with pleasure as he threw more wood on the fire.

Squeals of agony filled the room as blisters rose on the naked feet and then popped in a rush of liquid before being consumed by the rising flames.

Irritated by the delay, Capitán Mendoza prodded the Cañari with the hilt of his sword.

With a concealed scowl, the peasant shouted, louder this time, to make himself heard above the howling, screaming servants.

'Where's the gold? Tell us and we will cut you down.'

Princess Inkasisa and Maichu had stepped back to the wall and were now staring in horror at the torture of their servants.

'Stop! Stop! In the name of the Great Inti, Stop!' Dropping down to her knees, she looked imploringly at the conquistador captain.

The Cañari looked at his leader, who grasping what the Inca girl was saying, nodded his head.

'Tell us first,' said the peasant craftily.

'You will find what you want at the Temple of Inti at Qucha (lake) Titiqaqa,' sobbed Inkasisa while at the same time trying to keep Maichu from interfering. He was trying to persuade her not to tell.

Mendoza smiled when the Cañari translated for him. 'Put more wood on the fire,' he said, shouting to make himself heard above the wretched screaming of his victims.

'And bring those two,' he added, pointing to the crying princess and a surprisingly resilient prince who got a cuff round the ear when a Conquistador found his tiny knife.

Without a backward glance, the Capitán led the conquistadors and their two prisoners outside. The Cañari came out last, doing a sort of a victory dance, drawn from his tribal customs.

The odour of burning flesh was overpowered by the smell of burning thatch and soon that was lost as the conquistadors rode back along the Inca road, heading for the Temple of Inti, their horses' hooves ringing out as they clashed on the stone cobbles.

The prince, hands bound, attached to the last horse rider by a rope, stumbled along as best he could trying not to fall over. His short tunic would not offer much protection to his knees. Thank the Gods he was wearing his sandals. He felt a fleeting feeling of envy for his sister, draped over the back of the leader's horse but only for a moment. He was nearly a man. Then he could seek revenge.

Bringing up the rear the Cañari padded along, his bare feet toughed by a lifetime of using the Inca paved tracks. He was feeling happy and he gripped the severed ear of one of the servants more tightly. The Gods would be pleased if the sacrifice he had in mind took place. He looked along the line of horse riders and saw the bobbing form of the girl and his face twisted into a lewd grin of anticipation.

6

Makhassé looked over to Chuck, then at the other two.

'We have to go on. Obviously we can't stay here, the Conquistadors might return.'

The others didn't blink at the word.

'Well,' said Chaz, with an anxious look at the door.

'What do we do if we see them. I mean they're nutters aren't they? I...'

'Chaz,' Esha interrupted him, 'I don't really know why or how we got here but this is real. They are Conquistadors, Spanish soldiers. From what we have seen and what history tells us, they are ruthless killers, and I'm absolutely terrified of meeting them.' She looked over towards Makhassé with pleading eyes. 'Is there a chance for us, really a chance that we can stay safe?'

Makhassé threw his arms up into the air. A Quechuan curse spat from his mouth.

'How the hell do I know?' Then he added slightly more calmly, 'I'm just a local Indian with some education!'

Seeing the look of surprise on their faces, Makhassé apologized. 'Sorry! I'm in a state of shock about our predicament just as you lot are.' He looked over at Esha, 'I think we have to be on our guard from this moment on. If we hear the sound of a horse, jump off the path pronto. Okay.'

The others nodded in agreement.

'Right then.' Chuck, sprawled on an animal skin by

the oven, made the decision for them.

'Let's grab our stuff and make tracks, though this time keep it quiet.'

Chaz gave a shudder and with a quick glance at Esha, leaned over for his backpack and dragged it to the door as Makhassé led the way out.

7

Around two hundred and fifty metres above the Tampu, the small side pongo (canyon) had proved to be quite fruitful. Quylur Chaski had managed to find a Chacruna tree; the leaves she had collected would make a fine psychedelic brew. Then the lucky find of the Achiota plant, the seeds which when ground into a red powder and with the right incantations would protect her from malevolent spirits. A useful side effect was that it made an excellent insect repellant not withstanding her natural native resistance to them. It had been well worth the toil up to this pongo.

While stuffing another handful of seeds into her khapchos (woollen bag), a loud bang echoed through the mountains making Quylur Chaski jump to her feet.

A sense of fear clutched at her heart. A fire-stick had been fired, the Devil Riders.

'Noooo,' she screamed aloud and bent down to grab her Khapchos and staff. Making sure that her multi-coloured striped shawl was pinned securely around her neck, she hitched up her long tunic and began to clamber as fast as an old woman could, down the steep pongo slope.

A while later, pausing to catch her breath, a whiff of smoke drifted up from the valley below and she felt a stab of fear again.

The sun was high in the sky when she finally reached the Tampu, retching from the exertion and from the swirls of smoke and the stench of burnt flesh emanating from the charred ruins. Her face blanched with the thought of what she was going to find. She called out weakly, 'Inkasisa, Maichu.'

She croaked again, louder, her voice dry with emotion.

'Inkasisaaaa..... Maichuuuu.....'

The fire had died down long enough for her to approach close enough to see through the doorway and amid the ashes and smouldering embers, she could make out three charred bodies – *Three* - Praise the Gods.

8

'Are you sure there is a place to stop near here?'

Gasping for air, Chaz leaned heavily on his thick stick and looked hopefully at Makhassé.

His feet were killing him.

They were climbing, more like stumbling, along the side of a massive mountain on the Inca paved path, which had been zig-zagging upwards for at least two hours.

The thick mesh of branches which had provided welcome cover from the hot sun, was now starting to thin and Chaz for one had had enough.

Pausing in his stride, Makhassé looked round and grinned at Chaz.

'If I'm right, not far ahead there is a Tampu or at least a Tampus where we can stop for a rest and a meal. I can smell the smoke of their cooking fire.'

'What's the difference between them?'

Esha asked curiously, still looking quite fresh despite the stiff climb.

'Well, I believe the original ones and that is what we are going to see quite soon, were about status. The Tampu was built for the use of officials of the government and royalty. The Tampus were mainly basic feeding and resting stations for the Chasqui, you know the runners like the one we saw this morning.'

'Never mind the semantics, lets get on. I don't give a monkey's toss which one it is,' said Chuck as he bent down to loosen a bootlace.

'I'm with Chaz, the sooner I can rest my aching pegs

the better.'

Makhassé shrugged his shoulders and nodded, 'Okay, with luck we should reach it in about an hour. Are you ready?'

With that, he turned and began to climb the narrow path.

'Jeez, what a bloody carry on,' muttered Chaz to himself as he swished a huge caterpillar away with his stick.

Fortunately, the path peaked sooner than Makhassé had forecast.

On the brow of the next ridge the land flattened out in a kind of bowl set at the base of a large rock face. What they didn't expect to see was a small group of thatched huts and the largest, set in the centre, a burnt ruin.

Smoke was still swirling around before drifting upwards and away.

'Oh my God,' cried Esha, her hands to her mouth.

'Not again, please tell me it's not the Conquistadors?'

A side path led to the Tampu, for Makhassé had ascertained from its size that it was one and he led them down towards it.

'Hold on, there's some one down there. Can you see, by that hut,' Chuck said, pointing towards it.

A figure, half-hidden by a cloud of white smoke was kneeling by a small fire. It was an old woman, her long dark hair held in place by a coloured band from which several small bird feathers sprouted.

Her hands protruding from a striped shawl were held outstretched. A hoarse sounding voice was making some kind of incantation. Her eyes were shut tight and then she began to groan and wail.

Makhassé dropped to his knees.

'My God,' he said in a whisper.

'It's a Shaman.'

As he spoke the woman – shaman - began to move her arms. On each arm was a bracelet of small round chacapa nuts that rattled when shaken. As the arms waved around in ever increasing patterns, the bracelets began to make bell-like sounds, which transformed to the pitter-patter of rain on large leaves and then the coarse rattle of small pebbles falling on a drum.

To the amazement of the enthralled watchers, at each change of sound, a different coloured light formed around the bracelets.

Dancing ribbons of gold, green and blue shimmered and shone before turning into tendrils of energy that then disappeared into the smoke of the fire.

The smoke began to darken and in the middle of it, shapes began to form. Two islands could be seen. One with steep cliffs had a tall building perched on top of them, the other, an active volcano with a plume of steam rising from its summit.

The apparition then slowly disappeared, leaving just a column of white smoke, which lazily drifted upwards.

Suddenly the old woman-shaman s gave a loud shriek, and called out at the top of her aged lungs.

'KayPacha, KayPacha, KayPacha.'

Then she slumped to the ground in a shaking fit.

'Bloody hell, what was that all about when I'm at home,' said Chaz, rubbing his eyes.

'Did I really see that?'

Esha looked over at Makhassé who looked as though he had just seen a ghost.

'We must go down to see her. She is our only hope,' he said, as he got to his feet.

'If we help her she might help us in return. It's our only chance.'

'Hey, come back,' yelled Chuck as Makhassé raced off towards the old woman.

'What if he's right?' Esha said.

'I'm going too.'

Chuck looked at Chaz. 'What the hell, let's go and join the fun.'

'Not so fast,' cried Chaz, hobbling along as fast as he could.

Jeez, why the hell did I come to South America?

As Makhassé reached the old woman, she began to stir and looked around as though awakening from a deep sleep.

With a startled look when she saw him, the old woman grabbed her staff and slowly got to her feet. By then the others had gathered in a group on the other side of the fire, which was now little more than a heap of smouldering embers.

Hitching her shawl more tightly round her shoulders, Quylur Chaski leaned on her staff and stared at them, completely unfazed by their appearance.

She looked at Makhassé and said in Quechuan, 'Quylur Chaski greets you. You have travelled far to see Kaypacha,' and before anyone could move, she bent down and pulled out of her bag a short, narrow tubular root. With her other hand she removed a stopper of some kind and flicked her wrist. A puff of orange dust wafted over them. It was impossible not to avoid breathing in some of it.

'What the hell!' Chuck cried out in alarm.

'The she-devil has just poisoned us.'

Mama Quylur Chaski didn't wait for any more comments. She raised her arms and made an intricate pattern in the air. As she did so, her bracelets began to rattle, a gentle bell-like tone, more of a tinkle arose and then a shimmering glow began to emanate from them before turning into several streams of silvery rays. Then a ray picked an individual and as one penetrated the throats of each one of them.

'Don't be afraid,' Quylur Chaski said quietly.

'Now you will be able to understand me. Makhassé, your people's language has changed so much since my day.'

Esha gave a gasp of astonishment.

'I understood every word, it's impossible.'

'Not when you have the power of Qolqe Chunpi,' replied Quylur Chaski authoritatively.

As though coming out of a dream, Makhassé held the palms of his hands together in front of his face and bowed respectfully.

'Mama Quylur Chaski we are indeed from Kaypacha but not of yours. We have come here by accident.'

Quylur Chaski shook her head.

'I say,' interrupted Chaz. 'You're both talking in Quechuan and I understood every blasted word .....'

He stopped speaking.

'I mean,' he added. 'What is this Kaypacha? I know that it means - of today or the present time, but what's the significance of it?'

Makhassé looked over at Mama Quylur Chaski quizzically but she only nodded her head so he spread out his arms and shrugged and said, 'Well, I suppose you could say that we exist in two time dimensions or rather that we have moved or what I believe has happened, been brought to this one from our own time.'

He looked earnestly at the others.

'The helicopter – remember!'

'Much as I don't want to say it, I think that the recent events have proved that.' Chuck said, kicking at the dying embers of the fire in some embarrassment and turned away.

Esha plucked up the courage to approach the Shaman and knowing that she would be understood, copied Makhassé and said, 'Mama Quylur Chaski, what were you doing with the fire?'

Leaning on her staff, Mama Quylur Chaski took a deep breath and explained how her royal charges Princess Inkasisa and Prince Maichu had been taken by the Devil Riders and were in grave danger of losing their lives.

She had been *scrying*, looking into the smoke and had seen the Temple of Inti at Qucha (lake) Titiqaqa.

'That is where we must go,' she said in a tone that brooked no argument.

9

The overhanging vines and branches of the dense rainforest blocked the way again. Mendoza cursed and ordered the lead rider to use his sword and hack a way through. *The Inca road builders had never envisaged horse riders using them,* he thought.

He was covered in sweat, his armoured covered body allowing no respite from the incessant heat of the day. No thought of consideration passed his mind for the Conquistador up front, standing in his stirrups cutting and slashing as though there was no tomorrow.

Slapping his face as an insect bit, thus adding even more to his myriad facial sores, he gritted his teeth with foreboding.

He couldn't, daren't slow down.

The savages could be around him now. They were so good at hiding in the trees. No honour, they don't fight like soldiers.

The way was clear and he urged the party on. The road began to drop down towards the river and was seen occasionally through trees clinging precariously to the steep sides of the valley.

Another curse from Mendoza as it began to climb up again in a series of rocky stairways.

With a loud groan, Mendoza ordered his men to dismount and lead their horses on foot.

Sweat! His body now felt as though he was in the river itself. His boots squelched with each step and it was with a thousand thanks to St Christos when they staggered out of the jungle onto the edge of a cliff.

A narrow strip had been carved out of the face of it and three small thatched huts were perched on the far side of the road.

'A Tampus,' the Cañari called out knowingly from the back of the group.

Beckoning to one of his Conquistadors to tend to the horses, Mendoza pulled Princess Inkasisa off his mount and prodded her towards the central hut.

It proved to be the resting house, so he pushed her inside whilst ordering food and drink be brought to him and that the rest of his men could sort themselves out in one of the other huts.

The dark interior was sparse, an old llama skin lying by the central oven, which was full of cold ashes. Several earthenware cups and bowls were neatly stacked to one side of it.

He motioned to the far corner and pointed to the Princess.

'Sit,' he snarled.

Getting the message, Inkasisa sat down quivering with fear.

My brother, she wanted to ask. *My brother, is he safe?*

Unbuckling his sword belt, he suddenly jerked round when a commotion outside the doorway erupted. He grasped the hilt and rushed out.

'What is it?' he demanded harshly.

'What's going on?'

The Cañari danced into view holding the headless body of a long yellow snake.

'Master, Master, look what I found by the water hole.' He was grinning from ear to ear. It wasn't a pretty sight.

'Good food Master, good food.'

'By the Saints, get rid of it you fool. Now!'

The Cañari's face dropped and then he snarled

something in his own language and stalked away still muttering to himself, as Prince Maichu was roughly thrust past Capitán Mendoza into the hut, by his *'Guardian.'*

Maichu stumbled and then crept over to his sister and in the semi-darkness of the room accepted her urgent hug and hurried whisper asking if he was all right.

After a moment or two, he shrugged her away. After all he was nearly a man and then he squatted down onto his heels.

Inkasisa stared down at him, slightly confused. She had expected him to be afraid, so she slowly crouched down next to him whilst wondering what was going to happen to them.

More noises came from the doorway.

The Capitán stirred on the animal skin and flinging out an arm knocked his breastplates and greaves together adding to the noise. *My God*, he thought, *I was nearly asleep.*

'What now?' he growled. 'It had better be good.'

The Cañari stood there, an inane grin on his face. 'Master, look!' He was holding a large jar. 'Chicha, Master, chicha.'

Mendoza sat up. He knew about chicha, an alcoholic drink made from maize. He smiled and waved for the Indian to bring it in as he grabbed one of the cups lying by the oven.

The sound of laughter outside indicated that his men had a jar too.

A pleasant while later, at least for Mendoza and his men, (the princess and her brother were still cowering in the corner) the chicha had mellowed them all.

The Cañari brought in a bowl of stew for the captain. He had found the supply hut of the Tampus. It was full of different sized sealed storage jars containing maize, potatoes, (including potato flour) quinoa, various vegetables and fruit, dried guinea pigs and the jars of chicha that he had previously given out.

Mendoza grabbed the bowl and the proffered oven-hot baked potato bread and began to eat greedily, slopping bits of stew down his cotton shirt.

Waiting for a few moments for a word of appreciation or something, the Cañari scuttled out and returned with a bowl of roasted snake meat with a few hot sweet potatoes in it, a bowl of lulo fruit, (the Spanish call it Naranjilla – little orange) and a bowl of water.

Then, snarling at Inkasisa and Maichu, he thrust the bowls down onto the floor at their feet, spilling most of the water, before sniggering to himself as he went to get his own meal.

10

Shortly after Makhassé had collected an assortment of food from the supply hut, which had fortunately been left untouched by the conquistadors, they left the smoking ruin of the Tampu.

Mama Quylur Chaski, alongside Makhassé, led the way, leaning on her staff, khapchos slung from a shoulder. She set a good pace, obviously worried sick about the welfare of the prince and princess.

Chaz, following with Esha at the back of the group, had a firm grip on his own stick and laboured up the steep uneven paved Inca road under the long tendrils of the many kinds of vines and tree branches.

Pausing for breath after a particularly steep climb, Makhassé leaned on his machete and turned to Chuck who was behind him, mouth wide-open, panting loudly and said, 'I'm glad that the Conquistadors have done the dirty work and cleared the path for us. I reckon they have saved us a couple of hours at least.'

'Not us.'

Chuck sucked in a lungful of air and added.

'You mean you, Makhassé. None of us could match you with the machete and you know it. I for one am really glad that you are with us.'

Makhassé nodded and smiled, then glanced round and saw that both Esha and Chaz had taken a breather as well, so hitching his backpack into a more comfortable position, he began to follow the Shaman who, with a toss of her head when she saw him stop, had unbelievably, carried on.

With creaking joints, the others took the first faltering steps before settling into some form of rhythm and with a sigh of relief began to walk along a fairly level stretch of the Inca path, trying to catch up with Makhassé who could now be seen and heard shouting for the old woman to stop.

Breathing heavily, Makhassé cursed the old woman for not waiting, as he hurried along after her. He was, to his surprise, concerned about her welfare. A feeling of foreboding had recently begun to worry him and he was sure the Mama was leading them into a dangerous situation.

Wiping his brow, sweat dripping over his eyes, Makhassé felt his stomach tighten at the thought their very future and safety rested in her.

A turn in the path brought her into view. She was leaning on her staff both hands clasped tightly around it, looking through a gap in the rampant foliage.

'What is it Mama?' asked Makhassé as he reached her.

Without speaking, she pointed with her staff.

Far down the mountain slope, a plume of smoke rose from a small Tampus and the faint cries of foreign voices could just be heard.

They seemed to be singing, thought Makhassé.

'The Devil Riders,' said Mama Quylur Chaski, 'Have found some chicha. They won't be going anywhere until the morning.'

'What's up?' asked Chuck as he and the other two came along.

'I think we've caught up with the Conquistadors,' said Makhassé, indicating the smoke.

'Unfortunately they are several hours down the path

and it will be dark soon. We shall have to camp somewhere round here.'

Esha looked around, the rainforest hemmed in all about them.

'It's not very promising,' she said, waving a hand towards the jungle.

Makhassé smiled at her and said, 'We can make a camp a few metres from here, follow me.'

He turned left and using his machete, slashed a path through the thick undergrowth until he reached a level spot.

'Stand back please.'

He quickly cut down an open area big enough for each of them to lie down.

'Hang on a bit more,' he said, breathing heavily from his exertions before dropping his backpack.

Should have done that before, he thought.

Chas look on in amazement as Makhassé began to hack down medium sized branches about two metres long, which he trimmed with a few quick slashes of his machete.

Then he began to gather cut lengths of thin liana vines with which he tied the poles, about a metre apart, to suitable trees. Using the liana again, he wove a criss-cross pattern between the two branches.

He had made a simple bed, safely above the ground from any nasty creepy-crawlies.

Esha clapped her hands in admiration and joined in by helping with the weaving of the liana. Within the hour each one of them had a rough but usable bed.

Makhassé looked over to where Chuck, Chaz and Esha were sitting on the edge of their 'beds,' rooting in their backpacks.

'I suggest that you use your sleeping bags as a mattress. The night temperature around this height is not too bad, though of course you will need your mosquito nets. I have a ball of twine, just cut off what you need and hang the top of your net to the nearest branch. Don't forget to tuck your jeans into your socks, just in case an unwelcome crawler gets inside the net – oh! I've got a small folding shovel too, for you know what. Just remember not to hang around when you have finished – okay'.

Chaz looked puzzled.

'Why the shovel, Makhassé and why the rush to get back?'

'Come on Chaz, what planet do you live in?' Makhassé said with a grin.

'You must know about the main rule of *'wild camping.'* No litter or waste to be left at the campsite. The shovel is to bury the waste - you know what I mean!'

He raised an eyebrow, and added, 'Take my word for it, come straight back.'

Nodding to indicate that he had got the message, Chaz thought that Makhassé was being a bit fussy.

Jeez, we're in the middle of the jungle, for Christ sake and leaning forward he began to unstrap his sleeping bag and take out his mossie net from his backpack.

Esha and Chuck had been all ears as they listened to what was said and they too began to quietly sort out their stuff from their backpacks.

Meanwhile Mama Quylur Chaski had leaned her staff against a convenient branch and placed her khapchos bag by her bed before sitting down on it.

She let out a big sigh – her age was beginning to tell

– even for one such as she.

It was time for a little coca, she thought and delving into her bag, lifted out a leather pouch containing a wad of coca leaves and a small gourd of lime powder. Carefully picking out one leaf, she sprinkled a dash of lime powder onto it before putting into her mouth to chew.

A sense of calm passed through her aged frame, then the first tingle as a surge of energy flooded her veins. Another sigh passed her narrow lips but this time it was the sigh of contentment and with renewed vigor she pulled out a small gourd of achiota powder from the bag. Removing the wooden plug, she sprinkled some of the red powder onto her palm and began to rub her face and neck with the fine dust.

The local insects wont bother me tonight.

Then, pushing the half chewed coca leaf to one side of her mouth, Mama Quylur Chaski leaned down to grab a squat tube of bamboo from her bag and after removing the stopper, drank a sip of water.

'I'm going for a walk,' she said to Makhassé, as she replaced the water tube inside her bag.

'I won't be long.'

Makhassé nodded and placed his hands together, palms upwards and bowed towards her as she, unusually sprightly he thought, disappeared into the thick undergrowth surrounding the campsite.

Chuck had by now hung his mosquito net and crawled inside, his head resting on his backpack and actually feeling quite comfortable lying on his sleeping bag, with his rapidly emptying bourbon flask in one hand.

He took another pull and called across to Makhassé.

'I say, are you sure that the old lady has all her marbles.'

He saw Makhassé looking puzzled.

He hadn't understood.

'I mean, I know we saw some funny things at that Tampu and I know that I can somehow understand the local lingo but still, did she actually do what I saw or were we, well sort of hypnotized?'

Chaz and Esha lying inside their mosquito nets and both, funnily enough, chewing on an energy bar, looked inquisitively at Makhassé to see what he had to say.

How can I explain to these people that Mama Quylur Chaski is a real Shaman. A person who can see the future, one who can speak to the spirits and cast spells that can turn you into anything, even bring the dead back to life.

He shuddered at the thought.

'My friend Chuck, the Inca Shamans have been able to speak to the spirits for centuries. They have the ability to cross time and space and also change your sense of reality. Scorn them at your peril.'

'Hey! Steady on, Makhassé. I only asked if she could do what I saw. I'm not trying to ridicule her in any way. Hell, It's just that I'm trying to get my head round what I saw.'

Makhassé relaxed just a little. He knew that the last few hours had been traumatic for everyone, including himself but especially so for his new companions.

He looked across to Chuck.

'We must trust Mama Quylur Chaski. Don't forget, we are now in her time. Our destiny is bound up with her and her people and the Conquistadors – how it will end I don't know but without her help we are doomed to die here.'

Chaz groaned out loud. 'Jeez,' which drew a quick glance from Esha.

What he had just heard gave him the shivers but that was secondary.

He had realized that he had to go and quick. Squeezing out of his mozzie net, he walked stiff-legged to where Makhassé had put the folding shovel and picked it up.

The other three watched silently as he pushed his way through the undergrowth just as Mama Quylur Chaski came back into their little clearing from the other side.

Daylight was fading fast as he made his way further into the gloomy jungle.

The persistent buzz of insects was much louder off the path he noticed, when the sudden 'chuck-chuck' of several squirrel monkeys gliding from branch to branch high above, made him jump.

'Steady, Chaz, steady, they're only monkeys,' he muttered to himself.

He was glad to quickly find a fairly open spot, on what he thought might be part of an animal trail.

Better be quick, he thought. As if - he smiled to himself as he began to dig.

What was it – about twelve centimetres deep the rule-makers said, – arseholes!

Chaz sniggered at his feeble joke.

A couple of minutes later he pulled up his jeans with a big sigh of relief and began to backfill the hole.

A flicker of movement amongst the leaf litter on the ground made him stop. It was just light enough for him to notice something creepy.

'Ugh,' he stepped back, a line of huge ants had suddenly appeared and were marching straight to his hole.

Then a flurry of nasty looking hairy beetles scurried over his boots, making for the hole as well.

'My God,' he gasped in horror.

'Makhassé was right.'

And then he remembered the story about ants eating the corpse of a large animal right down to the bones in a matter of minutes.

He turned with a shudder of revulsion at the thought and crashed back to the campsite as fast as possible only just remembering to keep hold of the shovel.

On the edge of the camp, he slowed down and entered as nonchalantly as he could and as he walked over to his bed he saw Makhassé smile at him.

Chaz felt his face redden.

The bugger knows. He bloody well knows what happened out there.

Kicking off his boots, he unzipped his net and sprawled on his sleeping bag silently cursing Bolivia and its stinking rainforest.

11

The shrill cries of a nearby troop of squirrel monkeys passing the Tampus, jerked the Capitán awake. It was still early he could see. The sun had barely risen over the valley and shone through the cracks in the woven reed door in a scatter of weak rays of light.

He threw his rough llama wool blanket to one side and sat up.

By the Gods, he thought, rubbing his back, *these earthen floors don't get any softer no matter how thick the sleeping pelts are.*

Across the one room, by the far wall, he could just make out the prone forms of his two captives, bound back to back. His guide Serpienté, the Cañari, (it had amused him to give him that name after he had found out that the fool thought his people came from snakes and birds) had thrown them down to the floor last night. They lay, squirming in agony as their bonds restricted the blood supply to their limbs.

The oven fire was still smoldering but gave out no heat. With a shiver, Mendoza stood and stretched, uttering a groan as his saddle-sore backside reminded him that he needed to bathe, before picking up a boot.

He paused before turning it upside down and gave a big shake.

Nothing, he thought to himself. *You'd have no chance if a scorpion, a poisonous spider or small snake had taken possession during the night. It wasn't a pleasant sight watching a fellow Conquistador die in agony because he forgot to shake his riding boots.*

After checking his other boot, Mendoza pulled them on (he had slept wearing his shirt and breeches) and went to the door of the Tampus. Kicking it open, he stood to one side of it and relieved himself.

'Serpienté! Serpienté! Where are you, you lazy dog?' Mendoza growled.

'I'll skin you alive if….'

'Master, Master, I come.'

A grovelling Serpienté appeared carrying a jar of chicha.

Somewhat mollified, Mendoza took a long drink whilst at the same time aiming a kick at the Cañari.

Serpienté now wise to the ways of his master, jumped to one side with a hidden sneer on his face.

One day, one day, he thought, *I will stay where I am and you will get a thorn dart covered in frog-poison jabbed into that sickly pale-face. And I, Atuc, will watch you die a slow, painful death.*

Backing away, he grovelled again and said, 'Master, I get food now.'

Mendoza just nodded and went back inside the Tampus hut. The now open doorway allowed in enough sunlight to show the prisoners still writhing in pain on the floor.

'Gonzales! Gonzales! Get in here! Now!'

A short while later, his second-in-command stumbled into the hut.

'Where have you been?' growled Mendoza as he took another drink from the chicha jar.

A scruffy, unkempt Gonzales stood blinking his bleary-eyes in his shirt, breeches and boots trying his best to make out his captain in the gloom of the hut as he munched a piece of flat bread and wished he had not drunk so much chicha.

'Sí, Capitán, what is your wish?' he asked, his voice hoarse and croaky.

Too much singing last night, he thought to himself.

Ignoring the poor state of his second-in-command, Mendoza pointed to the two figures on the floor.

'Untie them and take them outside before they piss on the floor and see that they get some food and water. That is, if that idiot guide of ours has got anything ready yet. Tell him to get a move on or else he will feel the back of my sword.'

Swallowing the last of the bread, Gonzales nodded and crossed over to Inkasisa and Maichu and bent over to release them.

Separated at last from being bound together all night long, they tried to sit up. As one they both cried out in anguish as the blood in their veins began to circulate freely. It was agony at first but within a few moments the pain began to ease.

Maichu couldn't stop the tears so he vowed to himself to seek vengeance on his tormentors as his sister swallowed back her cries of pain and looked up at the two Conquistadors, wondering if she and her brother would live the day out.

Suddenly, Gonzales spat on the floor and pulled out his dagger and jabbed it at them, then pointed to the doorway.

They got his message and tried to stand up. It proved more difficult then they realized. Their leg muscles seemed unable to bear their weight. So, on hands and knees they began to crawl.

'Get up!' shouted Gonzales, before grabbing a

handful of Inkasisa's hair and dragged her upright.

When his sister screeched in pain, Maichu lost it. With a cry of rage he clenched a fist and tried to punch Gonzales in the groin. His limbs refused to act quickly enough and with a raucous laugh, the Conquistador twisted his knife- hand round and clubbed the prince with the hilt, knocking him back to the floor where he lay stunned.

'Enough!' the loud shout from Mendoza made everyone stare at him.

'If you can manage a boy and a young woman by yourself Gonzales, take these wretches out of my sight. And for God's sake get me something to eat.'

His face red with embarrassment, Gonzales kicked Maichu, who gave a groan but managed to stand and grabbing hold of his sister led the way to the door. The seething Conquistador followed behind, his dagger ready and eager to be used.

The rest of the Conquistadors had been given a smaller Tampus hut to bed down in.

It was probably clean when they arrived. (It was custom and practice to sweep out every hut in the land every day by royal decree. In fact, government administrators who travelled the Inca highway had a duty to check that it was done).

It now smelt of the stench of several men who had been on the road for days on end as well as the stale odour of spilt chicha mixed in with the whiff of cooking food.

Gonzales pushed Maichu and Inkasisa roughly into the gloomy hut. They couldn't help but stumble over a hotchpotch of armour, weapons and packs strewn by the doorway. The rest of the Conquistadors were sprawled around the room, some still half-asleep.

A prick from Gonzales dagger made Maichu jump forward, knocking his sister towards the smoking oven where the Cañari was preparing the morning meal.

Sensing a presence, he turned round and seeing who it was gave her a leering grin.

'Sit,' he ordered in rough Quechuan, pointing to one of the few remaining empty spaces by the oven.

Rather gingerly they sat down, their limbs still throbbing, intermittent spasms of pain making them wince and watched hungrily as the Cañari spooned some soup from a large bowl of quinoa, tarwi beans and peppers, which was bubbling away on the flat top of the oven, into a smaller one.

Then, from the embers of the fire, he picked out one of several roasting guinea pigs and put it into the bowl. Dropping the spoon, he reached over to pile of flatbread kept warm by the fire and grabbed one.

Grunting loudly, he stood up, barely stopping himself from spilling the soup. Pausing only long enough to snarl at Maichu to get two pieces of flatbread and on their life to stay where they were, he stomped off with the Captain's meal.

Maichu reached over and snatched the flatbread and gave his sister one. They broke pieces off and ate hungrily.

As they were eating, a Conquistador rubbing his eyes, stood and came over to the oven and bent down in the gloom for a closer look, particularly at Inkasisa.

Turning to his friends, he made a lewd comment about her, which raised a laugh with them.

He sensed that the boy was about to do something so he trod on the exposed foot of Maichu squatting by his sister. What with the night of being bound and the full weight of a grown man pressing down on it, Maichu howled in agony as a roar of laughter came from the rest of the Conquistadors.

Inkasisa was too terrified to move, let alone say anything. The fact was she couldn't hold her brother to try to comfort him. It was, she knew the last thing he wanted. He would feel ashamed to be seen seeking help from his sister - a woman. She felt so helpless; there was no one to help them.

Gonzales, who had gone to his own bed space, sniggered with them. Then he stopped. *Maybe the Capitán wanted these two in good condition, at least for the time being. I'd better be safe than sorry.*

He suddenly remembered that the last Conquistador who had upset the Capitán had had his tongue ripped out and then been tied naked to a fire ant nest.

'Enough! Let them be, Pedro, - for now anyway.'

Pedro scowled at Gonzales. *These Inca need teaching a lesson. After all, they're heathens aren't they?* Then he thought of his Capitán. *Well for now, so be it.*

So he grabbed a wooden bowl and dolloped some hot soup into it ignoring the squeal from Maichu who got splashed, before snatching a flatbread and went back to his place with a swagger and some more ribald talk with his friends.

***

Capitán Mendoza looked down at the last leg bone of the guinea pig. He had just picked it clean in less time than it took to have a good fart. *A rat has more meat on it,* he thought to himself as he threw it on the floor next to the empty soup bowl.

By now the sun was high enough to raise the morning temperature, enough to make him wipe the sweat from his face.

At least he felt more ready to face the day after having eaten. He reached inside his shirt and pulled out a roll of tanned skins.

All made from a stupid Inca warrior who had refused to say where there was a hoard of gold. Of course, he had to be flayed alive, the Inca had to know what happened if they didn't cooperate. The tanned skin made handy writing material, parchment, it was like gold and he chuckled to himself at the thought.

He removed one of the sheets from the roll and examined the rough map he had made with the help of the Cañari. To get to the Temple of Gold he reminded himself looking closely at the map, they had to cross the river. Not too far away now, the Cañari had said.

The Inca always built a bridge in the dry season (now), wide enough for llamas to cross and with luck, horses. It saved them four or five days of travel, so was worth the effort.

Mendoza stuffed the roll back inside his shirt and as he began to complete the job of putting on his armour, thought about Capitán Alfonzo De Orlando and his men who had been given the job of checking the right bank of this river and who had been ordered to meet up with him as and when it was practicable. Maybe this bridge was the place?

12

Esha woke and blearily looked up at the canopy of the rainforest trees, the early morning sunshine trying its best to dissipate the gloom caused by the rampant foliage.

Despite the early hour, the buzzing, chirruping and calls of the myriad insects, birds and monkeys was quite loud and she was amazed at how she had slept through it so well.

After one more languid stretch, Esha sat up on her narrow bed and lifted the edge of her mossie net and looked around the small clearing that Makhassé had made the evening before.

A grunt and snort from the recumbent form of Chuck drew her attention and she smiled to herself. He had turned out to be more than just a pilot. His steadfastness during the helicopter crash and the subsequent support he had given to her and the others during the strange events of the last twenty-four hours had really been first-rate.

She looked over to the curled up form of Chaz, one arm half raised in a kind of salute. It made her smile turn to a grin.

He was quite cute in a good-natured kind of way. A bit accident-prone she suspected, possibly a bit naïve but he was fun to be with.

Makhassé's mossie net twitched and he looked out across the gap and said quietly.

'Hello, Esha, I see that you are an early riser too?'

Esha nodded and as she pulled on her boots,

whispered back, 'I'll just go for a walk in the trees, okay.'

Sitting on the side of his bed, Makhassé copied Esha and shook his boots before putting them on, stamping his feet as he did so.

'I'll make a fire for a hot drink then,' adding, 'Hopefully those two will get the message when they smell the coffee.'

A rustle in the bushes made them both turn quickly but it was only Mama Quylur Chaski returning carrying the skinned carcass of a squirrel monkey.

Esha waved a hand in greeting and disappeared into the jungle as Mama Quylur dropped the carcass by Makhassé's feet and crossed over to her bed space.

'Are you expecting us to eat that thing?'

Chaz, his head poking through his net, said in a loud voice.

'Jeez…'

'Do you have to shout so loud, Chaz?'

Chuck interrupted, sounding quite peeved.

'I like to sleep in when I'm off duty.'

'Remember where you are, Chaz,' said Makhassé quietly, hoping to ease the situation.

'There are no super-stores selling fresh meat round here. Okay. We eat what we find and be glad that we have Mama Quylur Chaski to help us. That way we can save the food we found in the Tampus for later.'

A subdued Chaz withdrew into his net and lay down in a huff.

With a shrug of his shoulders, Makhassé proceeded to make a fire in front of his bed frame. He cleared a space of leaf litter and using his knife, dug a small pit.

He then turned and lifted his 'net' and gathered a

handful of small twigs he had placed at the bottom of his bed the night before along with pieces of liana vine.

They were nice and dry.

Chaz watched carefully, his moodiness forgotten as Makhassé gathered a couple of used tissues, suitably dry of course, to set the fire and then grabbed several small branches which he had also put inside his bed space to dry. No rubbing of two sticks together here, he saw.

Makhassé had fished into a pocket and brought out a gas lighter.

As soon as the fire was lit and he had placed two of the branches on top of the flickering flames, Makhassé stood and picked up his machete from the scabbard hanging on a nearby branch and walked over to the edge of their little clearing where some green bamboo plants were growing.

The whack of the machete striking the tree made Chaz jump and he was surprised to see that Makhassé had suddenly turned round holding a thick stem of bamboo nearly two metres long, one hand cupping the bottom of it.

'Chaz, Chaz, grab hold of that copper kettle – quick as you can please.'

Fortunately Chaz had put his boots on and not knowing what on earth Makhassé was doing jumped out of his net and picked up the small kettle, which had no lid but a handy folding handle.

'Thanks,' Makhassé said, panting a bit from his exertions. 'Just hold it out will you.'

Chaz did as he was told and got the shock of his life when Makhassé removed his hand from the bottom of the bamboo stem and a stream of water poured out of it to fill the kettle he was holding. It was a wonder he didn't drop it.

'Bloody hell, Makhassé, that's fantastic. I'm sure glad you're with us. I would never have dreamed of looking for water in a tree.'

As Makhassé put the water filled kettle by the edge of the fire, Mama Quylur Chaski had been quietly fixing the monkey carcass onto a wooden spit she had made with her bronze knife. She placed it carefully between the fork sticks set on each side the fire and after a word or two with Makhassé, went back to her bed space.

'She'll be with us when the monkey is cooked,' Makhassé explained to Chaz.

'What's cooking?' Esha asked, as she returned from her morning walk.

'That's just what I was about to ask,' said Chuck as he crawled out of his net.

'I couldn't sleep anyway, not with Lumberjack Bill here chopping down half of the jungle.'

Makhassé looked enquiringly at Chuck.

'Don't mind him,' said Esha with a laugh. 'He's only teasing.'

Sometime later, Chaz, squatting next to Chuck by the small fire, spat out a small bone into the still warm embers.

The roasted squirrel monkey meat tasted all right after all, he thought.

Licking his fingers clean, he raised a thumb to Mama Quylur Chaski to indicate that he appreciated her early morning hunting catch; she was however after eating, sitting engrossed on her bed, muttering some kind of incantation to herself.

Makhassé drained his coffee cup and poured a few drops of water from his water bottle into it, in order to rinse it out. Then making sure that they had all finished he collected an assortment of bones and any bits of uneaten meat and wrapped them in a large leaf.

Pausing only long enough to pick up the folding shovel, he nodded to the group, and said that he would not be long, before pushing his way into the undergrowth.

Esha finished the biscuit she was eating and since no one else wanted anymore, put the half-full packet back into a plastic bag, making sure it was well tied.

'Well,' she said, looking at Chuck and Chaz.

'I think Makhassé will want us to break camp as quickly as possible, don't you?'

'Yeah, I would say so,' agreed Chuck, getting stiffly to his feet.

'Come on Chaz, better get your gear sorted and packed. I reckon that we need to catch up with those sons of a gun as soon as possible.'

Catching the urgency of the need to get on with the chase, Chaz eased his legs out from under him and stood up, trying his best not to show that cramps were shooting up his calves quite painfully.

'Okay, okay,' he said, limping over to his bed space. 'I get the message.'

Makhassé was pleasantly surprised when he returned to the camp. They had packed their backpacks and Chuck had even cut down a couple of thick bamboo stems and they had each topped up their water bottles.

Mama Quylur Chaski, oblivious to what they were doing, continued her incantation in low guttural sounds, arms outstretched whilst sitting on her bed.

Keeping to one side of the small clearing, they watched as Makhassé quickly covered the glowing embers of the fire with damp earth and then picked up his sorted backpack.

'Mama! Mama!' Makhassé bowed and said more loudly, 'Mama we need to go!'

Mama Quylur Chaski jerked her head up from her breasts and smiled.

'I hear you Makhassé, don't shout. Anyone would think I am an old woman?'

She held out an arm towards Makhassé and he took it as she stepped off her bed frame.

'The Devil Riders are stirring. We must hurry. More are on the way.'

Without another word, Mama Quylur Chaski, grabbing her shawl, staff and khapchos led the way through the undergrowth and set off along the Inca path.

Esha looked over at Chaz and Chuck and gave a shrug and said, 'Well then, hadn't we better follow her?'

Makhassé waited until they left the campsite and gave one last look round. It was second nature to him to leave the rainforest in as natural state as when he had found it. A few slashes with his machete cut down the frame-bed liana ties and the poles fell to the ground.

Within twenty-four hours no one would know that anyone had ever been there.

13

The constant roar of the river as it cascaded and splashed over a jumble of jagged rocks some fifty metres below a precarious Inca rope bridge, captivated and at the same time held in awe, Capitán Alfonzo De Orlando.

He was sitting, well more sprawling, on a horse blanket by the entrance to a Tampus, enjoying the warmth of the morning sun as he idly picked at a scab in his beard.

Thank the Gods for these stopping places.

The stink of his men, fifteen of them crowded into the small one room hovel, had driven him out. A night spent with a troop of monkeys couldn't have been much worse but their mad rush to escape had exhausted them.

He had been so tired he had just kicked his way to a spot by the smouldering oven, the evening chill already apparent in the gloomy room and snarled over his shoulder to his Cañari guide Uchu to bring him a drink.

What a mess. One man lost to the barbarians in the escape from the ambush.

Then the long race along the treacherous Inca path in the vile heat, hell, they must have ridden for hours.

No time to notice the prick prick of the countless blood sucking insects, or the slashing branches of low hung trees in the mad panic to get away from the deadly Inca arrows.

He leaned on one elbow, black eyes searching again

over his sharp hooked nose at the rope bridge, some one hundred and forty metres wide.

He had been told that they were made of natural fibres woven together to make a strong enough rope. The walkway was reinforced with wood plaited into the weave.

Each side was attached to a pair of huge stone anchors with massive cables of woven grass. Two more woven cables acted as handrails connected by more woven fibres to the bottom cables Even though the bridge would sag in the middle, it was to the astonishment of the Capitán, quite capable of carrying the weight of a horse and rider.

Enough daydreaming.

'Uchu, you lazy cur.'

De Orlando sat up and as he turned towards the Tampus, added more loudly.

'Tell those pigs we mount up as soon as I've eaten, and tell them to make sure that all equipment is secure. We're crossing the rope bridge, pronto.'

Mendoza must be near by now.

***

'Mierda,'

De Orlando cursed.

The first horse had refused for the umpteenth time to step onto the rope bridge, despite the furious spurring and whipping of its rider.

'Stop!' De Orlando roared.

He was furious.

'Imbecile! Do you want to kill the animal? I'll string you from this bridge by your bolas if it is harmed.'

The Conquistador cringed in fear as the Capitán

urged his own horse past the waiting line of his troop and stopped beside the sweating mount, its eyes bulging, froth dripping from its muzzle as the terrified rider hurriedly dismounted, armour jingling and tried to comfort it.

'Use your bandana, dolt. Cover the eyes and give the beast a minute to calm down. Then lead it over yourself. *Comprender.*'

The Conquistador nodded and shuffled forward red-faced to comply.

On reaching the other side without any further mishap, he led his mount towards a Tampus similar to the one he had just left.

'Well done, Gomes,' De Orlando shouted sarcastically across the river.

Gomes waved in acknowledgement and let out a gasp of relief at being out of the reach of his Capitán.

Copying Gomes, the rest of the Conquistadors used their bandanas to blindfold their mounts and began the slow process of crossing the rope bridge, (including the four packhorses, which also carried extra supplies of gunpowder and shot).

Pedro, the last in line of the Conquistadors, urged his horse forward. He was annoyed that he was last.

Mierda, he thought, *what a time to get the 'trots.' His friend Carlos had snickered when he told him that he had to go into the bushes. By the time he had come out, the walkway was empty.*

By the Gods, the Capitán will flay me alive if I don't get a move on. Sodding armour.

He pulled on the reins to make his horse walk faster as he reached the middle and saw the sagging bridge arch up before him.

73

'Pedro! Pedro! Hurry!'

It was Carlos screaming at the top of his voice.

'For God's sake hurry.'

A thrup, thrup noise made Pedro crouch in terror.

Two long arrows flitted past him as another bounced off his back armour, A squeal of pain erupted in his ear as his horse leapt up onto its hind legs, an arrow sticking from its rump.

The rope bridge jiggled and swung to and fro as the horse jerking again as it was hit by another arrow collapsed onto the walkway, its legs splayed between the handrail struts.

Pedro dropped down into a crouch, partially hidden by his dying horse. Leaning over the wide-eyed twitching animal, oblivious to its screams, he grabbed his saddle pannier and began to crawl up towards his comrades, trying desperately to avoid entangling his legs with his sword.

A sudden blast from two arquebuses covered him in smoke; the noise of their discharge was deafening but it gave him time to climb up and over the end of the bridge.

'Over here, Pedro, over here,' Carlos shouted urgently from the entrance to the Tampus as a shower of arrows thudded into the trees around them.

Scuttling like a startled rabbit, Pedro reached the safety of the Tampus enclosure where De Orlando was shouting orders to his men.

They were scattered around holding their horses' reins, apart from Miguel and Anton who had taken positions by the edge of the Tampus and were in the process of frantically reloading their arquebuses as fast as possible.

'Rodrigo, Rodrigo,' screamed De Orlando, jabbing his sword at one of them.

'Take the horses; take the damn horses to the back. Diego for God's sake, wake up and help him.'

De Orlando cursed, wiped his sweating brow and took a deep breath.

Slightly calmer, he pointed to two more of his men and ordered them to cut down the rope bridge.

They looked blankly at him.

'Use your hatchets. Use your hatchets idiots before I cut you down.'

Nodding fearfully, the two Conquistadors handed over their reins to Diego and rushed to the bridge, pulling out their hatchets from their belts as they did so.

Kneeling on each side of the huge anchor stones, they began to hack at the thick woven cables.

At once a shower of arrows shot across from the trees on the other side of the river. The big stone anchors gave some protection and neither man was hit.

They crouched down lower in fear of being hit before furiously attacking the fibrous rope again when De Orlando screamed at them to get on with it or face being flayed alive.

Suddenly, a group of Incas appeared and began to cross the rope bridge whilst another shower of arrows peppered the two axe-men, one whom cried out as he was hit on the shoulder.

His body armour saved him as the arrow glanced off and fell to the ground.

Miguel and Anton rushed to the rear of the sweating axe-men and each fired his arquebus filled with lead shot at the approaching Inca.

When the smoke cleared, five bodies sprawled on the walkway.

The rest had fled back to the safety of the trees.

The rope bridge suddenly sagged on one side as the supporting cable on that side was cut.

De Orlando was nearly hysterical.

'Finish it off. Finish it off,' he yelled at the top of his voice.

Panting from his exertions, Miguel chopped down hard and with a large twang, the rope bridge fell down towards the river, one end swirling in the raging torrent, the other hanging down from its support anchors as the five bodies and the still twitching horse plummeted into the water to be dashed to a pulp by sharp rocks projecting up through the racing river like a set of fangs.

***

Mendoza thought something was wrong as soon as he saw the rope bridge hanging down into the river on the opposite bank.

He was leading the way along the tree covered paved path towards the Tampus where he hoped he would meet up with De Orlando.

A sudden noise made him rein in his horse to a stop.

A Conquistador, holding an arquebus, had appeared on a narrow side path partly hidden by the trees. He was looking anxiously around.

'Capitán,' he whispered.

'Thank God you have arrived safely. The heathen devils are just across the river. You must hurry and take shelter in the Tampus behind me before they start shooting their arrows again.'

Quietly urging his men to close ranks behind him, Mendoza spurred his mount into a trot and led them past the guard into the open area in front of the simple Tampus huts.

By the entrance to the largest one De Orlando stood, now composed and feeling more at ease with the situation. He acknowledged Capitán Mendoza's arrival with a casual wave of a hand and a brief nod. Then he said with a smile.

'Welcome to this rat hole, Vicente, I trust that you were more successful than I. The devious heathens have been on my tail for days now. Hopefully, cutting down that bridge will give us some respite.'

Mendoza slid off his horse and rubbed his aching back before handing the reins to Serpienté. He then ordered his men to dismount and see to their horses before settling in one of the huts.

Then he remembered.

'Oh! Gonzales, take those two bags of shit that we picked up and feed them.'

A little unsteady, his legs still stiff from the ride, he walked over to the Tampus entrance and slapped Alfonzo on his shoulder, saying in a friendly tone.

'You made it then. Good to see you.'

Turning as the Cañari led his horse away, he shouted after him, 'Bring some chicha for Capitán De Orlando and me - Rápido!'

Then with a wave of his hand, Mendoza added, 'Lead the way Alfonzo and tell me all about it.'

He had now quietly assumed command of the now quite large force of Conquistadors.

As they went into the hut, they were hit by the dank, odious smell of the group of men already in the gloomy, single room, who had suddenly gone silent at the sound of Capitán Mendoza's voice.

It mixed with ancient Inca odours and thick smoke from the ubiquitous oven fire, which someone had recently lit.

Stepping round several supine bodies, Mendoza and De Orlando squatted down by the oven in a space hurriedly vacated by some of the men, as a commotion in the entrance of the hut announced the Cañari's return.

'Shift. Out of the way,' he snarled at anyone blocking his way, as he came in carrying two pots of chicha for the two Capitáns, who took their drinks without so much as a glance at him.

They did not notice the venomous glance he gave them as he backed away.

He would have words with the other Cañari, - Uchu. Their time would come.

'Now then, Alfonzo, you were saying.' Mendoza took a big gulp of chicha and looked carefully at his new deputy.

'Well, Vicente.'

De Orlando hesitated and tugged his pointed beard for a few seconds and took a sip of chicha. He went on to describe the last few days, the ambush and the loss of a good man. Glossing over his terror of being caught by the heathens, he shuddered at the thought and went on.

He looked Mendoza in the eye and bragged how he had saved his troop by ordering the destruction of the rope bridge. The loss of the horse was unavoidable he added, hoping to the Gods that Mendoza would overlook that. (Horses were more valuable than men in this godforsaken country).

Draining his pot of chicha, Mendoza pondered for a while, then said in genial tone. 'You did well in the circumstances Alfonzo. Pity about the bridge though.'

Turning to the doorway he called out, 'Serpienté. More chicha and bring us some food pronto or you will feel the back of my sword.'

Mendoza smiled at De Orlando.

'Don't give the bastards a centimeter or they will think we are soft. Is that not so, Alfonzo?'

'Absolutely Vicente. Absolutely. A good whipping never does any harm. I mean, how else are we to get these heathens to do what they are told promptly,' he replied, much relieved by the turn of events.

A harassed Serpienté and Uchu appeared and scurried over to them carrying more chicha and bowls of chuñu gruel and hunks of flatbread.

After placing them on the floor they backed away bowing low and apologizing for the delay.

See what I mean, Alfonzo,' said Mendoza with a sadistic smile, as he broke off a piece of bread and dipped it into his gruel.

'Now, about my prisoners.'

14

Mama Quylur Chaski paused as the Inca path suddenly dropped steeply before her. The thick undergrowth arching out from the side had nearly caught her unawares as her staff poked through a tangle of ferns at her feet and touched - nothing.

Catching her balance just in time she called to Makhassé who had nearly caught up with her.

'Take care, the path has begun to drop down to the river and the morning dew will make it as slippery as a tree frogs back.'

Makhassé grunted in reply. He had already noted the change in the noise of the river some hundreds of metres below them and had guessed that they would have to start climbing down soon anyway.

Some way behind him Esha and Chaz were already struggling to keep up. The uneven stone slabs set at different levels made climbing awkward even though they had had a day or so of practice.

Chaz, as was his wont, was chuntering to himself. Brushing some flies from his sweaty face with one hand, he leaned on his walking pole, thankfully made for him by Makhassé the night before and said for the fifth or sixth time to Esha, 'Don't you think it's time for a break, I'm knackered.'

'For goodness sake Chaz, we've only been walking for about half an hour. If we keep stopping every few minutes we'll never get to the Princess and the Prince.'

'Well, I was really thinking about you.'

Esha smiled to herself. She was getting to know

Chaz and his habit of twisting things around to suit his own way.

'What the hell,' Chuck's voice suddenly called out in front of them.

The sound of a body falling into the bushes lining the path was heard.

'I say, could someone give me a hand. I'm friggin stuck.'

Makhassé was the nearest and he turned round to see Chuck sprawled between two large tree ferns, his arms and legs waving in the air, his heavy backpack jammed in the giant leaves.

'And for Gods sake be quick, I can feel some kind of a creepy-crawly on my leg.'

Machete in hand, Makhassé reached Chuck and with a swift flick of his wrist sliced the head off a small green snake.

'Aagh. Get it off me,' cried Chuck as he struggled to get to his feet.

'Don't worry Chuck, it was too small to hurt you,' said Makhassé as he helped him up. 'Good job it wasn't its daddy though.'

Chaz and Esha arrived just as Chuck kicked the headless snake off the path.

Makhassé turned to them and said, 'You saw what happened to Chuck, these Inca paths can be treacherous in the mornings, wet and slippery, so keep your eye open, okay.'

Esha and Chaz looked at each other and then at the severed snakehead bleeding by their feet and nodded at Makhassé, who then turned away to catch up with Mama Quylur Chaski.

'Will you just look at that,' Chuck said as he

81

tightened the waist belt of his backpack before bending down to pick up his own walking pole. 'I was nearly poisoned to death by that snake and Makhassé pisses off without a saying a darn thing.'

'I suppose he thinks you're okay, since you didn't say anything, did you,' said Esha quietly.

'Well....'

'Come on you two,' interrupted Chaz, who began to walk carefully down the now sloping stepped path.

'I know we can't get lost but let's keep up with them.' He looked back at them and suddenly grinned.

'What if daddy snake decides to take a liking to you Chuck, like that one over there.'

'Where,' said Chuck loudly, hastily turning round, walking pole raised, ready for action and seeing nothing but the empty path.

'You little....'

'Now, now, Chuck,' said Chaz laughing loudly.

'We need Makhassé more than he needs us, so I for one am quite happy to be with him.'

'I agree completely,' said Esha.

'Now for Gods sake can it you two and let's get a move on.'

15

Gonzales nodded to his Capitán and roughly pulled Inkasisa from behind the saddle of the horse down to the ground. He sniggered as she fell, crying out in pain. Her bound wrists were unable to protect her face from the stone cobbles of the Tampus yard, which made a gash in her left cheek.

Leaving her where she had fallen, Gonzales went to get Maichu who was still attached to the horse of Marcos, now on the other side of the yard with the rest of the conquistador horses in a kind of makeshift corral.

Untying the rope from the saddle, he gave it a yank and Maichu, not expecting it, fell to the ground with a squeal of rage. That was about all he could do. The 'walk' from the last Tampus had exhausted him.

Laughing loudly, Gonzales pulled on the rope and Maichu had no option but to struggle to his feet in order to prevent himself from being dragged over the rough stone yard.

There was a small hut attached to one of the larger buildings used to keep llamas, the Inca pack animal, so Gonzales led the now quiescent Maichu into it and tied his end of the rope to a post.

'Don't move,' he snarled at Maichu, who now lay with his back against the wall on a pile of dried fern leaves.

Maichu was too tired to answer back so Gonzales gave a short laugh and went outside.

He was back in minutes, pushing Inkasisa down to

the floor. Her wrists had been freed and she was rubbing them hard trying to get some circulation back into them and groaned with pain when it did.

Gonzales yanked on the rope round Maichu's hands and lifted him up before roughly untying them.

Then cuffing Maichu round the ears, knocking him down in the process, he growled. 'Don't make a sound, do you hear, or you will regret it. The Cañari will bring some food and drink if you behave.'

With that Gonzales went out closing a woven reed door behind him.

At the sound of the word Cañari, Inkasisa's heart missed a beat. The memory of her servants' screams came back and she shivered in fear as she gently touched the wound on her cheek wondering if there was any hope for them.

Maichu stirred, his anger coming back and slowly and painfully he crawled to the door and looked through the cracks in the weave. He saw a conquistador squatting on the ground holding an arquebus and squinting right back at him.

***

It was mid afternoon and the air was getting chilly.

Well, at least for this area of the country, which was quite high, thought Capitán Mendoza. *They must have been up and down the side of three or four mountains today.*

The Tampus oven fire was burning nicely and he was sprawled comfortably out in front of it on a fairly clean llama skin.

'Another splash of chicha Alfonzo, before we talk about the Temple of the Sun.'

Alfonzo, squatting by the oven, nodded. His eyes

were already beginning to glaze over. This drink, although rough to the palate, wasn't too bad after the first litre or two.

'Si. Gracias.'

Sitting up, Mendoza picked up a gourd and poured into Alfonzo's simple wooden qiro cup before throwing it into a corner, not bothered that it bounced off the wall and splatted a drowsy conquistador with the last dregs.

'Now according to that simpleton of mine, Serpienté, it will take another two or three days to get to the Temple of Gold.'

'Not good for the horses,' slurred Alfonzo.

'They are getting to the stage where we will have to rest them before we lose some of them through some mishap or other.'

'We have to risk it,' replied Mendoza, his eyes gleaming.

'From what we know, a kings ransom is there for our taking. Remember that the rainy season is not too far away and horses or not, we don't want to lose a chance of a lifetime.'

Alfonzo tried to concentrate. Drinking on an empty stomach had made him less alert and he sort of remembered in his fuzzy state of mind that Mendoza had a quick temper and that he needed to at least agree with him and fast.

'That's true,' he mumbled, as a loud belch erupted from his mouth.

He turned and spat a gob of phlegm onto the oven and watched it sizzle.

'Maybe a nights rest would be good for all of us, including the horses,' he added hopefully.

Mendoza looked at Alfonzo for a moment and then laughed loudly.

'I knew I had a good man when I first saw you, Alfonzo but take heed, this is not a job for the faint hearted. I will stop at nothing to get this treasure, understand. No man or Inca will get in my way or they will suffer, comprender.'

Alfonzo looked at Mendoza and saw the eyes of a zealot. He gave a shudder and nodded. Thinking that he'd better change the subject, he turned towards the door and shouted.

'Uchu, Uchu you lazy burro, bring us some charqui (dried llama meat), chuño (gruel), flat bread and more chicha, rápido.'

Mendoza nodded in agreement as he took out his roll of maps and pulled one free. He looked at it for a few moments and then said, 'After we have eaten we go on.'

'But Vicente the horses . . .'

'Sod the horses. We go on. Chopping that bridge down was the wrong decision Alfonzo and I won't forget it.'

De Orlando's face froze into a mask. Mendoza's fury was renowned for its savagery.

Mendoza stabbed at his map before putting it away.

'Lucky for you my friend, that idiot of mine, Serpienté, has told me that the river is fordable at this time of the year, not too far from here. So we press on. Any questions?'

Alfonzo wiped away the beads of sweat that had suddenly formed on his forehead.

'No. No Vicente. We can leave whenever you say. The horses will have been fed and watered by now and the men will be ready by the time we have eaten.'

'Good. Now where's that damn food, – Serpienté! Serpienté!'

16

Going downhill was more energy sapping than climbing as Chaz (at the back of the line) was now finding out to his cost. His calf muscles were burning and he had to really hold onto his walking pole to keep himself balanced while at the same time keeping an eye open on the stone steps as they dried out.

Then the damn insects were plaguing him like the devil. His face was full of bites and itched like mad. He cursed himself for not asking Esha for some of her insect cream. In the rush to leave the camp that morning, he had completely forgotten about it.

Enough was enough.

'I say,' he shouted. It was more of a croak but Chuck just in front and still a bit rankled with what had happened earlier, hearing him, stopped and turned round.

'What's up?' he asked before calling out, 'Hold on Makhassé. We may have a problem.'

Chaz breathed a sigh of relief and dropped his backpack before slumping down on a damp stone step, head between his knees, both hands tight round his walking pole, which stopped him from falling forward.

'It's my legs. They're locking up. I just need a minute or two.'

'Here, have a drink,' said Chuck, passing his water bottle over.

'Thanks.' Chaz took a big swallow.

'Hey, don't guzzle you'll get stomach cramps.'

'He's right.' Makhassé had just come up, leading

Esha and Mama Quylur Chaski.

'It's my legs, they're cramping up,' Chaz explained again.

'Okay, we might as well take a break now,' Makhassé said and turning to Mama Quylur Chaski asked her if she could help Chaz.

She nodded and as she squatted besides Chaz on the Inca path delving into her Khapchos bag, Chuck and Esha dropped their backpacks with gasps of pleasure, and sat down as well.

'I'll just go on a bit and keep an eye on things,' Makhassé said and with a brief nod to them, began to walk carefully down the steep path.

Chaz slowly stretched out his legs, his face twitching with pain as he watched Mama Quylur take out a wrapped leaf from her bag.

'This has some locoto seeds in it,' she said.

They saw it held about two or three handfuls of black seeds from which she took five or six, before putting the leaf-parcel back inside her bag and picking out a small smooth round pebble.

Before anyone could ask what the seeds were, Mama Quylur Chaski placed the seeds on a stone slab by her side and began to pound them.

'Ugh! What the hell,' cried Chuck, as a puff of fine black powder wafted into his face. 'It's darn pepper,' and it had made his eyes water.

Mama Quylur Chaski gave Chuck a look that said, *what is all the fuss about* and turning towards the edge of the path, leaned over to pluck a handful of big leaves from a shrub with pendulous-shaped flowers.

'Oh look,' Esha said, looking at the flowers. 'Aren't they pretty. We have some just like them back home in

Queensland. *Angel's Trumpets* I think we call them.'

Placing the leaves by the pile of pepper powder, Mama Quylur Chaski selected one and carefully brushed the powder on it.

Then, rummaging in her bag, she brought out a lulo fruit, which she first peeled, before squeezing its juice on the pile of pepper. She then proceeded to mix a paste with a twig.

With a small smile, Mama Quylur Chaski asked Chuck to cut down a length of thin liana for her.

Chuck had dried his eyes and had been watching curiously and wondering what was going to happen next. He nodded and got to his feet. Grabbing his machete from its scabbard on his backpack he pushed his way into the tangled jungle.

He was back in few minutes with a coil of thin rattan type liana.

'Will this do, Marm?' he asked hopefully.

'Just right, thank you,' she replied. Then, taking hold of her bronze knife, she cut the liana into short lengths.

Turning to Chaz, who like Chuck had been watching agog with interest at what she had been doing, Mama Quylur Chaski asked him to roll up his pants.

Thank God I didn't bring skinny jeans, he thought, as he rolled them above his knees wincing in pain as he did so.

But what in hell's name is she going to do?

He soon found out.

Taking one big leaf, Mama Quylur Chaski plastered some of the pepper paste on it and placed it on the calf muscle of his right leg, tying it on with two lengths of liana, then again on his left leg.

'There, that will make you feel better. Don't remove the leaves until tomorrow,' she advised. 'Or it will not work.'

Chaz looked at Esha and Chuck.

'Err, I'm not sure about this.'

He looked at Mama Quylur Chaski, and said, 'I don't want to seem rude but.....'

'Hey,' it was Makhassé. He had climbed back up unnoticed.

'I see that Mama Quylur Chaski has fixed your legs Chaz. It's an old Inca remedy for muscle cramps. The capsaicin in the pepper relieves pain and stimulates the circulation of blood around the inflamed area. The fruit juice in the paste takes the sting out of the pepper so that you wont feel any burning sensation. It's good stuff. I recommend it.'

'Well in that case,' Chaz said in a happier tone of voice. 'I vote we have a bite to eat and see how I get on.'

17

'By all the saints in heaven I'll skin Pedro alive if he keeps us waiting again,' muttered De Orlando to himself.

He was furious as he watched the conquistador rush from behind the llama pen, trying without much success to tie his sword belt round his waist and run towards his horse.

'Hurry you dolt, the whole company is waiting for your attendance.'

Pedro was sweating in fear. Not only was Capitán De Orlando cursing him, there was Capitán Mendoza the Beast, as he was called by his compatriots, watching as well. His foot slipped out of the stirrup and he nearly fell flat on his face in his anxiety to mount his horse. He was sure he heard a snigger from that bastard Gonzales as he eventually fell into his saddle.

Actually Capitán Mendoza was occupied at the front of his troop with the Cañari, Serpienté.

They were standing by the anchor stones of the destroyed rope bridge, looking down at the fast flowing river far below them.

'Are you sure, really sure, that we can cross this river lower down. If you lie, I'll dangle you head first into it myself.'

The Cañari cringed at the thought. 'Master, master, by the spirits of my ancestors the 'Kan' (snake) and the 'Ara' (macaw) I speak the truth.'

'By the Gods I hope so for your sake. Now go and tell Capitán De Orlando that we are leaving this shit hole now and that he is to bring up the rear with two men with arquebuses, then run back to me.'

Flicking at the cloud of ever-present flies hovering around his face, Mendoza marched over and mounted his horse as Serpienté scuttled back.

With a curt nod to him to lead the way, he turned and waved to his second-in-command the signal to move out.

The Cañari began to trot down the stone steps when Mendoza called out, 'Slow down, fool, you know the horses have to pick their way carefully when going downhill, especially when it twists and turns like this one.'

Serpienté slowed down, pushing aside overhanging branches when they dropped too low and made his regular curse.

Just you wait master, just you wait, I won't forget.

18

The meal was simple, a wedge of flatbread and fruit taken from the Tampu and water.

Then they began to sort themselves out. Some made a call of nature while the others checked their footwear and backpacks to their satisfaction.

Chaz took this moment to exercise his legs a bit. To his amazement the pepper 'patches' had already begun to work.

Apart from a faint tingle in his calves the cramps had gone. There was a bit of an ache but otherwise he felt fine. He couldn't believe it, so he climbed up and down the stone steps a few times before going over to Mama Quylur Chaski. He smiled at her and to her surprise gave her a big hug.

She looked a little startled, then smiled back as she gently patted his cheek.

After a quick check by Makhassé to see that everyone was ready, he asked Mama Quylur Chaski to walk with him at the front.

As they proceeded down the steep stone steps of the path, followed by a rather quiet Chuck, Esha beckoned to Chaz who went over to her.

'Did you want something,' he asked.

'I wanted to know if you are really fit enough to carry on. You had us worried for a while.'

He grinned back at her and said, 'If you want me to dance a jig I will but not on these lumpy stone slabs. I'm not that stupid. Seriously though, I feel fine. I don't know how Mama Quylur Chaski did it, but I think there is more to it than just pepper and fruit tied to my legs. Remember those funny lights at the fire when we first met her. I can't swear to it but I'm pretty sure that something like that happened when she tied the leaves to my legs. Little sparks seemed to jump from her fingers. It's unbelievable I know, but I think I could climb a bloody mountain right now.'

Esha looked at him, not knowing what to say. The problem was he was right about the strange goings on at that first meeting with Mama Quylur Chaski.

'Okay,' she said at last.

'Let's leave it at that shall we, at least for the time being. Come on, we are way behind the others.'

Esha then gave Chaz a grin and said, 'All right prove it, last one to reach Chuck is a . . .'

She left Chaz to finish the phrase.

Once they had caught up with him, they all followed Makhassé who cautiously led the way until the path reached a small pongo (canyon), which rose up towards a gap in the mountain but away from the river.

It was a steep climb, the path zig-zagging under a canopy of overhanging branches, some obviously showing evidence of being recently cut back by the conquistadors.

It took them about an hour to reach the top. By then even Makhassé was ready for a break. The air was cooler up here so he decided to make for the collapsed ruins of an old Tampus that he had seen half hidden by trees and bushes some way from the path.

A few minutes with his machete was enough to clear a space to make a small camp inside the walls of one of the old huts.

'About darn time,' said Chuck with feeling as he flung his backpack to the floor.

'I thought I'd never make it.'

'Me too,' said Esha, as she too slipped off her backpack and took a sip of water.

Chaz just smiled and joined them along the back wall of the ruined hut and watched in amazement as Mama Quylur Chaski put down her bag and staff and casually went back out into the trees.

Makhassé had left his backpack by the overgrown doorway and went back, squatting next to it for a few minutes looking around the ruin.

'Well, it won't get done by itself,' he said, picking up his machete and walking over to the collapsed oven, dropping his backpack by the wall on his way.

He cleared a space by stacking the broken pieces of clay tiles to one side and dug a small pit with the machete blade.

Then, using the bits of the old oven, made a hollow pyramid round the hole.

There was plenty of wood lying around from the collapsed thatch and Makhassé soon found enough dry pieces, which he chopped to fit the fire hole.

Soon it was blazing away, the smoke rising through the cracks in his clay pyramid and wafting around the open ruined room.

Mama Quylur Chaski, who had disappeared for a while as soon as they dropped their backpacks, returned with a collection of large leaves full of tubers.

Makhassé nodded when he saw the tubers and asked her if she would go back and find a tulumo gourd.

'Only if you peel the yuccas for me,' she replied with a big smile.

'No problem,' he said, knowing full well that the yucca skin was poisonous and had to be skinned before cooking.

As Mama Quylur Chaski went on her errand, Makhassé turned to Chuck, who like Chaz had listened avidly to the talk about the yucca and said, 'Would you and Chaz go and see if there is a bamboo grove around here and get a few stems. We need to replace the water we have been using.'

'Sure thing,' answered Chuck, grabbing his machete.

'I think Chaz here is ready for another hike aren't you old sport,' giving him a wink as he did so.

Chaz grinned. He was relaxing on his bedroll and he wasn't feeling as 'done in' as usual after a big climb and he was savouring the experience. He hoped that Mama Quylur Chaski's 'medicine' would keep working for a lot longer.

'Yeah, I'm ready grandpa,' and he ducked quickly as Chuck made a friendly swipe at his head.

They left the old hut chuckling together.

Makhassé looked across to Esha and said, 'I say, would you mind helping by peeling the yuccas. I need to tend to the fire.'

'Of course,' she said, and unzipping a side pocket of her backpack took out her all-purpose tool containing a knife blade.

Picking up a couple of the big leaves that Mama Quylur Chaski had brought back earlier, Esha knelt down and grabbed a handful of tubers and began to peel them, using one leaf to put the cuttings on, the other for those ready to cook.

'Will this do Makhassé?' asked Mama Quylur as she came in holding a gourd about the size of a soccer ball.

'Yes that will do fine,' he said. 'Thank you.'

Then he picked up his machete and sliced off the top. 'Would you scoop out the seeds as well, please,' he asked.

Mama Quylur Chaski nodded and carried it to a corner where she squatted and began to take out the seeds.

Makhassé went back to putting more wood on the fire which by now had heated the clay tile pyramid so much that it now radiated a fierce heat into the room.

'That should do it,' he said to no one in particular and went over to his backpack, taking out a plastic bag, which he had earlier filled with maize flour from the Tampus stores and put it on the floor by the oven.

'Are there enough?' asked Esha as she finished and pointed to a pile of peeled yuccas.

Mama Quylur Chaski came across.

'Plenty,' she said, handing Makhassé the scooped out gourd.

He nodded his thanks and placed it in front of the fire, hoping to dry the inside enough before Chuck and Chaz came back.

The inside of the ruined hut was quite warm now and Esha and Makhassé lay down on their bedrolls and gradually began to slumber.

Mama Quylur Chaski went over to the corner and squatted next to her bag from which she picked her bracelet of chacapa nuts and placed it round her right wrist.

With her left hand under her heart she then began to wave her other hand, which made the bracelet shake and rattle.

Very quietly, eyes closed, Mama Quylur began to

chant, her upper body swaying in time with the incantation. The smoke from the fire swirled about her and then formed into a thick cloud above her head. A scene appeared – of a river, rippling over a sand bar and then figures, mostly on horseback, beginning to cross.

Suddenly the cloud disappeared. Just the wispy remnants of smoke rising from the fire could be seen and Mama Quylur Chaski's body jerked and twitched. Then her eyes opened and she saw Chuck and Chaz in the doorway, each holding several leaking bamboo stems.

'I say, it's all right for some,' Chuck called out with a chuckle on seeing the recumbent forms of Esha and Makhassé and Mama Quylur Chaski looking a bit dazed in the corner.

When he had cut the bottom of the first bamboo stem they had had to figure a way to stop all the water from leaking out and he had come up with the idea of wrapping a big leaf over the opening.

It had worked quite well, Chaz had proved adept at tying tightly the leaves with a piece of liana but now water was oozing out of their makeshift stoppers.

Makhassé sat up at the sound of Chuck's voice and when he saw the dripping bamboo stems, he turned and called to Esha.

'What?'

'What is it . . .?'

'Would you collect everyone's water bottles, we need to fill them up.'

She rubbed her eyes and looked around more carefully and noticed Chuck and Chaz holding several dripping bamboo stems.

The penny dropped.

'Oh, the water, right,' and she got up and went to the backpacks gathering the water bottles.

Chuck nodded at Chaz and they placed their bamboo stems against a wall except for one.

While Chuck held it at an angle to avoid more water leaking, Chaz untied the leaf.

Esha passed Chaz a water bottle and once he had refilled it, it didn't take them long to do all the others.

Meanwhile, Makhassé had picked up the gourd and the bag of flour left by the oven and was pleased to see that the inside was dry. He asked Chuck to half fill it from one of the remaining bamboo stems left with water and carried it to Mama Quylur Chaski, together with the flour and asked her if she would mix some dough for them.

Now completely aware of her surroundings again, she was happy to oblige and sat down with the gourd between her knees and began to drop handfuls of the maize flour into the water before kneading it into dough.

Makhassé went to the doorway with his machete, saying that he needed some green branches.

Chaz and Chuck decided to tidy up a bit and threw the empty bamboo stems over one of the walls into the bushes surrounding the ruined Tampus. After Esha returned the filled water bottles to the backpacks, she went to have a word with Mama Quylur Chaski, still busy kneading the dough.

Makhassé returned with five sticks of green wood each with one end of the bark shaved off. He asked Esha if she would bring the peeled yuccas to the oven as he put the sticks to one side. Then using the end of his machete he levelled the glowing embers of the fire. The oven tiles were now very hot and it was uncomfortable to be too near it for long.

As he moved back, Mama Quylur Chaski, knowing full well what Makhassé had in mind, carried all of the peeled yuccas in one of the big leaves to the oven.

She had already sprinkled over them various spices and herbs taken from her bag and with practiced ease placed them one by one in the embers of the fire. Then glancing at them with a slight smile, she went back to her corner.

While she had been doing that, Makhassé had spread a few of the big leaves on the floor and taking out the ball of dough that Mama Quylur Chaski had made earlier, proceeded to take a piece of it and roll it on a leaf until he had a thin sausage shape. He made four more before he took each one and wrapped it snake-like round the carved end of the stick. When all five were ready, He stuck them in a row in front of the fire. What with the radiant heat of the hot tiles and the embers, the rolled dough was soon baked.

A meal of hot bread and yucca was on the menu.

While they were eating Mama Quylur Chaski told them of her vision and it was taken at face value. She had more than proved that she had extra-ordinary powers.

Makhassé was a little puzzled though. Mama Quylur Chaski had already told them that there was a rope bridge not too far away. Why this vision?

Then Chuck said, 'Remember when we saw that conquistador killed with an arrow by those Inca people? I assume that's who they were. What if the conquistadors had got as far as the bridge? What then?'

'Well,' Makhassé paused for a moment. 'We know that there is a group of conquistadors on this side of the river. Maybe they we going to meet up, possibly at the bridge.'

'Yeah,' said Chuck. 'That sounds about right.'

'If that's the case then, why did Mama Quylur Chaski see them actually crossing the river?' Esha asked.

'Good point,' replied Chuck.

'Maybe something happened to the bridge,' Chaz said rubbing one of his calf muscles, which had worryingly, suddenly started to ache.

'If that is so,' Makhassé said, 'I think that we had better get over this ridge as soon as possible and see if the bridge is still there. If not, it means one, that they have been delayed and two, we might have some friends on the other side of the river.'

'What about three?' said Chuck, grimly, 'There are twice as many conquistadors now as before, aren't there?'

It was quickly agreed to move on, so Makhassé damped down the fire before throwing on enough dirt to make sure it was completely out and buried the litter they had made.

Then, after everyone had sorted out their backpacks and made a necessary if needed visit behind a bush, Makhassé took one last look round and led the way back to the path.

It only took a few minutes to reach the brow of the ridge and in a way they saw a mirror image of the pongo they had already climbed. This one though, double-backed around the mountain ridge towards the river, the path's rough stone steps zig-zagging down through the forested canyon.

'Well, I'm darn sure,' said Chuck, to no one in particular.

'That this sort of terrain will slow any horse down. Yes sir, it sure will.'

19

Mendoza was having similar thoughts. The path, now a ledge, had reached a rock face. Small bushes perched haphazardly all along it, their overhanging branches a problem because of a horse's mass and height. They would have to be led, blindfolded.

A tedious business at the best of times, but with a huge drop by your feet it was made much worse.

This would really slow them down. By the Gods, he would be glad to see the back of this country and it's heathens.

But first, the gold, he must get the gold.

'Serpienté! 'Serpienté! Where the hell are you? Serpienté!'

'Master, Master,' the cringing Cañari darted forward to Mendoza's horse, crying out loudly.

'I was here, Master, here.'

"Never mind that drivel. Lead the way quietly or you will be flogged. If I lose one horse, you will follow it all the way down to the bottom of this ravine, understand? Now get going. And check the way.'

It took a while for all the Conquistadors to dismount, tie a bandana round their horse's eyes and make sure that all equipment was securely tied.

Then Mendoza turned, one hand on his mount's muzzle, the other holding the reins and said to his second-in command – Gonzales, 'Pass the order, quietly mind, we don't want to spook them, so keep one horse length apart. And say that if a horse slips over, the man had better jump after it. It will be a damn sight quicker than what I will do to him.'

Two nerve racking hours later Mendoza and his men reached the end of the treacherous switchback path.

It joined a narrow pongo, which dropped down towards the river.

In a convenient gully set to one side of the path, he ordered a short rest, as much for his benefit as for his men. Riding boots were not made for walking and he led a rush to bathe his feet in a stream.

'Back, keep back,' he screamed to the nearest Conquistadors.

'Water the horses first.'

Gonzales restored order with the back of his sword and soon the horses had been watered and let loose, though hobbled, to eat the scrub grass of the gulch. Only then did Mendoza allow his men to eat whatever they had brought with them.

Serpienté brought both of them (De Orlando had gladly dropped beside him with a big sigh of relief as he removed his boots, before dipping his feet into the freezing water), pieces of flatbread and strips of charqui and more importantly, two small gourds of chicha from the supply packhorses.

As soon as they had finished, Mendoza ordered Gonzales to get the men ready, no matter how much they grumbled and cursed.

Once mounted, the mood of the men changed. They were doing what they did best. Ride.

And the chitchat up and down the line was heartening to Mendoza.

He well knew the success of his mission depended on them.

They expected tough times and harsh decisions from

him but at the end of the day they were Conquistadors, soldiers of fortune – gold seekers – like him.

20

Mama Quylur Chaski was transmitting a sense of urgency. It was obvious from her demeanor that she wanted to press on as fast as possible.

She had begun to utter a chant. *Asking the Gods to help*, thought Makhassé.

Taking the hint, *more a blast from a loud speaker*, Makhassé chuckled to himself as he quickened his pace as best he could, terrain permitting.

Eventually the tree-lined path levelled out and ran high above the river. The steep gorges and rocky scrub-strewn slopes were a death trap for the unwary traveller.

'I say,' Chuck called out.

'Can you smell smoke?'

Makhassé stopped and sniffed the air. He had been concentrating on the path in front of him and it rankled him that he had missed it.

'You're right Chuck,' he said and noticed a half-hidden track leading into the trees not too far ahead.

It must lead to a Tampus, he realized.

Then he saw the top of the rope bridge anchor rocks half hidden by bushes. He turned, pointed and said, 'Look, across the river.'

They saw the dangling ends of the bridge twisting and bobbing up and down in the fast flowing water before they turned and walked up to the Tampus.

They were met by the stench of horse ordure. It was overpowering.

On the far side of the yard, a makeshift stockade

made of cut branches could be seen. The dung piles were swarming with flies and a myriad different types of beetles and ants.

'Ugh, what a stink,' Chaz said holding his nose. 'Let's get inside.'

Esha was first. She went to the nearest hut. The reed door was open so she entered before rushing out again coughing and spluttering.

'My God, it's even worse in there,' and she pulled out a tissue and pressed it to her nose.

Makhassé went and had a quick look and said when he came out, 'Chuck was right about the two groups of Conquistadors meeting up. The mess left in there could only have been made by a large group of men.'

'Have a look at this Makhassé.' Mama Quylur Chaski had stayed behind to take another look at the damaged bridge and had almost tripped over the long arrow shaft that had buried its tip into the base of a tree-fern.

'This proves it. The other group of conquistadors must have made it safely from the other side of the river whilst under attack from the Inca,' Makhassé explained. 'Then they destroyed the bridge.'

'Yeah,' drawled Chuck. 'That makes plenty of sense to me. But what are they going to do now?'

'I think that Mama Quylur Chaski has already told us,' Esha said. 'Remember her vision.'

They all turned to look at her.

'The sand bar,' cried Chaz excitedly. 'That's where they're going isn't it.'

Mama Quylur Chaski nodded her head.

'Let's get away from this stink and find a spot to eat,' Chuck pleaded, 'I'm starving.'

Makhassé agreed that they should move on and as

quickly as possible and stop at the first convenient place.

Unfortunately, the steeply descending path, dictate otherwise. The stone steps twisted and turned around every rocky outcrop and often climbed back up the mountainside just to annoy them, it seemed.

Then the mountain decided to test them again.

They were still high up when the stone path merged into a small platform before turning into a wicked looking ledge just wide enough for two slim people.

It crossed one of the biggest mountain buttresses Chaz had ever seen. The drop from the rock face to the river at the bottom of the ravine was mind bending. Then there were the sodding bushes, sticking out all over, ready to force him to lose his balance if he edged past them.

'Hey, if you think I'm going to walk along that bloody path, you must be out of your sodding skulls,' Chaz exclaimed, white faced and trembling at the very thought.

'Can we have a rest here Makhassé?' Esha asked, pointing to the platform they were standing on.

'It's big enough for all of us, don't you think.'

'Well it's sure big enough for me and I'm still pesky hungry, you know,' said Chuck, dropping his backpack where he was, before sitting on it.

Makhassé looked over at the path-come ledge and nodded his head.

'Okay, it will do and it will give us time to think about how to safely cross this part of the path, especially for those who might be a little bit anxious. How about some lovely llama charqui strips and a handful of dried papaya fruit.'

Makhassé added, with a grin.

'Just what I wanted, how did you guess?' Esha replied, smiling back. 'Come on Chaz, you will feel better after a snack.'

'You want to bet,' he said with feeling.

Esha was proved right. Not only Chaz but everyone seemed to recover their spirits and Chuck just to prove that he was friends again with one and all, brought out his mouth organ and played a tuneful melody before suddenly stopping.

'Oh. Go on Chuck. That was lovely,' said Esha, clapping her hands.

'Err, I'd like to,' Chuck replied with a rueful look, 'But I didn't realize what high altitude can do to the lungs. I've run out of puff. Sorry folks.'

And he put it back into his pocket.

'Many Inca play the flute or reed-pipes, what you would call panpipes,' Makhassé said.

'Of course being brought up in the Andes means they have no problem with playing wind instruments.'

He looked over at Mama Quylur Chaski and she smiled and nodded at him before she rummaged in her khapchos bag and took out her bamboo *quena*.

The quena is a flute open at both ends with six finger holes in the front and one in the back.

Holding it with both hands, Mama Quylur Chaski began to play a simple harmony, repeated several times.

Then, smiling at them, she quietly put it back into her bag.

'That was a musical prayer to *Pachamama,* (Mother Earth),' said Makhassé, as he held his hands together in front of his face and bowed his head to her.

She nodded and made the same gesture in return,

including the head bow.

Chaz, Chuck and Esha didn't know whether to clap or not so they all put their clasped hands in front of their faces and bowed their heads as well.

They were rewarded with a lovely smile and nod of her head.

Then Makhassé turned serious. 'We need to do something to slow the Conquistadors down but how, I haven't a clue.'

He looked earnestly at them as they sat or squatted together on the last open patch of land big enough to fit all of them before it turned into the start of the formidable ledge across the bare rock face.

Mama Quylur Chaski broke the silence. She looked at Makhassé and said, 'It is time I called on the spirits of the Gods. Wait here until I have finished.'

Picking up her staff and khapchos bag she stood and walked back along the path until she arrived at a small gully, which reached up into the mountainside. The vegetation was thick and difficult to pass through.

Mama Quylur Chaski used her staff to beat a way in before stopping.

A huge tree towered over all the others overlooking the gully, casting its shadow over her.

It was a kapok tree.

With more swishes of her staff, Mama Quylur Chaski cleared a space so that she could examine the ground more easily.

The Gods were on her side. Several yellow fruit pods could now be seen, two of which were open. The fluffy, yellowish fibre protecting the seeds was what she wanted.

Putting down her staff and khapchos bag, she picked

a big leaf off a handy shrub and wrapped a handful of kapok fibres in it before putting the package into her bag. Then she picked up an armful of dry leaf-litter, again using a large leaf as a wrapper and feeling more relieved than anything else, made her way back to the path.

The others watched curiously as Mama Quylur Chaski emerged from the gully and walked towards them.

'Makhassé,' she called out. 'Would you make a small fire pit for me, please. This side of where you are now.'

'What has she in mind?' asked Chuck.

'We won't know until she tells us. Excuse me Esha, I need to get to that clear bit of space behind you,' said Makhassé quietly.

'Oh sorry, just a minute, I'll move my backpack,' Esha answered, getting up.

Using his hunting knife, Makhassé quickly dug a small pit and placed some small rocks round it to stop the fire spreading.

Nodding her thanks, Mama Quylur Chaski squatted down in front of the new fire pit.

'This will do fine,' she said as she placed the leaf-litter beside her and then took out her parcel of kapok fibre and put several strands of it into the middle of the fire pit after shaping them into a little ball.

Then to the amazement of all the others except Makhassé, Mama Quylur Chaski delved into her bag again and brought out a bronze concave mirror, small enough to fit into the palm of her hand.

Moving sideways a little so that the she was facing the sun, she leant down holding the mirror close to the kapok fibre ball.

The sun's reflection was focused onto the kapok in a narrow beam of intense sunlight and in a matter of seconds the kapok began to smoulder. Leaning much closer, Mama Quylur Chaski began to blow, gently at first, then harder.

The kapok fibres burst into flames and she quickly put some of the leaf-litter gently on them, blowing continually until that too began to burn. She added more leaf-litter and leaned back as the fire now took hold and returned the bronze mirror to her bag.

'Well I'll be...,' Chuck was gob-smacked.

He wasn't the only one.

Chaz clapped his hands and said loudly, 'Bloody 'ell, does that take the dog's biscuit or what? Who needs a gas lighter now? Right on. Right on,' he yelled even louder and he gave Mama Quylur Chaski the thumbs up.

Esha held her hands to her face in surprise at what she had witnessed.

Makhassé just smiled.

Then Mama Quylur Chaski put on her coloured headband with small bird feathers attached and the pair of bracelets made of chacapa nuts before taking out several other items from her bag and indicating that they should all move back, as she placed them by her side.

Wondering what was going to happen next, they complied by shuffling to the far side of the area and sat down to watch.

Picking up a small gourd, Mama Quylur Chaski removed the stopper, before shaking a white powder over the flames of the fire.

There was a hiss and the white smoke turned yellow

and it began to writhe and twist in the air before forming a small cloud that hovered above the fire.

Mama Quylur Chaski then picked up her quena flute and began to play a series of notes that changed pitch as she began to weave her body too and fro.

Dropping the flute, she then began to chant an incantation, pausing briefly to pick up another small gourd which had two openings from which she sprinkled equal amounts of a dark brown powder – vilca and lime powder - onto her other hand.

After putting the gourd down, Mama Quylur Chaski mixed the two powders together and sniffed the resulting snuff.

In moments her invocations became erratic and she began to twitch and convulse, her arms waving to and fro and her chanting even more incoherent. Her eyes bulged and her mouth drooled saliva.

Then the chacapa nut bracelets began to chime and emit a series of shimmering, darting beams of energy, which connected with the cloud.

The writhing yellow apparition began to lighten and turn into a whitish phantom like emanation.

As if in a dream, Mama Quylur Chaski picked up a bundle of leaves.

No ordinary bunch these.

They were known as the *wairachina*, the wind spirit creator.

She began to shake the leaf bundle and all around her she felt a wind but her hair and clothes remained still and the cloud above did not stir. Then dropping the leaf bundle Mama Quylur Chaski picked up her quena flute and began to play a whistle song.

Immediately, the colourless cloud above the fire

stirred and began to swirl into a revolving, twisting shape.

Mama Quylur Chaski stopped playing and said loudly, 'I see you, *Yacumama*, the snake of the water.'

The cloud shuddered and quivered before reforming into an emanation of a monstrous snake with two horns, which made an anaconda look like a sand eel.

The writhing serpent-like creature in the cloud, circled above Mama Quylur Chaski's head and it appeared as though they were communicating to each other in a silent conversation.

Then Mama Quylur Chaski collapsed in a heap in front of a dying fire and the cloud containing the apparition disappeared.

A moment of silence, then Chuck burst out, 'I don't, I won't, I can't frigging believe what I just saw.'

He turned to Chaz....

Esha interrupted and said, 'For God's sake Chuck. Can it for a moment will you? Can't you see that Mama Quylur Chaski needs help.'

Before Chuck could respond, Makhassé and Chaz had already rushed over to see how she was.

They were pleasantly pleased to see that she was stirring and seemed little the worse for her ordeal.

'I have something to tell you,' she whispered, as she sat up.

Esha knelt down and handed Mama Quylur Chaski her opened water bottle.

Gratefully, she took a sip and explained that she had spoken to the Yacumama in her dream sleep.

'He has agreed to help us,' she added, 'But only if he can claim a sacrifice. I could only say yes. We have no other way of trying to stop the Conquistadors. Is that not right Makhassé?'

He nodded.

They were powerless at the moment, maybe the spirits were their only hope, he thought.

Chuck interrupted them by asking how the apparition could help them. He was still more than a little chastened by Esha's outburst.

'It has something to do with the sand bank and the river. That is all I know,' she whispered.

'In that case, we have no choice. Are you up for another trek, Chaz?' Makhassé asked.

Chaz stood up and bent his knees. His calf muscles did not complain.

'I feel okay. Let's go.'

21

The pongo like all the others they had passed through, was steep sided and covered in vegetation. The stone paved path was uneven and the horses, now well experienced, still had to pick their way carefully, especially when descending.

The switch-back nature of the path, together with the regular, sudden climb for a time, then back to a descent, was very tiring, particularly when the rider had to dismount at the very steep parts of the terrain unsuitable for riding.

As expected by Mendoza, the mood of the men changed after a while. The on-off the horses back, the walking in riding boots, took its toll on the men's well being.

So it was good news when his Cañari scout returned, covered in dust and panting heavily, from lower down the path.

'Master, Master, the river is near.' Serpienté turned and pointed.

'Soon Master, soon.'

Mendoza was so pleased; he forgot himself by lunging into his saddlebag and pulling out a lulo (a little orange type fruit), which he tossed to the Cañari who scampered quickly away, frightened that the Capitán might change his mind.

Turning in his saddle, the path acquiescent for once, Mendoza called to his second in command, Gonzales.

'Tell the men that we are near the river and ask Capitán Alfonzo De Orlando to make his way up to me as soon as he can, path permitting.'

I must be getting soft, he thought.

It was only when the rock strewn river came in sight and the stone path became more of a rough dirt track wide enough for two horses to ride side by side, that De Orlando came up to Mendoza.

'Vicente.'

'Alfonzo.'

They greeted each other politely, both happy that they had reached the river safely.

'My friend,' said Mendoza effusively, 'I just wanted to clarify what we are going to do.'

De Orlando nodded whilst privately thinking, *what's the bastard up to now?*

'As you can see, the track passes down through those trees to the riverbank,' Mendoza said, stating the obvious.

'The river upstream is still flowing too fast for us to ford, assuming it is shallow enough,' he went on.

'But this bend in front of us where it has widened has slowed it down considerably and would you believe it Alfonzo, that idiot of mine Serpienté, has been proved right about the sandbank.'

De Orlando had the sense to smile and agree that it had all turned out for the better, and said so.

'Well,' said Mendoza agreeably, 'I intend to send the two Cañari over first, just in case.'

He sniggered at the thought.

'Very wise, Vicente,' De Orlando said diplomatically. 'My man Uchu is over there now talking to Serpienté.'

And he pointed to the two squatting scouts.

Mendoza twisted in his saddle, 'Gonzales, Gonzales.'

His tone had changed as he barked a command.

118

'When we get to the river, dismount the men and allow them to clean themselves up.'

He turned back.

'Okay. Now let's go Alfonzo. A dip in the water for my aching feet is just what I need.'

'Just so,' said De Orlando. For once he was in full agreement with his leader.

The riverbank had a swathe of scrub grass alongside the water and the conquistadors soon had their mounts hobbled and grazing whilst they sank to the ground for a well-earned break, heads resting on their saddles.

While Mendoza was sitting on a rock in a state of bliss, his feet nicely cooling in the river shallows, Gonzales was pointing to the middle of the river where a large sandbank had emerged at some time. The river flow had slowed naturally because of the extra width of bend and a freak of nature had allowed the sand bar to emerge, which also covered most of the rocky bed. A natural ford had been made.

'See the big tree fern that is leaning over the river, the one with liana vines trailing in the water.'

Gonzales was getting more and more annoyed. It was on the far side of the river, opposite to where they were standing. The place Mendoza wanted to go was straight across the sandbank. Anyone could see that.

The two Cañari nodded their heads and pointed to a spot lower down the river.

'No. Damn you. No. By the saints, give me strength,' cursed Gonzales.

'The big tree fern,' he pointed again. 'The big tree fern, you go now.'

Then he drew his sword.

Uchu let out a wail and ran to the edge of the river

and began to wade across to the sand bank. It was only waist deep and he made good progress because the river current was flowing more slowly at this point.

'Good. Good. Well done Uchu, keep going,' yelled Gonzales and he turned to Serpienté, sword point at his throat.

'I go master, I go,' shouted Serpienté as he jumped into the river.

By then Uchu had reached the sandbank and had walked to the middle before squatting down to wait for his friend.

Half way across Serpienté felt a tingling in his legs and to his horror the water began to turn milky white. He turned round to go back but a mist had started to move downstream towards him and he panicked and instead waded as fast as he could towards the sandbank.

'Hurry. Serpienté, hurry,' called Uchu in a voice quivering in terror before he turned and ran to the far side of the sandbank, away from the strange mist.

A sudden surge in the river current knocked Serpienté over and he sank below the surface, arms and legs waving and kicking as he strove to get back to the surface.

He was terrified. He had never been under water in his life. Then he was buffeted by a huge body rushing past him at such a speed that he began to tumble and roll so much he felt dizzy.

One roll pushed his head above the water and he managed to suck in some air before he was back underwater, his legs and body scraping against bits of rock projecting from the sandy bottom. Then a tree root growing from the riverbank, which had been exposed by erosion, snagged an arm.

Serpienté jerked to a stop, a stab of pain shooting through his arm as the rest of his body was pulled down river. It was a chance, his only chance and Serpienté took it.

He grasped the root with his other hand and eased the trapped arm free. Despite the pain of his injury he pulled himself to the surface.

Gasping for breath, Serpienté, still clutching the root, looked around. Milky white water was swirling about him and he could now see that he was well past the sandbank because the strange mist was dissipating fast. Then he saw it.

An apparition from the spirit world.

Serpienté nearly let go of the root at the sight of it.

Yacumama, it must be. The biggest snake-like creature ever, he thought, as it circled the sandbank.

It was so big. The two horned head, large enough to swallow a fully-grown llama, was nearly up to it's own tail.

The wash from the huge swimming body was making waves that smashed against both the sandbank and the riverbank.

The squeals of terrified horses could be heard as the fearful Conquistadors tried to lead them away from the river and the horrifying sight of the monster.

Uchu was petrified with terror when the monster first reared up out of the mist.

The two-horned head stared at him. A mouth that could swallow him whole opened and a giant forked tongue flicked in and out as it swayed to and fro.

It was so high up he nearly fell over backwards looking up at it.

He turned to run but he was far too late. Mouth wide, Yacumama spat down an explosive jet of water, which knocked Uchu flat to the sand.

The giant monster snake struck so fast that Serpienté did not see it snatch up Uchu in its huge jaws and swallow him alive in one gulp.

The monster snake continued to circle the sandbank, now almost completely clear of mist as the milky white waves continually crashed against the riverbanks.

A nearly hysterical Gonzales, wielding his sword, was rounding up the last of the horses with the reluctant help of several conquistadors. 'Forget the monster,' he kept repeating, sword waving, his voice getting croakier by the minute.

'It won't leave the water, see.'

The Yacumama, *the snake of the water* obliged by doing another high-speed circuit, waves included.

Once he was satisfied that everyone had been accounted for, including the packhorses, Gonzales could relax a little.

Higher up the mountainside, Mendoza now somewhat calmer after he had nearly soiled himself when first he saw the monster snake, was conferring with a still white-faced De Orlando.

'Has anyone seen that Cañari simpleton of mine since he fell into the river? He must be found. He is the only one who knows the way.'

'Not quite Vicente, Not quite,' replied De Orlando confidently.

'Have you forgotten your prisoners?'

'By all the saints, Alfonzo, I had.' Mendoza was all smiles again. For one horrible moment he had thought that he had lost his gold. He looked over to where the princess and her brother were being guarded, bound back to back and jammed against a tree fern. He gave no thought to their well-being. Just keeping them alive was enough for him.

'But find that cur, he is more handy at getting information from anyone I know.'

De Orlando would dispute that. He knew who was the master of extracting info from any man and he was sitting opposite him on his horse right now. His reverie was interrupted by a shout.

'You, yes you. Come here at once,' commanded Mendoza.

A quaking conquistador, leading a hobbled horse to the temporary camp, turned round and looked in fear at Mendoza and said with a bowed head, 'Si Capitán.'

'One of yours, Alfonzo I see. His equipment leaves much to be desired.'

'I say Vicente, that's a bit harsh after what we have just seen. To be honest I think the men behaved remarkably well under the circumstances.' De Orlando was determined that his men should not be made scapegoats for the recent events.

Mendoza paused; he was about to reprimand De Orlando when he suddenly recalled the tightening of his buttocks not too long ago.

He managed a tight smile. 'Of course, Orlando, thank you for reminding me of it. We will let it go for now, eh.'

De Orlando nodded but knew there would be a payback time in the future, for sure.

Taking the opportunity, he called down to the conquistador before realizing it was the clumsy oaf from the bridge.

'Now my man, here is your chance to please Capitán Mendoza. Leave the horse and your sword with Carlos and go along the river to that boulder sticking out of the water. That was the last place we saw the Cañari. Your job is to bring him back alive. Understand?'

Pedro's heart froze. He was a walking dead man. How could the Cañari still be alive and how was he to get to the edge of the river with that monster thrashing about here there and everywhere. He knew he could not come back if the Cañari was dead. So he just stood and stared at his Capitán.

De Orlando felt a tinge of compassion. For all of his faults Pedro had tried his best during the time he had served under him. He was just one of those awkward clods who couldn't help themselves.

'All right Pedro. I know you think it's madness to go down there but it has to be done. To make it a bit easier for your chances, take off your body armour and helm, then stuff some grass and leaves in your shirt and hair and keep low at all times. Now go, we have no time to waste.'

22

Pedro had obeyed the order and was now squirming along the edge of the river, keeping under any kind of cover he could find. Unfortunately, the blasted grass stems and the bit of fern leaf he had stuck in his hair, kept drooping over his eyes, so that he could hardly see anything in front of him.

He was too afraid of being caught by the monster to do anything about it and so his progress was tortuously slow.

He paused. The leaves of a giant fern screened him well enough, so he pushed them to one side and saw that he was level with that large rock jutting out of the river.

Breathing a big sigh of relief, now that he knew he was relatively safe from the hellish monster, he crossed himself for luck. It was still going round and round the sandbank as though that was its only purpose in life.

Pedro decided to quicken up a bit but just in case, kept as low to the ground as possible. So, hunched over, with frequent glances over his shoulder, he carried on.

The body, feet still in the water, was at the foot of a huge tree, sprawled over a big root that had been exposed by river erosion, part of which was still immersed in the river.

Pedro's heart rate went berserk.

He had just crawled round the base of this massive tree when he saw Serpienté. He began to tremble violently at the sight of him.

There was no way he could go back. Capitán Mendoza would have him flayed alive.

Pedro cried out in anguish.

The body stirred and groaned.

Pedro stared. His mouth dropped in astonishment and he stood unsteadily, not quite believing that Serpienté was still alive.

'Praise be to God,' he cried, crossing himself three times.

'Serpienté. Serpienté,' he called again.

'It's Pedro, let me help you.'

Pedro gently lifted Serpienté off the tree root onto his shoulders and carried him to a patch of scrub grass next to the trunk of the tree and then crouched down next to him.

Serpienté's body was covered in small cuts and bruises caused by the rocky projections in the riverbed catching him as he was pitched and rolled along the bottom of the river. His loincloth offered pitiful protection.

A short while later, Serpienté opened his eyes and carefully looked around. He shivered. The river coming down from the snow line had had no time to warm up at this height and he clasped his arms around his body hoping to keep his body heat in and flinched. His cuts and bruises had begun to ache.

Then he saw Pedro and it all came back.

His eyes opened wide and he tried to get to his feet but Pedro gently held him down.

'Rest, you need to rest, Serpienté....'

'The monster, Yacumama.... Uchu....'

'The thing from hell is still here,' Pedro said, looking up river, and he crossed himself and then kissed his fingertips several times.

'Your friend is dead. The beast swallowed him alive. I'm sorry, there was nothing we could do.'

Pedro omitted to say that all of the Conquistadors had fled in terror into the forest before the Capitán and Gonzales forced them back to save the horses.

He spat on the ground. *They needn't have bothered, the beast just stayed in the river chasing its tail,* he thought to himself.

Serpienté groaned, partly at the loss of his friend and because his wounds were beginning to hurt. He sat up and painfully examined the area around him.

On the edge of the patch of scrub grass where Pedro had placed him, there was a splash of colour – a bush with reddish - purple leaves with yellow and pink flowers.

'Chamisa,' he whispered.

'Pedro, Pedro,' Serpienté looked agitated, 'I need…. you get flowers….., they I want.'

'Flowers! Flowers! What do want them for? Are you sure?'

'Need water as well.'

Pedro scratched his head, perplexed, but decided to humour Serpienté and went over to the bush and collected two handfuls of flowers and a large waxy leaf from a nearby shrub. Dropping the flowers besides Serpienté, he went to the river and using the leaf as a bowl, filled it with water, before carefully carrying it back.

Squatting in front of Serpienté, Pedro held out the leaf filled with water.

'Now what?' he asked.

Serpienté painfully sat up and leaning over, picked

up the flowers and put them into the water filled leaf.

Wincing in pain, Serpienté kneaded the flowers and water until he had made a mushy mess.

He sat back and said weakly, 'Pedro. You rub on me,' and pointed to the mush.

Pedro was astonished, 'This, this stuff, it will make you better?' he asked.

'Yes, good, good,' Serpienté replied slowly, as Pedro began to apply the mixture.

23

Once on the narrow ledge, Makhassé took the lead. Mama Quylur Chaski, who was quite perky after her séance experience, followed him, leaning on her staff confident and unfazed by the drop near her feet, chattering on about the various shrubs and plants that they passed.

Not too keen on heights, Esha kept in touching distance of the rock face. Unfortunately, the overhanging branches of some shrubs and trees made for many moments of anguish for her as she edged her way past them.

Chaz felt wonderful, well at least his legs did. There had been no sign of cramps but the sight of the river, down the sheer drop one short pace away, scared the shit out of him and he wasn't afraid to say that to anyone.

So, like Esha, he kept well away from the edge when he could, flora permitting and he was glad that he had his walking pole as it helped him keep his balance when the path became too steep and stopped him rushing down a sloping part.

Chuck just couldn't get enough of the views. It was a good job he was at the rear of the group otherwise his frequent stops would have really delayed them.

As a pilot he naturally had no fear of heights and he revelled in every turn that brought new vistas to gasp at.

He was actually disappointed when he turned a bend in the rock face and found the group had stopped.

The ledge had petered out.

It had actually dropped down into a small pongo and they hurried down it trying to make up for lost time.

Before long they reached a side gully that reeked of recent horse ordure.

'They stopped here for a while,' said Makhassé, after a quick look round.

'See, over there.'

He pointed to several piles of dung near a patch of flattened scrubland by a stream.

'Not a bad spot actually,' exclaimed Chaz, going a bit further upstream before flopping down in the scrub grass. 'Let's take five as well.'

Makhassé and Mama Quylur Chaski both gave him a look of, *what did you say?*

'He means just a short rest,' said Chuck helpfully.

Chaz nodded.

'My dogs,' went on Chuck..

He saw that look again.

'My feet could just do with a paddle in that cool looking stream.'

Esha took the initiative by dropping her backpack and removing her boots and socks before sitting on the edge of the stream and dangled her feet in the fast flowing water.

'Oooooh!' she squealed, 'It's freezing.' Then she smiled and said, 'Aaah, that's lovely, you just have to get used to it.'

Chuck and Chaz needed no more excuses and they were soon extolling the benefits of relaxing in a 'cool' stream, until Chaz jumped back away from it.

'Bloody hell, look at my feet they've turned blue.'

'I suggest that is long enough,' said Makhassé

quietly, 'You don't want to get hypothermia do you?'

'Darn right,' said Chuck, 'I surely don't. Come on Esha let's dry our do.... feet, pronto, okay.'

'Good idea, I think I've lost some feeling already.'

A few minutes later as she finished tying her bootlaces, Esha said, 'It was well worth the shock of that freezing water. I feel ten times better.'

Chaz wouldn't have put it quite like that.

***

They didn't stay long in the gully. After a meal of charqui, fruit and water they were on their way down the pongo.

The twisting nature of the path was a bind. It slowed them down. Every second lost was seen as a setback.

'What the hell.'

For once Chuck was in the lead when the river came into view. They were still high up the pongo and the elevation enabled them to see a long stretch of the river.

It was fast flowing. Spray splashing up from rocks that jutted up was evidence of that. Then he saw a big bend that widened out the river considerably, thus reducing the rate of flow.

That was when Chuck saw it.

A huge monster of a snake was swimming around a big sandbank in the middle of the river, which for some unknown reason was of a milky-white colour.

The swell from the moving creature crashing against both banks of the river had apparently uprooted trees and bushes, some of which were stuck on the sandbank.

'*Yacumama! Yacumama* has come,' cried Mama Quylur

Chaski excitedly.

'He kept his promise.'

'Err, I don't want to spoil the fun,' Chuck interrupted her. 'But how is this going to help us rescue the Princess and the Prince?'

'I think I can help answer that,' said Makhassé to Chuck, pointing to the river.

'Can you see any Conquistadors?'

Chuck shook his head.

'The monster has forced them to change direction by stopping them crossing the river here. They will have to take the longer route to get to the Inti Temple of Gold. It will take them through the Valley of the Moon. They have no choice, not one of them will ever come near this place again I can assure you. The Spirit of the Yacumama will see to that.'

'Well,' said Chaz. 'That certainly helps us a lot doesn't it. I mean, we can get there first can't we by crossing here. From what you say it will save us tens of kilometres, won't it.'

'Don't get sarky Chaz, it doesn't suit you,' said Esha trying to defuse the situation. 'That monster isn't going away soon, am I right?'

Esha looked over towards Mama Quylur Chaski, who nodded in affirmation.

'Okay, okay,' said Chuck.

'The Conquistadors are now on their way to the Valley of the Moon, wherever that is. We have to follow because of that overgrown worm swimming in the river over there and I for one am not going to say hello to the darn thing. So I vote we keep to the chase, all right. Anyone who disagrees can go for a swim with our new friend.'

Nobody had their swimming togs on, so Makhassé took the lead again, following a wide swathe of cut shrub and fern branches made by a hasty retreating group of Conquistadors.

24

Mendoza called a halt. He and his men were in a small ravine about a kilometre from the river and its hideous monster. It was cut into the shoulder of a mountain that seemed to go up to heaven.

A passing cloud shrouded a snow-capped peak. The steep sides were divided by a dried up watercourse, which meandered down the middle.

The leading conquistador had spotted it through a gap amongst the tree ferns and thick shrub, which were making riding difficult, and he had taken the easier route, the rest naturally following.

There had been no need to urge their horses to climb away from the water creature but it took brute power and the use of a short whip to keep them from bolting away in a panic.

In a small clearing, he called to De Orlando and Gonzales and went over to them.

By the Saints, he thought, *I must be going soft in in the head. They should come to me.*

He needed to know if there was another way to the Inti Temple of Gold.

Neither of them had any idea where they were.

'As you well know, Vicente we have always relied on our Cañari guides. Pity we have lost one,' De Orlando added dryly.

Mendoza's eyes narrowed at the remark. He would remember that comment.

This one will need watching, he thought.

'Yes it was, Alfonzo,' replied Mendoza, cracking a

thin smile as his whitened hands clenched hard on the reins.

Then, turning to Gonzales he snapped at him, 'Find Serpienté. I believe Pedro did something sensible for once and brought the Cañari back alive from the river.'

Gonzales raised a hand in salute and went to find him, glad to away from the bickering Capitáns.

***

'You wanted see me, Capitán.' Pedro had ridden over as quickly as he could through the makeshift camp. He kept his eyes fixed on the level of the Capitán's sword belt, hoping not to be noticed.

'Of course I don't want to see you, dolt,' snapped Mendoza.

'Is the Cañari fit to talk yet.'

Pedro let out a silent sigh of relief. Earlier, it had taken him ages to carry Serpienté back up the mountainside to the new camp, whilst at the same time trying to keep an eye open in case the monster snake thing came out of the river.

Nearing exhaustion, he had found his friend Carlos, who had saved his kit and after a quick drink of chicha, began to don his armour as Carlos gave the Cañari a piece of flat bread and a drink as he lay on a patch of scrub grass.

Pedro noticed that Serpienté had a graze on his cheek and when he groaned and writhed on the grass Pedro went over and gave him another drink of chicha.

'Take it easy, you've had a tough time,' he had said.

'Are you deaf, dolt?'

Pedro jumped and looked at the Capitán.

'I'll have you whipped if you don't answer me.'

'Sorry, sorry, Capitán,' Pedro cringed, 'The Cañari is wounded but he can speak.'

'God must be on your side, Pedro. You have been spared again,' Mendoza sneered at the wretched Conquistador.

'We ride as soon as everyone is mounted. You and the Cañari are to ride in front. Tell him we are going to the Inti Temple of Gold and if he doesn't get us there he will writhe on a stake through his belly. Make sure he knows that.'

He turned to Gonzales.

'Gonzales. Go and tell Capitán De Orlando that we are moving out now.'

Then Mendoza noticed Pedro.

'Why the hell are you still here? Go and get the Cañari or you will be on a stake too,' he snarled.

Pedro spurred his horse and went back for Serpienté as Gonzales could be heard screaming his head off at the Conquistadors to mount up.

It took a while for the camp to get organized. The recent experience was too much for many of the men to comprehend and they couldn't focus as clearly as they usually did, despite Gonzales' efforts.

Eventually Pedro got the signal to lead off. He felt a shudder from Serpienté who was sitting uncomfortably behind him, his small legs astride the broad back of the horse. He could only stop himself from falling off by holding onto Pedro's equipment belt.

'Go up water,' said Serpienté, pointing to the gap in the tree ferns. 'We go to top of it.'

Pedro guided his horse to a watercourse that had dried up and let it find it's own footing in the rocky streambed.

He gave a jab with his spurs and the climb up the ravine had begun.

Though the narrow sides were steep and well covered with shrubs and ferns, the winding nature of the stream was more like a zigzag, enabling the horses to make good progress.

Mendoza was more than pleased with the way things were turning out.

25

The trail of hacked shrub and tree fern branches was leading them away from the river up the side of the mountain and to a dried up watercourse that had made its way through the trees and had left a gap through which a ravine could be seen.

It had very steep sides covered in trees and shrubs so it made a rocky but serviceable path.

Unfortunately it was slow going. Mama Quylur Chaski began to struggle quite quickly, so Makhassé took her khapchos bag, which helped.

After an hour or so, Chuck said, 'There's no way we are going to get to the top today at the rate were going. It can't be far off nightfall, either.'

Esha agreed. She had just seen Mama Quylur Chaski put one of her chewing leaves in her mouth, a sure sign that she was suffering.

'Okay, let's bivouac here,' said Makhassé, as he looked around. They were standing in a bend of the watercourse which was fairly level, with only a few big pebbles amongst the gravel.

'I'll cut some fern branches down and we can lay them on the gravel and then put our sleeping bags on top.' He looked over to Mama Quylur Chaski and said, 'I have a roll of latex rubber that you can use. It's better than nothing.'

She nodded her thanks.

'Hang on,' said Chuck drawing his machete, 'I'll give you a hand.'

A while later, they had sorted themselves out.

Several layers of fern leaves had made a rough and ready base for their bedrolls and they sat or lay down, each finding something to eat and drink and making idle chatter.

Makhassé suddenly said, 'I know it's a bit mundane but as you may have noticed, there is not much water around here.'

Chaz gave a polite snort at the droll humour.

'Anyway,' continued Makhassé with an appreciative grin to Chaz. 'Just be careful. We don't know how soon we will find some more, okay.'

Nods all round and in the ensuing silence the buzz and the chirping of insects and the shrieking cry of some squirrel monkeys was almost drowned by the screaming *pi-pi-yo -- pi-pi-yo* of the piha bird.

'Looks like a finger in the ears night folks,' Chaz said laughing, as he poked a finger into each ear.

'Come off it, Chaz,' said Esha, smiling, 'I bet you will be in the Land of Nod inside of five minutes of your head hitting the pillow.'

Chuck paused in his nightly pull of Bourbon from a small hip flask and said, 'Five minutes, you must be joking, make it two.'

'Whatever,' Makhassé said, standing up, the folding shovel in his hands. 'As long as you don't snore, then on the other hand please do. It might keep the jaguars away.'

'What,' cried Chaz.

'Just kidding, just kidding,' laughed Makhassé making his way to the bushes.

'Oh, and set up your mozzie nets. Don't take unnecessary chances thinking its all right because we're high up, okay.'

26

When the Conquistador troop reached the top of the ravine, they crossed through a small pass, which led to a forested, verdant valley. The air was more humid and several small streams plunged down the slopes through trees and giant ferns, making their own miniature valleys.

Mendoza realized that it was getting late and they would have to stop soon, so he sent Carlos ahead to tell Pedro to find a suitable place to make camp as quickly as possible.

To Serpienté's relief, Pedro soon spied a sort of glade with a series of small terraces going down to a stream. It seemed suitable so he sent Carlos back with the news. As they went into it, Serpienté realized that it was in fact an abandoned ayllu.

Pedro dismounted and tied the reins to a shrub and then helped Serpienté off the back of his horse. It had been a long ride and the Cañari had never been on one before. In fact, he had never sat on anything other than the ground or his sleeping mat and he found to his amazement that he couldn't stand upright without Pedro's steadying hand.

Serpienté was so wobbly on his feet that Pedro had to ease him down onto a patch of scrub grass.

Then it struck. Stabs of pain shot through Serpienté's body. He did not know that because of his short stature, the spread of his legs across the horse's back would eventually cause pain in his thigh muscles.

He was also unaware that things could have been a

lot worse. He had fortuitously sat on his loincloth and thus avoided a very painful rubbing of his groin that the rocking gait of the horse might have inflicted on him.

Added to that, his cuts and bruises although a lot better, were nevertheless still painful.

He felt bad, unhappy and in great discomfort.

Pedro had noticed that the nearby stream had a pool, more of a deep spot where the bank had collapsed sometime long ago. The current over the years had scoured the landslip away and had left a hollowed out depression that had become the small pool.

'You need to rest in the water. It will relax your muscles and ease the pain,' Pedro advised in a friendly voice as he half carried Serpienté to the edge of the stream.

'No, no,' cried Serpienté, as he tried to struggle free of Pedro's grasp. He didn't want to go into the water. The recent experience with the Snake of the Water was too vivid in his memory.

Pedro half understood Serpienté's reluctance so he said a prayer to all the saints and just wearing his shirt, got into the pool as well.

By the Gods, it's freezing, he thought, *I must be mad.*

Serpienté lay in the cold water, holding tight to one of Pedro's arms. He was shaking, not from the cold water but of being immersed again.

The Cañari do not go in water. He could not swim and he was petrified that Pedro would let go of him.

Then, just as Pedro had said, he did feel better. The gentle tingling of the water as the current passed over his body, made the aches and pains disappear like a shaman waving a sacred Condor feather. He sent a silent prayer to the Spirit god.

Suddenly he felt his shoulder being shaken. Pedro was shouting but he couldn't hear him.

Go away, he thought, *let me sleep.*

A blow to his face made him jump.

Then he heard Pedro shouting, 'Serpienté. Get up, get up.'

Why, he thought, *it's so peaceful here.*

Another blow hit his face and this time he felt it.

What, what are you doing, Pedro. Why are you hitting me?

'Get out of the water now,' Pedro was screaming. 'We're freezing to death,' and he grabbed Serpienté by the arm and dragged him out of the stream.

'Stay here,' croaked Pedro, as he half dropped Serpienté onto the scrub grass and went to his horse and somehow dragged one of his saddlebags off its back.

Trembling with cold, he took off his wet shirt and grabbing his spare one from the bag, dried Serpienté as best he could before rubbing himself down.

'By the Gods, that's the last time I go in a stream in this God forsaken country,' he stammered through chattering teeth.

'Pedro, Pedro, are you all right,' Carlos called out, as he came riding up.

'I heard the shouting.'

Jumping off his horse he ran over to them.

'Is he dead?' he asked, looking down at the huddled form of Serpienté.

'If he is, we're both done for.'

Pedro paused in the process of tying his breeches and looked down.

'Praise all the saints in heaven,' he said, clapping Carlos on the shoulder and then made three signs of the cross before touching his forehead. 'He lives, the little runt lives.'

Then Pedro frowned. 'Help me put up the tent, Carlos, before he gets sick from the cold.'

He gave Carlos a knowing look. 'The Capitán mustn't know about this.'

Carlos nodded. Being eaten alive by fire ants would be preferable to Capitán Mendoza's special ways.

With a quick glance around the glade, he was glad to see that no one had taken any notice of a Cañari having a bit of bother. They were too busy sorting out their own gear.

So, pulling his small hatchet from his belt, he chopped down a few straight branches from the nearest suitable tree and made a tripod of them with a strip of thin liana. From the back of his saddle he untied a roll of thin canvas and wrapped it round the tripod he had just made.

With the help of Pedro, he soon had a compact shelter into which they put Serpienté, who was now complaining that he was hungry.

***

Mendoza was lying in his hastily erected 'tent' on a vicuña cloak he had 'borrowed' from an Inca noble who no longer needed it, ever since he had 'accidently' fallen over a cliff when he couldn't remember where he had got his extra large gold earrings from.

It was erected in the middle of the clearing near some ruined huts, well away from the trees and tall ferns and especially any troublesome creepy-crawlies -

he hoped.

He was in a filthy mood, stiff from the ride and thinking, *only one Cañari left and he's unfit. That idiot Pedro had said that he needed at least two days to recover from his injuries.*

Who would have thought that he would miss the little runt and how the hell would he survive the next two days eating the llama turds that Gonzales brought as food? And those strips of leather they call dried meat were not fit for dogs.

He took a big gulp of his drink.

At least this alpaca piss is better than nothing.

'Gonzales, Gonzales, bring more chicha and be quick about it.'

27

The usual monkey morning chorus, a natural alarm clock that tripped soon after sunrise, was enough to wake the devil. Howlers in particular, sounded as though they were in your sleeping bag when in fact they could be over two thousand metres away, so powerful were their cries.

Chaz sat up on his bedroll, rubbing his eyes. He couldn't believe that he had slept so well. Of course the hike of the day before was naturally tiring, but it was the way he had slept through the nocturnal chit-chat of the night creatures that amazed him. It would seem that some things were now so normal that he hardly noticed them.

He slipped out of his mossie net, dragging his boots with him before giving them a tap to see if anything had paid a visit during the night and bent to put them on.

'Nice to see you up and about so early,' Makhassé said quietly. 'Do you fancy a walk?'

Chaz jerked upright. He hadn't noticed that Makhassé was not in his sleeping place. 'Err, why not,' he said and picked up his walking pole and walked over to the other side of the watercourse towards Makhassé.

'Here, catch. Breakfast.'

Chaz was just quick enough to catch a lulo fruit that was thrown at him.

'You can eat on the way up. I want to see if the Conquistadors are still near. Oh, you can stop on the way for you know what. We need to set off right away.'

'Right,' said Chaz, a bit bemused at this sort of action so early in the morning.

Well over an hour later, Chaz wasn't so sure that it had been such a good idea to agree on accompanying Makhassé on this recce. The top of the pongo was half covered by a low-lying cloud. It drifted past them in small eddies driven by a cool breeze which left gaps through which they could see another well-wooded steep-sided valley with a meandering stream coursing down the middle.

It was Makhassé who spotted it first. Far down the valley, wisps of smoke were swirling up through the trees.

'Look,' he exclaimed excitedly, 'It must be their camp.'

Chaz had thought that it was just another cloud when he first saw it, then as he looked more closely he heard a loud report echoing around the valley.

'By the Gods of my ancestors,' cried Makhassé in alarm.

'That's cannon fire.'

28

The arrow was fired shortly after dawn.

The Inca warriors had spent the day before making their way down river on the opposite bank to the 'devil riders.'

At the sight of Yacumama swirling round and round the sandbar, the Inca leader Atiq called a halt and the whole group fell to the ground, bowing and chanting to the spirit for guidance in their quest.

When he noticed that the Yacamama was not listening to their plea, he stood and called for them to follow him.

Atiq had decided that the Great Spirit had meant to tell him to proceed at once further down the river, where they were to make a sacrifice.

Without question, the rest of the Incas picked up their weapons and set off in single file through the undergrowth alongside the river.

As they left the area, Atiq gave one last bow to the Great Water Spirit racing by in the river and saw that on the other side many tree and fern branches had been cut down, making a pathway through them.

'The devil riders were over there,' he whispered and stopped for a moment, thinking hard.

Then he smiled.

He knew where they were going and he was going to be there to meet them.

Sometime later, Atiq stopped in the middle of a glade mostly covered by scrub grass, which overlooked the river.

He pointed the tip of his long bow at the youngest warrior.

'Tie him to the nearest tree,' he ordered.

The indicated youth, Kusi, froze and then he smiled as he dropped his weapons and walked calmly over to a tree saying, 'Make it quick Atiq I want to see the Great Inti in person, not as the ball of fire in the sky.'

'Spoken like a true warrior, Kusi,' Atiq replied and then said to the rest of his men.

'Let him be. There is no need to tie him. The Great Inti will be proud to receive his spirit, as will we.'

Then before anyone could react, Atiq dropped his bow and ripped off Kusi's tunic before drawing a bronze knife and plunging it into his side.

Blood spurted out from the wound as he lowered him to the ground still breathing.

Then with a savage thrust, Atiq opened the ribcage of Kusi and pulled out his still beating heart.

Kusi widened his eyes in shock and gave a loud groan. It sounded like Intiiiii.

All nine of the remaining warriors watched keenly as Atiq cut slivers off the still pulsating heart and passed them to each warrior to eat, before swallowing one himself.

'May the Spirits of Kusi and the Great Yacumama give us the strength to drive the devil riders away from our lands,' Atiq said hopefully, as he put the remains of Kusi's heart on top of his body.

It took the rest of the day to reach a narrow rope bridge stretched precariously over the river. Atiq had remembered that it was only suitable for people and gave thanks to the Great Inti that it was still there.

After successfully crossing it, Atiq decided that it

was too late to go on. It was nearly time for Inti (the sun), to go to sleep.

As quickly as they could they each tied two or three giant tree fronds together with thin liana vines, making a simple off the floor sleeping-platform.

It took only a few more moments to gather some fruit and cut down a large bamboo stem full of water, all of which was then shared equally between them.

Just in time, for Inti slipped out of sight.

It was now completely dark. Each warrior had wrapped himself in his cotton tunic and then said a silent prayer to his favourite spirit for a safe nights sleep.

The next morning as dawn broke, Atiq urged his warriors through the undergrowth. Apart from a drink of water they had stopped for nothing.

A pongo rose up high above them. The fast flowing stream had opened a gap, which allowed him to see that it lay in the direction from which he knew the 'Devil Riders' must come.

'Not long now my loyal warriors,' he whispered.

A climb along the side of the stream had led them higher and higher up the pongo, through thick bushes and shrubs until at last Atiq saw his quarry.

A spur of the pongo had been exposed by what appeared to be an old ayllu.

The larger trees had been felled and terraces made overlooking a bend in the stream. Several shrubs and bushes had been cut down and Atiq saw a collection of makeshift tents dotted around the cleared central area.

Of the original ayllu huts, only the piles of stones marking the walls remained. The interiors were now being used as pens for the diabolical monsters that the devil riders rode.

Atiq paused.

The only way he could attack was from the wooded area he was now watching from. He frowned in frustration. It was a long shot for his bowmen.

With an angry glance at the enemy camp, he ordered his warriors to spread out and hide beneath the fern fronds.

Unfortunately, one of his warriors was a little slow in hiding and a shout came from the camp.

'Inca! Inca!'

The reaction was swift.

A fire-stick boomed and a parrot squawking on a branch above Atiq fell to the ground silent, in a mess of blood and feathers.

Terrified, Atiq scuttled away to hide behind a rocky outcrop and watched as the devil riders rushed to one of the ayllu ruins and snatching several things from it, ran behind a giant tree-fern stump.

He watched uncomprehending at the assortment of strange objects.

A black tube of metal, he thought. *It seemed to be very heavy. Then a long piece of thick wood with a big groove along the middle of it together with two strange shapes, like a bronze mirror but with bits taken out of it and a short piece of wood.*

The mirror shapes were put on the ends of the short piece of wood and the other longer piece of wood was placed between them.

What were they making? Puzzled Atiq.

The black tube was then put on top of the long piece of wood. It slid snuggly into the groove.

The Falconet was ready for loading.

As Atiq watched in wonder, the Conquistadors

poured in a black powder down the tube and then pieces of cotton before a long pole with a thick end was rammed down the tube.

It was when a round stone, small enough to fit inside the tube was inserted that Atiq suddenly felt a stab of fear. *It must be magic,* he thought, *like the firesticks.*

Grabbing his bow, Atiq stood and fitted an arrow. He took aim and let fly just as a Conquistador touched the fuse taper to the end of the cannon.

A blast of thunder echoed round the pongo and a cloud of smoke drifted up into the sky as flocks of birds rose up screeching and monkeys raced away through the trees, hooting in alarm. Atiq and his warriors turned to flee.

29

The arrow hit the ground in front of Mendoza's tent, the shaft point burying itself in a tuft of scrub grass, the flight feathers quivering from the shock of the impact.

The sight of it hitting the ground just as he leapt out of his tent holding a riding boot in one hand, almost made him lose his balance.

With his ears still ringing from the boom of the cannon shot and the throbbing of his head from the previous night's drinking, Mendoza hopped one more step and roared.

'Gonzales! Gonzales! De Orlando! For God's sake someone answer me?'

A figure came rushing into view. It was Gonzales, his face white with shock, waving his sword in the air.

'Capitán! Capitán! We are being attacked.'

Still hopping on one foot trying to put his boot on, Mendoza cursed again.

'I know that fool.'

The cannon boomed again, deafening everyone within range.

'Go and tell those dolts to stop firing before I stick that ramrod up their rears.'

Then he realized that they had already stopped firing.

Since no more arrows had been shot at them, Mendoza assumed the Inca attack was over.

Now fully shod, he looked around the camp as he buckled his sword belt on.

Order was just about restored by a hysterical Gonzales. He was rushing about, shouting and cursing at anyone who appeared to be unprepared for action.

Then De Orlando came over to confirm there was no sign of any Inca in the immediate area. They must have fled when the cannon fired he surmised.

Hearing that, Mendoza calmed down somewhat. He was worried because he did not know how many Inca there were in the attack.

The next ambush might be his last. They had been lucky this time, he thought. *It was a good job De Orlando had persuaded him to post those lookouts. Maybe he had been a bit too hard on him lately. Yes, I shall try to be more interested in what he says in the future.*

Mendoza then smiled to himself. *I can always cut his legs from under him, whenever I want.*

And he smiled again at the thought.

Now that the camp was awake, he decided to have a conference talk with De Orlando, maybe make more use of his talents. He now realized that Alfonzo might prove to be more useful than he had previously thought.

After a quick meal of that sodding charqui, fruit and a weak chicha, Mendoza sent for De Orlando.

They sat on their saddles, having had them brought over for this occasion and they spent some time discussing ways of getting to the Inti Temple of Gold without fighting the Inca.

"It's impossible,' De Orlando said, for the tenth time. 'With our horses, there are only the Inca paths through these mountains which we can use.'

'Just so, Alfonzo, just so.' Mendoza was at his pleasing, condescending best, which did not fool De

Orlando for one minute.

'And .....'

There was a disturbance behind them and they both turned round.

De Orlando saw one of his men, Pedro, holding the wretched figure of the Inca noble boy by one of his ears.

Mendoza was annoyed at the disruption.

'What do you want, simpleton?' he snarled, recognizing Pedro and knowing full well he was De Orlando's man.

'Capitán, I beg your indulgence. I caught this one trying to escape when we were being attacked.'

Maichu was wriggling, trying to get free but Pedro squeezed harder and Maichu squealed in pain and stopped moving, He stood still, tears in his eyes but with murder in his heart.

'For God's sake.'

Pedro suddenly realized that it hadn't been a good idea to bring the boy to the Capitán.

'Just chain his legs. Now go.'

Pedro bowed and tightening his grip on the boy's ear, which caused him to scream again, dragged him away, thanking the saints for getting off so lightly as Mendoza and De Orlando laughed behind him.

Mendoza suddenly had an idea.

This Pedro was friendly with the Cañari. Well, he knew how to get on with him. More than any other Conquistador he had noticed.

'Wait,' he commanded.

Pedro's heart froze and he turned to look at the Capitán.

'When you have finished with that carrion, bring the

Cañari to me. Carry him if he can't walk. I need to speak to him,' he snapped.

De Orlando raised a questioning eyebrow.

'Sorry, Alfonzo but I've just had an idea. The Cañari might be of help to us with our little problem.'

A gourd or two of chicha later, Pedro returned with Serpienté, who could just about walk on his own.

Not handsome to begin with, his face was full of patchy pinky blobs, which covered his wounds.

Mendoza cleverly put his servant at ease by giving him a small gourd of chicha and then began to question him about their problem of avoiding the Inca warriors.

Squatting in front of his master, Serpienté thought for a while and then smiled. His green, many gapped teeth appeared in his open mouth.

'Uchu....'

De Orlando jerked up, suddenly alert. That was his Cañari guide/servant.

'Uchu, what did he tell you?' he asked urgently.

Serpienté nodded and turned and pointed back up the pongo.

'Inca masma, masma. Near. Soon.'

'What in the name of the Gods is he talking about?' Mendoza asked in a petulant tone.

De Orlando pointed to Serpienté and said, 'Masma. Where?'

Serpienté put his gourd down and scrambled around until he picked up a small broken branch and started to dig a hole in the side of the depression that they happened to be sitting in.

Mendoza was about to clout the Cañari round his ear for wasting his time, when De Orlando clapped his hands and shouted out.

'I don't believe it,' he cried.

'Don't you see, Vicente, he's digging a tunnel.'

Mendoza stared for a moment and clapped de Orlando on the shoulder.

'By the Gods, you're right.'

Jumping to his feet, with a big grin on his face, he yelled at the top of his voice, 'Strike camp, we leave as soon as we are ready.'

Mendoza looked down at the still squatting Cañari and called to Pedro, 'See that he gets a horse. He leads us to glory.'

Serpienté got the message and flinched. His thighs were still not healed from his last ride.

30

Chaz dropped to the ground and crawled behind the nearest tree.

'What are you doing?' laughed Makhassé at the sight of Chaz peering anxiously down the valley and he laughed again.

'They must be an hour's walk away at least. Get up you look like.... Well, just get up. There's no danger up here.'

His face flushed, Chaz didn't rightly know how to respond, as he stood up.

'Err, I slipped on a stone,' he said, and he bent down and rubbed an ankle.

Makhassé realized that he had made a mistake laughing at Chaz so he said in a friendly tone, 'It's a good job you have ankle boots on then. A bad sprain or worse could be deadly up here, especially if you were on your own.'

Chaz nodded and decided not to take it any further, so he replied casually, 'Oh, it's feels okay. What are we going to do now?'

Then he ducked down as a loud boom echoed around the valley again.

They both turned and saw another cloud of smoke climbing up into the sky.

'You stay here and keep an eye on things whilst I go down and tell the others. Are you okay with that Chaz? I'll bring up your stuff, probably with Chuck's help. It will take some time though. It will be a lot slower than what we did carrying the backpacks.'

Makhassé paused for a moment, 'Hey, I bet you're as hungry as me?'

'Now you mention it, I am,' replied Chaz.

He looked around. 'There doesn't appear to be much round here though.'

'It's a good job I'm here then,' grinned Makhassé and he walked over to a big shrub, covered with conical, manky-looking fruits. 'This is a chirimuya tree,' he called.

They had a greenish-yellow knobby wart-like skin and he picked half a dozen of them before coming back and sitting on a convenient rock, cutting one in half with his knife.

'This will keep the wolf away from your door, isn't that what you say at home, Chaz?'

Chaz nodded and took the two halves of fruit while Makhassé cut into another one. He saw that the inside was creamy-white and dotted with large black seeds.

'Oh, one thing I should tell you.' Makhassé looked across to Chaz now perched on another rock.

'Don't eat those black seeds. They're poisonous.'

'What!' Chaz nearly dropped the pieces of fruit in his hands.

'Hey, hey, take it easy. You can eat it, no problem. Just the seeds, all right.'

And picking out the seeds in one of his fruit halves, Makhassé took a bite and began to eat it.

Chaz wasn't quite convinced.

Makhassé wasn't rolling around in agony holding his stomach, so he flicked out the seeds and tentatively took a small bite out of his.

It was delicious. A sort of pineapple-banana taste and nice and juicy as well though it was a bit sticky, so he wiped his hands on a tuft of grass.

A few minutes later Makhassé did the same after finishing off his other two fruits.

'I'd better be off then,' he said. 'You should be okay up here. We'll try to be as quick as we can, all right.'

Chaz nodded and sat down with his back against a rock, where he could keep an eye on both sides of the pongos.

31

Mendoza walked back and forth in front of the ruined ayllu huts. He was frustrated. It was taking too long to break camp. However, he had been in command long enough to know that sometimes you had to bend a little, even he. It was annoying to say the least but he knew that this was one of those times.

What with the attack, especially with the firing of the canon, the men were over excited and could soon become unmanageable if pushed too hard.

At last, Gonzales came over and bowed.

The cheeky little..... Mendoza swallowed hard and enquired with a sardonic smile, 'I trust that we are ready to move on?'

Gonzales hurriedly took a pace back. He had got the message.

'Capitán. Yes, we are ready for your esteemed order to mount.'

'Well then, what are you waiting for, idiot? Give Capitán De Orlando the signal to go.'

The plan was for the Cañari and Pedro along with De Orlando to lead the troops, with him in the center and Gonzales to take the rear position, behind the packhorses with the prisoners.

Mendoza hoped this arrangement would protect him best if the Inca attacked on the journey.

Seeing Gonzales waving his sword, De Orlando, who was already mounted next to Pedro and the Cañari, gave Pedro's horse a nudge with his boot.

'All right you two, lets get going.'

Pedro gripped the thin rope he held in one hand more tightly. It was connected to Serpienté's horse reins and he whispered quietly, 'By all the saints don't fall off or you will wish you hadn't.'

'Move it,' snarled De Orlando. He too didn't want to hear the wrath of Mendoza.

With a big sigh, Pedro spurred his horse into action and led the troop off back up the pongo, dodging trees and shrubs as best he could, using his sword to cut down low hanging branches when necessary.

Serpienté, despite the pain in his thighs, was looking out for a sign that would lead them to the masma (tunnel).

The horses found it difficult to weave in and out of the close undergrowth, especially when they climbed higher and had to scramble over uneven ground as well.

Mendoza soon realized that he was losing more time riding this way and called a halt. He ordered everyone to dismount and lead the horses by foot.

This actually suited Serpienté better since he hated riding the devil animals and had spent most of his time ducking branches and trying not to fall off.

He could see the lie of the land much better though he worried that he might not be going in the right direction. He might have missed the sign already. Fortunately for him, his mount followed docile and surefooted so he had no problem there.

Then he saw it.

A narrow fissure half hidden by large fern fronds was visible in a vertical rock face away to his right. A small stream dribbled down from it through a jumble of rocks, before disappearing into a muddy hollow not far from where he was standing.

The fissure, he could see, was wide enough for the devil animals to pass in single file, so he pulled hard on the reins of the suddenly reluctant mount and began to scramble up the rocky incline towards the opening.

Then Serpienté gave a gasp of surprise as he saw a carving on one side of the opening.

It was of a disc with waving lines radiating from the edges.

He dropped to his knees before the image of Inti the sun god and touched his forehead three times before uttering a prayer that no one could hear. Then he turned and called down to Pedro.

'Masma! Masma! Soon, near.'

Pedro had just made the sign of the cross for luck when he heard the Cañari call. He turned excitedly and waved to De Orlando and called out, 'Capitán, Capitán, pass the word, we have found it.'

Between the two, near vertical walls, the fissure zigzagged long enough for Serpienté to start wondering if he was in the right place. The trickle of water was hardly sufficient to wet the rock-strewn streambed and when it disappeared through a slot at the base of one of the walls, he felt a stab of fear.

He edged slowly to the dead end, the fissure narrowing somewhat. It also began to get darker and he looked up and saw that the gap at the top was nearly closed too.

In the gloom, a bat suddenly appeared out of nowhere and flew past his head chittering loudly. That can't be, it had to come from somewhere, and as he reached what he thought was the dead end, Serpienté gave a gasp of relief.

The fissure made a sharp left turn. In the dimness he had not realized that possibility.

A nudge in his back made him stumble. His mount had nuzzled him, probably as anxious as he was so he went on.

The floor of the fissure was now dried up and cracked in places, with plenty of rocks sticking up to trip the unwary, particularly those who found it difficult to see clearly in the shadowy cleft.

Apart from the clip-clop of the devil beasts and the odd clatter of the Conquistadors boots hitting a rock, there was no sound and Serpienté was starting to feel uneasy again. The fear of the wrath of the Capitán made his face sweat and he made a silent prayer to the Great Inti.

Then out of the gloom, a darker patch appeared. It was the mouth of a cave. The light from above was just enough for him to see that it had been lined with stone blocks.

This must be the masma, he thought, dropping to his knees in relief. *Uchu had been right about them.*

Suddenly a hand gripped his shoulder and the other patted his back.

Serpienté nearly collapsed in shock before he saw that it was the other Capitán.

'I don't believe it,' cried De Orlando, who had pushed his way forward when he too had seen the cave.

'Pedro, Pedro, go and tell the Capitán we have found the tunnel and to send three men with torches.'

32

Chaz was bored out of his mind, Makhassé had been gone for a couple of hours and it was getting warmer as the sun rose higher. He was also getting stiff. The rock he was leaning on seemed okay at first. He had actually dropped off for a bit. Well, hadn't he got up at some godforsaken hour.

He glanced up and down the valleys, nothing to shout home about.

Jeez what a life, he thought.

He picked up a small stone and tossed it wearily at a line of ants making a beeline for something or other that lay behind that strange fruit tree.

Not bad fruit though, then he remembered the black seeds, *Jeez, I could have bloody died.*

The stone was ill aimed and bounced off the tree trunk and fell behind another large rock with a funny sound, a sort of clink noise.

Chaz was bored enough to be intrigued and slowly got up to investigate what had made that unexpected sound.

Behind the large rock was a shallow pit in which a shiny object was half buried in leaf litter, it was some sort of helmet with what looked like some broken feathers attached to the top.

'Hey,' he said to himself, 'That looks like a good souvenir.' And he scrambled down in order to pick it up, jumping the last few feet.

To his dismay, the floor of the pit collapsed as he landed on it and with a scream of terror, Chaz fell through and down a dark hole, tumbling head over heels for what seemed ages.

Then, with a sudden breath-taking jolt he landed on a pile of dried up leaves as bits of the rotten woven matting that had covered the opening ages ago fell all over him.

He lay for a while gasping for breath before sneezing from the fine dust that swirled around his body. A gleam of daylight bounced off the sides of the narrow hole he had fallen through which he now saw had a series of ledges jutting out. These had prevented him from plunging straight down. Fortunately, his anorak and hat had protected him from serious knocks as he fell down.

Chaz got gingerly to his feet. Only his chest felt a bit bruised so he thanked his lucky stars for that and looked up at the hole above him. There was no way he could get back up through there.

A glint of light by his feet made him look down. It was the sodding helmet. He gave it a kick, 'Bloody hell,' he yelled aloud. It was heavy and hurt his toe.

Chaz bent down and picked it up. It was made of copper and gleamed in the weak light. It was heavier than he thought and when he tried it on, (a tight fit for him) he said, 'Jeez they must have had neck muscles like bulls.'

Then he sat down with a jerk remembering what had happened to him. Chaz had to bite his lip to stop it trembling.

This is getting too much, he thought. *To stay here was a big gamble. The odds of the others finding him were huge, so do something.*

To take his mind off these thoughts, Chaz had a

more thorough look round. He was in a tunnel that was dry and the floor relatively smooth with well-laid slabs of stone. The roof as he had surmised earlier, was too high to reach, so that was out.

The actual tunnel sloped down and that sort of made up his mind for him. *It is easier to walk down than up – QED* - he thought.

'Okay McDuff let's go.'

Then he paused. 'Idiot, idiot,' he scolded himself.

How the hell was he going to see when he left this part of the tunnel? It had the only light source for miles for all he knew.

He looked down at the pile of leaves and bits of woven reed. *Not much here,* he thought.

Then he noticed several small strands of green liana that must have blown into the pit. Picking up a piece, Chaz found that it was still pliable. *Maybe, just maybe,* he thought. *Why not, I've nothing to lose.*

So Chaz began to pick up the bigger pieces of reed and tied them into a bundle with the liana.

A lucky find of a thick stick but that will burn as well, was the obvious answer to that. Then he paused and smiled to himself and said, 'Why not.'

Even though there was no one around, Chaz went to a wall with the stick and holding it under one arm, unzipped his jeans. Then positioning himself, he didn't want to waste a drop. He urinated onto the stick.

Sure that it was saturated, he went back to where he had left the reed bundle and carefully shoved the wet end of the stick into it.

He sat back on his heels, feeling quite proud of what he had made. Then with a bit of a groan, (that fall was beginning to tell on him) he stood up.

Feeling his anorak, Chaz unzipped a pocket and took out his camping fire making stick. Small enough to hold in one hand, the ferro rod and steel striker was all he needed.

First though, he collected as much of the bigger pieces of reed as he could comfortably carry. He didn't know how long he might be in the tunnel, so just in case, tied them up with the remaining strand of liana.

Then ruefully he put the copper helmet on after stuffing his hat into his anorak pocket. He wasn't sure why but he did.

Holding the torch between his knees, Chaz struck the striker to the spark rod and in seconds he had a nice flaming torch.

33

'Are you sure this is where you left him?'

They had just arrived at the top of the pongo and had been shocked to find that Chaz wasn't there.

'I mean,' continued Esha, 'There is no sign of him at all is there?'

Makhassé nodded in agreement. Shouting had brought no response so he was as perplexed as anyone.

Mama Quylur Chaski had walked, somewhat wearily, to an open patch of scrub grass and squatted down, placing her bag and staff next to her. Then she closed her eyes and began to quietly chant a prayer for the safe return of Chaz.

'See,' Makhassé said, pointing to a flattened patch of scrub grass in front of large rock.

'That's where he was when I left him.'

''Yeah, I can see that someone has been here,' Chuck said, as he wandered around.

'Hey, look. I reckon that must be his walking pole,' and he walked over and picked it up.

The pole was by the big rock where they thought Chaz had been waiting for them.

'Now we know that he was here, what do we do?' Esha asked.

Makhassé beckoned to them to move over to where he had suddenly sat down, after taking off his backpack and leaving a polite distance from Mama Quylur Chaski who was still chanting.

'Come and make yourselves comfortable,' he said, patting the ground.

When they were all settled as best they could on the hard ground, Chuck threw out the question that had been puzzling them.

'Why the hell did he go off without leaving a sign or something?'

'Well we know he didn't come back down our way,' Esha said quietly.

'So, the obvious thing to do is go down this other pongo.'

'That's right for sure,' agreed Chuck.

'I reckon that if we start right away we might just catch up with him.'

'Right then,' Makhassé got to his feet.

'If everyone agrees, we go down the pongo, okay.'

Not expecting an answer, Makhassé picked up his backpack and slipped his arms through the straps and waited for Chuck to do the same.

To make it easy for them to carry Chaz's backpack, Makhassé had utilized an age-old method of carrying a heavy load, a thick pole through the backpack straps and long enough for the carriers not to crowd each other when each had one end of it on a shoulder.

The climb up the first pongo had sorted out the teething problems such as speed and how to navigate tight turns.

Esha had the role of using the machete when required, so she had led the way. Makhassé had agreed with that but said that she probably wouldn't need it as the Conquistadors had done a good job so far in clearing the way.

Mama Quylur Chaski quietly took up the rear position.

Makhassé had proved to be more adept in finding

the best way along the track made by the Conquistadors so he took the lead when Chuck called out that he was ready, happy with the added stability that Chaz's walking pole gave him.

34

'Go on, it won't bite,' yelled De Orlando, at the leading Conquistador who held a flaming torch in front of the tunnel opening and who stood hesitating, not sure whether to go in or not.

'Do you want to feel my sword up your backside? Move, dolt.'

The Conquistador cringed and glanced back to make sure the Capitán wasn't there behind him.

Reassured, he took a deep breath and slowly edged deeper down the dark tunnel.

The flickering, smoking torch cast a series of jerky shadows along the walls and caused a sudden eruption of thousands of sleeping bats to flee from their roosting area along the roof of the tunnel.

The chittering, flapping mass of flying bodies, all trying to escape by the tunnel entrance, totally unnerved the Conquistador and he turned and fled himself, dropping his torch in his panic.

He was fortunate that De Orlando was also so surprised by the sight of a cloud of bats streaming towards him, just as he was about to enter the tunnel.

Several of the nearest horses although blindfolded, heard the chittering and felt the rush of air of the passing bats and started to rear and kick in fear.

This also occupied De Orlando as he screamed orders to the men to calm the horses down.

Things settled down fairly quickly and the same Conquistador was ordered to proceed once again.

Knowing what to expect and holding his torch at a

better angle than before, well away from his body. He hoped this time it would stop any hot bits dropping down and burning his hand.

He went in again.

The torch was made from a short piece of bamboo, thin enough to be held comfortably and the top hollow part plugged about one third down with a blob of mud. Then shredded pine bark was pressed firmly down on top of it. He carried two more under his other arm as replacements.

The torch flickered in the air current and the smoke from it wafted up to the roof where countless smudges of soot gave witness to the passage of many other travellers. It gave enough light to see that the tunnel was quite high enough to walk upright.

De Orlando followed the light-carrying Conquistador, leading his horse by the reins. He had issued the order that all the mounts be blindfolded with bandanas, otherwise they would never have entered.

Pedro and Serpienté came next with the rest of the troop as before.

Not knowing how long the tunnel was had become a source of worry for De Orlando. He knew that Mendoza would not take any excuses for failure to find an exit from this diabolical passage. He also hated being in a confined space at the best of times.

'How long now, Cañari?'

'Soon, soon,' answered Serpienté with trepidation.

'You said that ages ago, cur. We have had three stops already to rest the horses and you still say soon.'

'Capitán! Capitán!'

The torch carrier had stopped.

'Look, look Capitán, another tunnel.'

The flickering torch cast shadows but towards the left, a much darker patch could be seen. A smaller tunnel, much narrower and less well made than the one they were following and it seemed to rise up away from them.

'What's this Cañari? You never mentioned another tunnel did you. Is this a trick?'

Serpienté gaped at the sight of it and fell to the floor.

'Capitán, I swear on the word of the Great Inti Uchu never said there was another tunnel. I swear I ....'

'Stop the drivel, cur ....'

'Capitán! Capitán!' the torch carrier shouted out hysterically.

'A monster, a monster.'

De Orlando sprung round, sword in hand as a sort of apparition appeared down the side tunnel.

It held a smoking torch that flickered so much it seemed to go out before a burst of flame shot up again in a puff of smoke.

Then they realized the figure was holding it well away from its body and they could see that it was a man, but what kind of man.

It was dressed in a magical costume, the like of which they had never seen before but the head was protected by an Inca noble's helmet.

Then it spoke.

'Can you help me, I'm lost,' Chaz said, trying to keep the smoke from the flaming torch from choking him to death.

Behind De Orlando, Serpienté gave a gasp of surprise and dropped to his knees, arms outstretched.

He had seen the bright red hair of the strange man.

'By the Great Inti, it is the Special One,' and he bowed his forehead to the ground several times.

De Orlando was at a loss. He looked down at the idiot Cañari bowing before this, this.... What?

The stranger had spoken like the Inca so the Cañari had understood what he had said. Probably like he understood and spoke Spanish, though not very well.

'Ask him where he came from?' demanded De Orlando.

Serpienté plucked up enough courage, to stand and in a quavering voice passed on the message to Chaz.

On hearing that the man had fallen into the tunnel, De Orlando relaxed. This was no spirit from the gods.

It was some buffoon or juglar that had come from afar.

Keeping his sword pointing at Chaz, he shouted loudly, 'Pedro! Pedro! Come here and take this el payaso to Capitán Mendoza and say that I think he should be put with the prisoners.'

Chaz cringed when a hulking Conquistador holding a great big bloody sword came forward into the torchlight and indicated that he go back down the tunnel, past what seemed to be hundreds of horses jammed tight one behind the other.

'Jeez, what the hell have I got myself into now,' he muttered to himself as he squeezed past a local native who suddenly started to protest to the big guy in charge.

De Orlando turned and snarled at Serpienté, 'Don't ever tell me what to do again,' as he used the hilt of his sword to knock him to the ground.

The Cañari squealed in pain as he fell and lay in a collapsed heap, out cold.

***

Mendoza was slowly building up to explode. The troop had been held up for ages and he didn't know why.

Added to that, the smell of the horses in the confines of the tunnel, combining with the acrid smoke from the torches and with practically no air circulating to clear the dank atmosphere, it was no wonder that he felt ready to run through the next one that crossed him.

He could just make out the shadowy figures and shapes of the men and horses in front and behind him, outlined by the flickering torches.

A commotion up front drew his attention and he saw two figures trying to squeeze past the line, the one in front lifting his torch up as high as he could to avoid catching either man or beast with the flickering flame.

Mendoza was astonished to eventually see Pedro, sword in hand, behind a strangely clad figure, wearing an Inca noble's helmet on his head.

Holding up a hand, Mendoza stopped the outlandishly dressed man.

'By all the saints in heaven Pedro, who the hell is this?'

'Capitán De Orlando sends his respects,' Pedro said as he sheathed his sword.

'This el payaso (clown) appeared out of nowhere.' And Pedro explained what had happened.

Mendoza looked at Chaz, who by now had realized he was in deep shit.

These buggers must be the ones that had killed every inhabitant of that village and of course the ones in that burnt out hut.

'So,' continued Mendoza, with a nasty smile forming around his lips. 'We have another prisoner to entertain us. Eh, Pedro.'

'Si, Capitán.'

Pedro was no fool and he gave a lopsided grin in agreement.

'All right then Pedro, you take this ... this,' he looked at Chaz and shrugged, 'To Gonzales at the back of the line and tell him what has happened. Oh, and tell him to make sure that this one can't escape.'

Pedro nodded and drew his sword before prodding at Chaz who promptly jumped away towards the back of the line, nearly dropping his torch in the process and joining somebody he knew as Gonzales. He was picking up Spanish quite fast.

Mendoza gave a sinister laugh and called out, 'Pass the word to Capitán De Orlando, we move on now.'

35

Who said life was easy. Chuck felt the sweat run down his face and couldn't do a thing about it. They were about half way down the pongo when Makhassé in the lead called out.

' I'm about to stop, Chuck, okay.'

'You bet, ready when you are.'

And they both slowly lowered the long pole threaded through Chaz's backpack onto the ground, before dropping their own.

'Aah, that's better.' Chuck had let go of his walking pole and flung himself down on to a patch of grass after a couple of stretches with his arms.

'I'll tell you one thing, Makhassé, I'm not coming back as a burro (pack animal) in the next life I can tell you.'

Makhassé smiled as he sat down, 'I think you're right. I shall be a truck driver.'

Chuck stretched out and put his hands behind his head. 'Yes siree, I might just join you.'

Mama Quylur Chaski and Esha came down the slope and sat with them.

'I have a few biscuits left and some lulos if you want some,' Esha said, and opened her backpack to get them.

They were gratefully received and after they had eaten, Makhassé passed his water bottle around.

They rested for a while, then Chuck went for a short walk. Nature calls wherever you are.

He was back in double quick time.

'Come and look at this,' he called.'

Through a gap in the ferns they saw a tree with a half cut branch hanging down and by the base of the tree was a pile of horse droppings.

'They must have been here,' Chuck said excitedly.

'Yes, but why are they going towards that mountain?' asked Esha, pointing to more cut branches leading to a steep rocky face in the distance.

That was when Mama Quylur Chaski went into a trance and collapsed down to the ground.

'What the heck,' said Chuck, looking round, then at her body which had begun to twitch and shake.

He and Esha watched with worried expressions as Makhassé walked quickly over to her and placed a finger gently on the side of her throat.

'Her pulse is okay.' He looked steadily at them and added, 'I think she is connected to Kausay Pacha, the spirit world.'

Esha and Chuck looked at each other but neither said anything. They had seen enough of Mama Quylur Chaski's special 'gifts' not to question Makhassé's explanation.

As they watched her, she suddenly sat up and opened her eyes, which were sort of glazed over. Then she smiled at them before looking up at the sky. A dark cloud of birds appeared out of nowhere and then Esha squealed, 'Look, they're not birds they're bats, millions of them.'

Chuck twisted round and saw them. Of course there were nothing like millions of them but it sure was a big cloud of them.

They flew around in a dizzy frenzy just above their heads until they all suddenly flew away.

That is except for one. It swooped down and to the surprise of everyone but herself it landed on the side of Mama Quylur Chaski's head, the hind claws gripping her headband so that the bat's mouth hung next to her ear.

'I don't believe what I'm seeing. No siree, I sure don't,' whispered Chuck. 'I wish I had my camera ready.'

Esha clutched Makhassé's arm thinking the same thing, as Mama Quylur Chaski nodded her head as though she was talking to the bat. Then in a blur of movement the bat had gone.

Mama Quylur Chaski reached for her bag which she had dropped a few minutes ago and took out her bamboo water container, removed the bung and had a drink. After replacing it back in her bag, she turned to them and said.

'The Special One is in the tunnels below us. He is safe for now. We must go that way,' she went on, pointing to a gap in the mountain away from where the Conquistadors had gone.

'I say, marm, begging your pardon but are you sure about that?'

Mama Quylur Chaski nodded.

'The mashu has seen him and saw which way he was going.'

'Mashu, you know. The bat,' Makhassé explained.

'Oh. That's all right then,' Chuck said doubtfully.

'Chuck!'

Esha glared at him.

'Err, sorry, I didn't mean to infer.....'

'Don't worry, Chuck,' Makhassé said gently.

'I know Mama Quylur Chaski hasn't been offended.'

'Now that's been settled, I vote we get on with finding Chaz. Oh, and what's this about him being the Special One?' Esha added.

36

Gonzales sneezed and wiped his nose with the back of his hand. The infernal smoke from the torches had thickened so much by the time it reached him and the others trailing the troop, that it made his eyes water.

What with the flickering shadows cast by the torch held by the last man in the troop just behind him, his smarting eyes and the two shuffling prisoners, their legs now hobbled because of that mad Capitán's orders and who kept falling behind, so that he had to keep prodding them to keep up with the packhorses, he was fed up to the back teeth.

A noise up ahead alerted Gonzales that something was happening and he squinted to see what it was.

A wavering torch, held high to avoid horse's heads, was approaching him. A comrade who was holding his sword materialized behind the outlandish figure as they squeezed past the line of men and mounts in front of him.

'Don't worry, Gonzales it's only me, Pedro, with a gift from our esteemed leader, some sort of an el payaso.'

Gonzales stared in astonishment at Chaz and his strange garb.

'Oh and make sure he can't escape or else our esteemed leader will not be amused.'

Pedro grinned as he passed on the message and took hold of Chaz's torch.

By all the saints in heaven, what have I done to deserve this, Gonzales thought as he turned to get a piece of thin rope from his saddlebags.

Inkasisa and Maichu, squatting on the floor, exhausted by lack of food (for all his faults that nasty Cañari had at least fed them regularly) and the amount of walking they had been forced to do, watched as the new prisoner's legs were hobbled by Gonzales.

Then he snarled, 'Get up.'

Chaz just looked at him, not understanding Spanish.

That was all Gonzales needed. All his frustrations were vented in the vicious kick that landed in the small of Chaz's back.

'Agh, you....'

Another kick in the same place silenced Chaz for a second and wincing in pain he rolled over and got to his knees before standing, holding his hands out in front of him.

'All right, all right, I get the message,' he said in Quechan.

He didn't let on that under his anorak he had earlier stuffed a wad of scrub grass because the rock he had leaned on was, as all rocks were, damned hard. He had forgotten all about doing it, what with all that had happened. The kicks had hurt but nothing like they could have done.

As Chaz moved away from Gonzales and more into the flickering torchlight, Inkasisa gave a gasp and nudged her brother.

'Look,' she whispered and pointed over towards the tall, pale-faced redheaded man.

'It's the Special One.'

Maichu just gawped, speechless, as a noise ahead indicated the troop had started to move again.

Pedro had already left to get back to keep an eye on

Serpienté. So Gonzales, somewhat mollified by his outburst and release of tension, snarled at the prisoners.

'Keep up or else,' before he turned to the last Conquistador in the line.

'And you keep that damn torch out of my hair, do you understand, cretin?'

37

Once they had agreed to continue the search for Chaz, they set off at a tangent to the track the Conquistadors had already made, towards the gap in the mountain that Mama Quylur Chaski said was the right way.

It was slow progress until Makhassé decided that a better way to carry Chaz's backpack was to pull it.

Chuck was dubious at first until he had seen what could be done with the bits and pieces of an A–frame made from different sized poles lashed together with thin plaited liana, made in double quick time by Mama Quylur Chaski along with a shoulder harness of the same material.

After a session in which Chuck had covered three times the distance in half the time as before, Esha had a go and was really surprised that she could do it, though not at quite the same pace as Chuck.

This left Makhassé the machete expert, free to clear a path through the trees and shrubs and this suited everyone fine.

They reached the gap in the mountain around mid-day and stopped for a well-earned rest and some food on the edge of a steep drop, more of a cliff that faced a low lying wetland glistening in the sunlight.

After a while Makhassé decided to go and examine the edge of the cliff. He wanted to see how awkward it was going to be to get down to the valley.

He was pleased to see that because it was the dry season, it would be possible to use the bed of a stream conveniently running in the direction they wanted to go, as a ready made, if uneven path.

This time Makhassé split the portage duties with Chuck and Esha kept company with Mama Quylur Chaski.

Fortunately the streambed, though rocky, had enough patches of small pebbles and suchlike amongst the larger rocks and boulders for them to pick their way without breaking their necks, though the poles that Chuck and Makhassé were pulling rattled and banged enough to make their hands and arms ache fairly quickly.

They found adopting a routine of swapping over every ten minutes helped.

After an hour or so of descending the switchback streambed, they stumbled onto a grassy bank and as one sank down, breathing heavily.

'Hey,' Chuck gasped, after taking a big swig from his water bottle.

'That sure was a heck of a trip. Yes siree. It certainly was.'

Esha was too busy taking off her boots to answer. The rocky walk had taken its toll on her feet. They ached like mad and it needed a liberal rubbing of a skin moisturizer to make her feel like her old self again. Only then did she nod her head in agreement before she too had a long drink of water.

Mama Quylur Chaski and Makhassé looked at each other and smiled.

Mountain walks came relatively easy to them though she did make a small concession and delving into her bag and took out her coca leaf and lime pouch and selected one.

A moment or two later a look of peace crossed her face as she chewed slowly and deliberately.

Makhassé just leant back on his backpack and closing his eyes, slowly relaxed.

It was only when Chuck decided to stretch his legs that he noticed a change in the landscape. The valley had levelled out and amongst the trees and ferns he saw a series of pools.

Makhassé, hearing Chuck get up, had followed him and said, 'The ground around here is much less rocky and so the land is holding the water longer. It's a good job that it's the dry season otherwise we would need a boat to cross this valley.'

Chuck pulled a face and said, 'From the look of things I think we should have brought our rain boots.'

'Well as long as you tuck your jeans in your socks you should be okay from leeches.'

'See, I told you we should have brought rain boots,' Chuck replied with a grin.

The others were now ready to carry on and Chuck followed Makhassé down to the streambed, still harnessed to Chaz's backpack A-frame.

Scrub grass up to their knees grew between a series of pools, some quite large and well wooded so that they seemed to go on into the distance towards a strange looking range of hills.

The humidity rose and the number of insects became noticeably more of a nuisance, the pools adding their share of nasty flies and mossies.

'I say,' Esha called out. 'Can we stop for a minute. I need to put some more anti-insect cream on.'

'That's a purty good idea, Esha,' Chuck called out, his sweat strewn face red from his pulling.

'If you have any to spare .....'

''Don't be silly, Chuck. As soon as I've finished you can help yourself.'

The brief pause was a welcome breather and they continued to make good progress across the now, rather soft ground. The continuous chatter of squirrel monkeys that seemed to inhabit most of the larger pool islands, echoed loudly across the water.

That was when Chuck, trying to cut a corner by a big tree fern that Makhassé had gone round, made his mistake.

A smooth green swathe of grass was on his side of the tree. It would save about one hundred metres Chuck estimated.

His foot went straight down into a sticky, smelly mud bog, cunningly hidden by the smooth green grass.

Chuck lost his balance but had the presence of mind to fall backwards. The A-frame, fortunately on the side away from it did its bit to save him as well. The weight of the backpack pulling him down helped to avoid a nasty situation.

Makhassé rushed back to help Chuck back to his feet.

'Hey, are you all right?' He asked in a worried voice.

Chuck slipped out of the harness and looked at his muddy foot and said, 'Well it sure could have been a lot worse. I suppose I was a bit lucky.'

He bent down and pulled up a handful of grass and cleaned off as much of the mud as he could.

Esha and Mama Quylur Chaski came up both showing concern.

'Sorry, Chuck. I should have told you to keep an eye open for these smooth green patches. They hide pockets of bog, some big enough to swallow two or three horses and leave no trace.'

'I think we should take five,' said Esha. 'Let Chuck recover from his fall.'

'Well....' Chuck began.

'Good idea,' Makhassé agreed, 'We could all do with a break anyway.'

So, moving away from the smelly hole Chuck had made in the bog, he slipped out of his backpack and sat down beside it.

The others sat or crouched as Mama Quylur Chaski invariably did, in a loose circle as she handed out sticks of charqui to them.

As they chewed on their snack, Mama Quylur Chaski pointed to the nearest pool, which like many others was big enough to have at least one island in it.

'Do you see those birds in the trees?' she asked, pointing.

'Oh yes, I can,' replied Esha.

'Aren't they pretty.'

They were quite big colourful birds, pheasant like, with long necks and small heads with a hairy crest. The unfeathered blue face had red eyes. The upper body was brown and yellowish below.

'They stay in the trees most of the time,' Mama Quylur Chaski added. 'Feeding totally on leaves. This means that they have a very smelly odour. Not nice at all.'

Makhassé looked over and said, 'Many people say they smell like cattle manure. Not for nothing are they known as the stinkbird or the flying cow.'

'And noisy critters too,' Chuck exclaimed, as a variety of hoarse calls, including groans, croaks, hisses and even grunts came from the island.

'Maybe that's because of those.' Makhassé pointed to several logs floating by the island.

Then, as they looked, one of the 'logs' opened its jaws. It was a caiman.

'They're probably on the lookout for chicks wandering near the waters edge,' added Makhassé.

As they watched them, there must have been at least twenty odd birds in the colony scrambling up and down branches. Mama Quylur Chaski casually picked up several hoactzin feathers, which lay in the grass by her feet and put them in her bag.

Makhassé suddenly leaned over and grabbed his machete.

'There's a bamboo grove over there. I'll cut a few down to top up our water bottles while we have the chance.'

'I'll give you a hand,' Esha said, getting to her feet.

'I'm glad that you can think ahead like that. If it were left to me, we'd all die of thirst.'

'I'm sure you're not as bad as that,' he replied, pleasantly pleased.

After they had replenished their water containers, Chuck had a good stretch and did a few knee bends.

He had decided that he was okay to carry on.

'I reckon it's time to hit the trail again folks, though I think we need to keep a bit further away from any pools we come across, just in case any of those critters fancy a bite of somebody's leg.'

Mama Quylur Chaski glanced quizzically at Makhassé, who smiled and gave a shrug.

People, he seemed to say.

She had got the message though and collected her

things as the others sorted out theirs.

'I know I don't need to remind you Chuck about nice flat green places,' Makhassé said, 'But keep in line with my track, okay.'

Chuck nodded as he adjusted the A-frame harness round his shoulders and looked down at his muddy boots.'

'I sure will,' he said with a grin.

'I don't want another mud bath today.'

After a while the terrain began to change again. The ground began to rise and it was much drier. The pools had gone and the trees and ferns were more spread out.

'Well, at least we don't have to worry anymore about those pesky insects,' Chuck said, wiping his sweaty face.

Makhassé nodded and began to explain why so little vegetation was around. It was because the rocks in this area were more permeable and so held little of the rain that fell.

They carried on, each one in deep thought until a turn in the valley brought gasps of surprise from Esha and Chuck. For the last hour or so, the vegetation had been getting much more sparse. Trees and shrubs had all gone.

Down the valley was a vista as from another planet. The terrain had totally changed again. Valleys and pongos were now largely clay and had been formed into a surreal landscape by eons of erosion caused by wind and rain. This erosion had also exposed hues and coloured minerals of beige, yellow and orange that glittered as they caught the sun.

'My God,' Esha said, 'There's no need to go to the

moon. Its here right before us.'

They were standing next to a dried up stream, which meandered down the slope. The rock hard mud-like bed, with hardly any stones or pebbles in it, was the best looking path they had come across for ages. It weaved amongst the towering spires and jutting turrets before disappearing round a bend in the pongo.

'I bet this is a raging torrent in the rainy season,' Makhassé said, 'And....'

He stopped speaking.

'Look, look,' he shouted excitedly. 'There. Right down in the valley, a dust cloud.'

'So, its a bit windy,' Chuck said smiling, 'I wouldn't mind a cool breeze myself either.'

'No, no, its not the wind. Horses have made that dust cloud. The Conquistadors are there, right there below us.'

38

The torch was burning low and the Conquistador holding it began to fret. It was the last one he had. The Capitán would have his hide if it burnt out before the end of the tunnel.

He began to hurry around a bend and sparks fell onto his gauntlet-covered hand but he wasn't too bothered by that. It was a change in the gloom in front of him. His shadow, bouncing and weaving from rocky nodules sticking out from the tunnel walls was suddenly more difficult to see.

He stopped and stared, then turned and shouted out excitedly.

'Pedro, Capitán, we are here. I can see daylight.'

'Out of my way, dolts'

De Orlando ran forward and pushing Pedro and the Cañari out of the way, saw for himself.

The tunnel opening was at first too dazzling for him to make out what lay outside.

Then he saw.....

By the saints in heaven, have we come to hell?

What else could he think? A grey mass of towering spires and pinnacles riddled with nooks and crannies lay before him, with not one bit of greenery in sight.

The exit of the tunnel sloped downwards, a track of crumbly dried clay between two sheer rocky walls, which was just about suitable for the horses to negotiate. It had a series of steps or ledges that had been worn away on the lip by rushing water at one time or other.

De Orlando had to make a decision and fast.

Pedro was standing behind him in the opening with the Cañari. They were holding his and their horses, all still blindfolded and they were blocking the exit.

Mendoza will go mad if there is an accident with the horses, he thought.

He called to the Cañari to remove the blindfold and lead his horse down the track making sure to be careful. If the animal was injured ... well.... he left the rest unsaid.

Squeezing against the tunnel wall, De Orlando watched as the Cañari and then Pedro went slowly down the stepped track and breathed a sigh of relief when they reached a more or less level part of it.

He looked up at the towering sheer walls the track threaded its way through and called out.

'Pedro, Pedro, if you reach a space big enough for the troop to sort itself out, stop there, all right.'

Pedro turned and waved in acknowledgement of his order and continued to follow Serpienté and his horse.

They plodded along the twisting, winding track between the soaring pinnacles and towering cliff faces split by erosive forces into countless vertical cracks all devoid of any plant life.

A feeling of sudden desperation struck Pedro. They had been walking for what seemed a long time. The long reach of Capitán Mendoza's wrath made him feel anxious so he called out to Cañari to stop.

'Are we near the type of place the Capitán wanted?' he asked hopefully.

All he got was a spiel of Cañari curses.

'What do I know. Uchu only told me a few things. After the tunnel he said there was a water hole, that's all I can remember. By the Great Inti, that's all.'

Pedro's heart sank.

'We go on then, maybe a little faster.'

Serpienté just shrugged and pulled the horses reins.

'We go,' he said and walked on.

Pedro sighed and made three signs of the cross and whispered to the Holy Mother of God to help him one more time – please.

Miracles do happen, thought Pedro as Serpienté stopped so suddenly that Pedro had no time to prevent his nose from being tickled by the backside of the Cañari's horse.

'Is this place Capitán wanted?' Serpienté asked.

The sheer sides of the pongo - gulch, Pedro didn't care what you called it, had widened into an open space, a kind of amphitheatre more than large enough for all of the troop to bed down in if they wanted.

'Praise be to all the saints in heaven.' Pedro smiled for the first time in days and issued a command to Serpienté.

'Go, go and tell the Capitán that we have found the place he wanted and go as fast as you can.'

Serpienté let go of the accursed animal's reins and with a brief nod of his head sped back the way they had come.

39

Mendoza had made his way forward when the troop stopped moving and stood with De Orlando at the exit of the tunnel, squinting in the daylight.

He was not pleased to see a narrow passage that threaded its way between high vertical walls that were a mass of cracked, jagged fissures, barren of vegetation.

The track was largely in shadow and the grey rocks were a depressing sight though he was amazed to see that where the sun shone on exposed rocks, a clash of vivid colours flashed and twinkled brilliantly.

'I see that you have brought me to a delightful part of the country, Alfonzo.'

Half expecting something sarcastic like this, De Orlando just nodded. Then he said, 'I'm expecting to hear from Pedro soon, Vicente.'

'Talk of the devil, I think I can see that little runt approaching,' Mendoza sneered.

Turning, De Orlando saw a begrimed figure covered in grey dust.

'Master, Master,' Serpienté called out, 'We found place. You come now? Yes.'

'Give the order, Alfonzo. I'm going on ahead.'

'As soon as you have gone, we will follow, Vicente.'

Mendoza stared at Serpienté. 'Lead on cur.'

Nodding, Serpienté cursed silently, mentally adding another poisoned dart to stick up the Devil Riders ..???

The dusty passage between the towering craggy walls twisted and turned but always journeyed downhill.

Mendoza was happy that he could at least ride, the

passage plenty wide enough for his horse. Then he realized that the animal was faltering. Its walk was becoming unsteady and breathing ragged. His mount was in need of water.

'By all the saints,' he cursed. He needed his horse alive so he called out to the Cañari to stop and dismounted.

The animal stood trembling, nostrils flared and the head dropped as Mendoza pulled the reins over its head and tried to coax it to follow him.

Water, we must get some water, he thought. God, if we lose the horses we are all dead.

'How far cretin, how far to Pedro?' He yelled at the Cañari.

Serpienté had got the message. He had seen animals suffer of thirst many times and he knew that his very future was at risk if the place where he had left Pedro was dry.

'Master, soon. Much soon, master.'

Mendoza gave the Cañari a withering look but said nothing.

Gently patting the horse's head, he pulled on the reins again and the animal responded and began to follow him.

By the saints I shall burn a hundred candles to the Blessed Virgin, when I get back to Saville, he promised himself, *if we get to a stream or pool.*

Serpienté led the way, more slowly this time and was mighty relieved when the narrow track opened out into the open amphitheatre shaped depression where he had left Pedro.

Along one side of it, the track continued down towards another narrow passage between more towering crags. Away from the track was a dip or hollow, which filled most of the place. On the far side several large clusters of prickly cactus were a welcome sight of colour, their bright green tubular stems around two to three metres high.

What interested Mendoza the most was the sight of Pedro sitting by a small pool that seemed, from where he was standing, to bubble up from the ground, then to run away as a small stream towards a fissure in the rocks.

'By the saints,' cried Mendoza at the top of his voice, 'I'll make it five hundred.'

Pedro looked over with a puzzled expression on his face.

Serpienté grinned a semi-toothless smile and did a little hop and a skip before going over to Pedro to get a drink from the pool.

He had to be quick. Mendoza's horse smelt water and with a jerk of its head pulled the reins out of his hands and eagerly trotted to the pool.

Pedro had already watered his and Serpienté's mounts and had moved them away from the pool and hobbled them next to the rocky wall where some of the cactus grew.

Mendoza watched with amusement as his horse, in its eagerness to get a drink, nudged the Cañari aside. He, his face buried in the water, had not heard the animal and so got the shock of his life when he nearly went for a swim, the last thing ever he would have wanted to do after his recent experience in the river.

The sound of many hooves clattering on the track made Mendoza look up from drying his feet. He was sitting on a convenient rocky lump by the pool, using his spare shirt as a towel and looking across the open space. He saw De Orlando leading the troop. *A scruffy lot too*, he thought as they appeared out of the dust cloud the horses had made.

He gave a casual wave and called out in what for him was a friendly tone.

'Alfonzo, tell Gonzales to make sure the men water the horses first and for God's sake don't let them stampede when they smell the water. Better put the bandana blindfolds back on, that should help.'

De Orlando waved back in acknowledgement and stopped where he was and shouted for Gonzales to move up from the rear with the prisoners.

Pedro was right. There was plenty of room for a camp and once the horses were watered and fed (the last of the feed, Gonzales pointed out to De Orlando), the men sorted out their own needs and necessities.

40

'What a place,' Chuck muttered as he spat out a mouthful of dust.

He was the last in line, dragging/ pushing the A-frame.

(Memories came to mind of having worked on a Wyoming dude ranch during his student days as a chuck wagon driver – a mobile kitchen - hence his nickname. That was where he learnt a few things about horses including the fact that a horse actually pushes with the harness (collar) round its neck above its shoulders.

The harness was beginning to chafe his shoulders. His idea of putting his backpack on it as well as Chaz's now seemed a bit stupid and he resolved to find some sort of packing to ease it. So he looked around and saw nothing that might be of use. In fact there was sod all as far as he could see.

The narrow clay track hemmed him in. It was obviously a water runnel in the wet season but dry as a bone now.

He gobbed another mouthful of dust.

'Mustn't have a drink yet,' he told himself.

He spied another group of spiky cactus growing at the base of the cliff-like walls.

Now they would sure make good padding and he chuckled to himself at his feeble joke.

His boots kicked up another cloud of dust and he began to have doubts about what they were doing.

How could they fight against a group of well-armed soldiers, yes siree, this sure is a mighty kettle of fish to solve.

'Hi Chuck.'

Esha had dropped back to see how he was doing.

'Here, have a drink.'

Chuck jumped, his musings over. The sound of Esha speaking had startled him.

'Oh, hi Esha. Sorry, I was miles away.'

Chuck stopped and took hold of the water bottle, sipped a little to rinse his mouth out and had a long pull.

'My, that sure was good. Thank you.,' he said, as he handed the water bottle back.

'Actually, I came back to tell you that there is a sort of bluff ahead.'

'What's that then, when it's at home?' asked Chuck wondering what it meant.

'I said the same thing to Makhassé and he said that it was either made by erosion or was maybe a landslip caused by an earthquake.'

'Yeah, but what is it?'

'Whatever caused it, probably yonks ago, made part of one side of the pongo fall down and disappear. Only God knows really. Anyway, you can now see forever over this part of the land. Well, not forever but you will see what I mean when you get there. Makhassé thought it might be a good place to have a rest as well.'

A short while later Chuck saw what she meant.

A towering, near vertical craggy side of the narrow pongo had gone, leaving a shelf like gap.

He did a double take as he dropped the A-frame harness not too far from where Makhassé and Mama Quylur Chaski were standing.

They were right on the crumbling edge of the track, a drop of at least two hundred metres by their feet.

There was a fantastic view over a mass of crags and

spindly spires that seemed to go on and on before rising up again.

'Sure is a mighty view,' Chuck said, rubbing his aching shoulders. He was definitely going to make sure that Makhassé did the next trick.

'What are you looking at?' Esha asked as she walked over to them.

Makhassé turned to her and pointed.

'Can you see an open space behind that funny shaped rock on top of the tallest pinnacle?'

Esha squinted and saw a deep depression amongst the tall jagged crags and what appeared to some animals moving around what might be a water hole.

But that seems unlikely in this area, she thought.

'It's too far to see properly,' she answered. 'What do think it is?'

'I'm pretty sure that is where the Conquistadors are camping.'

'How the hell could they be the ones we've been following. They're on the other side of the mountain, aren't they?' Chuck interrupted them.

'It's impossible for them to get here so quick.'

'There is a way,' Mama Quylur Chaski said quietly.

'I told you Chaz was safe in the tunnel. They have come out and they are down there.'

Chuck took a deep breath and decided not to say it. Too many strange happenings were going on and he found it difficult at times to get his head round them.

'Okay, okay,' Esha looked at each of them.

'Maybe Chaz is down there. Let's eat and rest a bit and think about what we have to do next.'

Chuck was already at his backpack before she had finished speaking, rummaging for something to eat.

They sat with their backs against the rock face as they ate, looking over towards what they now accepted was the Conquistador's camp, in a somewhat subdued manner.

A few ideas had been banded around for a rescue attempt but no one had come up with anything that was feasible.

Then Mama Quylur Chaski opened her Khapchos bag, took out her bronze knife and walked over to where a clump of cactus was growing out of a cleft in the rocks.

Choosing one of the smaller stems, she wrapped one end of her shawl round it to protect her hand from the sharp spines and cut it free. Then squatting down, she proceeded to shave off the spines.

The others were watching curiously, wondering what she was doing as she begin to cut the outer skin off one side of it.

Mama Quylur Chaski then began to cut several thin slices from the dark green flesh.

Satisfied that she had enough, she went back to her bag and took out a bundle of green leaves, picking one out and wrapping the slices of cactus flesh in it.

Placing the parcel of the sliced cactus on the ground, Mama Quylur Chaski went back to the cactus plant, rummaged around the base of it and grunting in pleasure, returned with three withered cactus stems.

Stopping to pick up her bag and the leaf parcel, Mama Quylur Chaski went to the edge of the bluff and placing them on the ground, squatted next to them.

She half turned and said to the now completely attentive group behind her.

'We have to make the Devil Riders move on. It

would be too dangerous to go to their camp. In these narrow pongos their fire-sticks would kill us. I am going to call on the God Apu to help us. Do not be afraid of what you see happening to me. Mama Pacha will protect me.'

'What the hell....?' Chuck began.

'Please Chuck,' Makhassé said quietly, 'Don't say or do anything from now on, okay.'

Chuck felt his face redden, so he just nodded.

They watched as Mama Quylur Chaski broke up the dry, withered cactus into small fragments and placed them in a hole she had made.

Then from her bag she brought out two small gourds and a handful of feathers and placed them next to her on the ground.

Next she took out her coloured headband with tiny feathers attached and fitted it on her head and then her chacapa nut bracelets which she slid onto her wrists. Finally she brought out her bronze mirror.

Satisfied she had everything ready, Mama Quylur Chaski used the bronze mirror to set the cactus kindling alight.

Chanting a short prayer to the Great God Inti, she opened the gourds and sprinkled a yellow powder from one and several drops of blood from a sacrificial virgin onto the flickering flames.

A plume of white smoke rose high up into the air and Mama Quylur Chaski began to shake her arms, rattling the bracelets, pausing only long enough to pick up the slivers of cactus. Putting them into her mouth she began to chew them.

Immediately her eyes rolled to and fro and her back arched. A loud cackle of laughter came from a foaming mouth as her body spasmed and writhed.

A loud exhortation came from her as she suddenly stood, arms wide and then a scream from a mouth dribbling red gobbets.

Mama Quylur Chaski collapsed back to the ground, writhing and chanting before she stopped to throw the handful of feathers into the fire.

A cloud of dense black smoke jetted into the air, filling the area and from it came a huge flock of birds.

Big birds and they were making such a racket. Caws, hoots and croaks. It was deafening.

Then they turned and flew unsteadily towards the Conquistadors camp.

'Goddamn,' cried Chuck. 'They're hoactzin birds. How the hell did they get here?'

'Let me check Mama Quylur Chaski first,' Makhassé said, as he bent down and felt her forehead.

'She's okay, though in a deep sleep, more of a coma really. The slivers of cactus contain mescaline and when she chewed them caused her to enter a state of elevated awareness. She became transcendent. Her spirit went beyond the physical existence. When she called up Kausay Pacha, the spirit world, her inner self was able to talk to Apu the mountain spirit and ask for his help.'

Chuck shook his head but said nothing.

Esha was fascinated by what she was hearing and nodded. She wanted to hear more.

'As you saw,' continued Makhassé, 'The hoactzin birds came to help.'

'Now come on folks, how on earth are those pesky birds going to help us against those Conquistadors?'

Makhassé smiled at Chuck and pointed across

towards the jagged peaks.

'Crikey, just look at that Chuck,' cried Esha.

A dark cloud was swirling over the Conquistadors camp.

41

De Orlando sat by the pool as the last of the troop watered his horse and led it to the temporary pen made of chopped down cactus stems.

The rest of the men had found nooks and hollows to settle down in and grab something to eat, what little there was being shared in a good-natured way. They were happy to be out of that diabolical tunnel.

He looked across the pool and saw Mendoza talking to Pedro.

That wasn't a good sign, he thought. *His man was becoming too close to Vicente.*

Pedro was not happy to be in the company of the Capitán, especially in the open like this. He wanted to be with his friends. Even the Cañari was better than not knowing whether he was going to be humiliated or not.

'I was saying,' Mendoza said impatiently, 'Where is this track going to?'

Pedro shook his head, *better to say nothing,* he thought.

'Well go and tell that Cañari piece of dog turd that I need to know if it will get us to the Inti Temple of Gold.'

Pedro turned pale. Serpienté had not said anything about where the Inti Temple might be and now the Capitán was demanding that he find out. By all the saints, if he couldn't get any answers he was doomed.

Suddenly there was a whirring in the sky above them. A dark cloud began to descend to the ground before turning into a frenzied swirling mass of birds, big birds that swooped and shrieked as they darted among both men and horses.

Then it hit them.

A stinking, putrid and nauseating smell enveloped the camp. It was so strong that men began to gag and wretch. Horses reared up kicking despite their hobbles and neighed in terror.

Mendoza jumped off his saddle and screamed, 'Clear the camp, mount up and clear the camp. Gonzales! Gonzales! For God's sake, get the men out of here.'

Slipping on his own vomit, Mendoza had to duck as several hideously smelling birds flapped awkwardly around him.

He picked up his saddle and scampered towards the horse pen, screaming orders to anyone he passed.

It took some time but it was only when the birds rose up and remained circling over the camp as though they had been told to keep watch over them, that Mendoza and De Orlando finally got the men to settle the horses enough to saddle up and load their equipment so that they could leave this foul smelling, vile place.

For the next hour or so the troop fled down the narrow pongo track, hemmed in between the near vertical sides.

Serpienté clung to the neck of his mount as it picked its way along the twisting track.

It was breathing hard and white froth oozed from its muzzle. The neck was sweaty and slippery and he was terrified that he might fall off and get trampled by Pedro's horse just behind him.

Gradually the pongo began to open out.

The sides were a lot lower and the track wide

enough for Pedro to ride alongside the Cañari, as they zig-zagged through a jumble of craggy outcrops down towards the end of it.

Behind them, De Orlando like many of the others was still trying to make sense of what had happened. His first need though was to get rid of the horrendous stink from those birds that somehow still clung to clothes and skin.

A shout from Pedro jerked him to the present.

'We can see a river head,' his voice echoed.

'It's in a new, bigger pongo.'

De Orlando looked down a slope that was covered with scrub grass and small shrubs and which levelled out alongside a wide rock strewn riverbed. The river was more of a trickling stream.

Then he remembered it was the dry season.

Praise be to the Gods, he thought and spurred his still skittish horse forward.

***

Mendoza lay sprawled on his vicuña cloak, head against his saddle, chewing on a charqui meat stick.

A wash in the freezing water of the river and a change of clothes had worked wonders for his moral. It had even tempered him enough to allow his men to do the same and get rid of that stinking smell on their clothes and wash them as well.

He sniggered as he threw his own stinking clothes to the Cañari and ordered him to wash them not once but twice.

'Alfonzo,' he called across to a similarly reclining figure, 'I think we can camp here for a while. Eh.'

'Excellent idea Vicente, the horses need to recover

too. Luckily there is fodder for them as well.'

Mendoza leaned back on the saddle. Then he began thinking. *The Inti Temple of Gold, how far away is it?*

'Gonzales! Bring the woman prisoner. I want to question her and tell Pedro I want to see the Cañari.'

42

Gonzales heard the shout and hurried to obey as soon as he had told Miguel to give Pedro a message. He drew his dagger and went over to where Inkasisa, Maichu and Chaz were lying on a mossy mound beneath a leafy shrub with their feet bound.

They were soaking wet. Like the others, they had picked up the stinking smell of the hoactzin bird and not taking any risks with them trying to escape, Gonzales and a couple of his friends had thrown them in the river to get rid of it.

'Ha, my wet fishes are still squirming. I give you a knock on the head, yes.'

He cackled at his own joke.

They looked up at him shivering in their wet clothes.

Maichu spat at Gonzales and said in Quechan, 'By the Great Inti, your turn will come, I swear...'

A cuff behind his ear put an end to his curse.

'Maichu, Maichu,' Inkasisa, cried out and leaned over to comfort him but he shrugged her away, his eyes burning with hatred.

Chaz looked on in amazement. He still couldn't get his head round the fact that he was a prisoner of a vicious group of mercenaries.

He had only spoken a word or two to others, a princess and a prince. Jeez, who would believe him, hobnobbing with them.

Then he saw the knife held by the hulking Conquistador poking at the princess.

Now he saw reality.

'You,' Gonzales pointed to Inkasisa.

'Are to come with me,' and he untied her feet before roughly dragging her away to the Capitán.

'Ah. The Princess. I see that you are getting well looked after, though I would recommend taking your clothes off before bathing, eh, Gonzales.'

Mendoza sneered his usual leering smile.

Gonzales looked at his Capitán and saw the nod that meant that it would be all right to join in.

He laughed like a hyena.

Mendoza nodded again.

'Now go and tend to the other carrion, Gonzales.'

Gonzales face dropped.

'Of course, Capitán, right away, right away.'

'Well then. Go, go.'

Mendoza sniggered as he watched him scuttle away.

Just like a caiman, thought Inkasisa, looking at his teeth with a shiver, not all caused by her wet clothes.

'Sit,' he indicated the ground in front of him.

Inkasisa knew enough Spanish to comply.

That white-faced shaman with the ring of hair, wearing a hooded punchu and a string of beads with a cross on it, had taught the noble's children in the palace for the past three seasons. She had done her best not to let this devil rider know that.

Mendoza went on, 'We wait for the Cañari.'

Inkasisa squatted (like most Inca she never sat). At the word Cañari she looked up and nodded.

Well, at least she got the word Cañari, thought Mendoza. *It's a start anyway.*

Serpienté arrived cowering as usual.

Mendoza pointed to Inkasisa.

'Ask her to tell me the way to the Temple of Gold.'

With a little bow Serpienté repeated the question in rough Quechuan.

Inkasisa now knew that there was no point in trying to lie. The way this white-devil had tortured her servants was proof of that.

So, taking a deep breath and praying for forgiveness from the Great Inti, she told him.

'You need to follow this pongo for most of a day and then you will see that the valley becomes much wider. The river there goes around a hill on which the Inca have built a pucará (fort). The river then passes through another pongo and enters a qucha (lake). The temple is on an island in the middle of it.'

Inkasisa then flung her arms to the sky, crying pitifully, 'May all the Gods save my spirit from darkness.'

Immediately Serpienté had finished repeating the directions, Mendoza jumped to his feet and shouted, 'Bravo, bravo,' with a big grin on his face.

'Take the prisoner back to Gonzales,' he ordered and turned and shouted to De Orlando who was dozing by his saddle.

'Alfonso, Alfonso, get over here, we have some planning to do.'

Then he called to Gonzales who hurried over with a worried expression on his face.

'Tell the men we are here for the night. We will break camp as soon after dawn as you can get the lazy louts on their feet. Oh and make sure that all the horses are well fed. It will be a long day tomorrow and I don't want any delays. Or else....'

Gonzales grinned in relief.

'Understood Capitán,' he said, as he walked away.

Now I wonder if Pedro has a gourd of chicha hidden away in his kit and his pace quickened.

43

'Should we go and see what's happening.' Esha asked, 'I mean. Would it be dangerous?'

'I would say not,' Makhassé replied thoughtfully.

'Not dangerous as such because I think the Conquistadors will have gone by the time we get down to their camp. From what I have heard about stinkbirds they are bad enough even in small numbers. Apparently people can't stand the smell if they get too close. From what we saw, the flock must have been of several hundreds at least. So just imagine what a stink that lot would make. Yes, I'm pretty certain they will be gone.'

'In that case I vote we saddle up,' Chuck said, 'Err, you know, make tracks. Move out.'

'Okay Chuck, I think you've made your point,' laughed Esha picking up her backpack.

'Right then, can you give me a hand with the A-frame harness Chuck?' asked Makhassé, a slight smile appearing around his lips.

Chuck bounded forward grinning, 'You bet. Just hang on a second while I adjust the straps for you.'

Once Makhassé was fixed up and Mama Quylur Chaski had checked everything was in her bag. Chuck took the lead, making good use of Chaz's walking pole as he adjusted to the different weight of Makhassé's heavy backpack.

They left the open bluff and entered the narrow track, squeezed between the two near vertical sides of the pongo.

Like before, it twisted and turned as it went down the mountain, sometimes in shadow and sometimes passing beneath a glittering kaleidoscope of colours as the sun reflected off the different minerals in the rock face.

Eventually they reached the Conquistadors campsite. It came as quite a surprise, a large open space among the jumbled mass of crags and jagged pinnacles.

There was a pool to Esha's amazement. Of course they wouldn't have stayed if there had been no water she realized.

By now there was no obvious smell to indicate the stinkbirds had ever been near there, to everyone's relief.

In fact there was little evidence that a camp had been here at all, the ground being rock hard.

Then Chuck spotted a metal gauntlet by a pile of cut cactus stems, bits of fodder strewn around and several tell-tale piles of horse droppings.

'That must have been the paddock for the horses,' Chuck announced confidently and then he smiled at them.

'I bet you got that too.'

Makhassé dropped the A-frame harness and stretched his arms out wide. 'Now I know why mules don't want to go anywhere with a load on their back.'

'Practice, practice, that's all you need Makhassé,' said Chuck with a big grin. 'I feel a lot better for what I did yesterday, so don't knock it.'

'Well in that case you can take over the next shift.'

'Hey, I'm not falling for that one. You obviously need a bit more exercise Bud and I for one am sure that you will get it.'

Makhassé waved a friendly hand in defeat and said, 'Okay, you win. Now can we get on with something to eat, I'm hungry.'

Mama Quylur Chaski had been looking around and came back and said that some of the cactus stems were suitable to make a fire and that she would make some stick bread.

Not too far from the pool, Makhassé scooped out a fire pit and while Mama Quylur Chaski took out a couple of the big leaves and a small skin sack of corn flour from her bag and went to the pool to mix a dough, he used his knife to slit some of the cactus stems to the central hardwood core. These would be used to hold the dough near the flames and to the surprise of many, cook tasty bread, especially after Mama Quylur Chaski included some of her herbs.

'Ummm, it's so nice to eat something hot,' Esha said, blowing on the nicely browned stick bread and taking another bite.

Chuck nodded in agreement as he finished off his share and bit into a strip of charqui.

Mama Quylur Chaski rounded off the meal by passing around a handful of lulos, the juice of the fruit gratefully appreciated by them.

It was decided to spend the night there and Makhassé reminded them that since they did not have much daylight time left, they had better be quick in setting up their bed-space etc.

44

The air was damp, a cool mist hovering over the riverbank and the Conquistador camp as the first rays of the morning sun tried to punch a hole in it.

Mendoza stuck his head out of the simple tent Gonzales had made between two shrubs and shivered before retreating hurriedly back inside it to finish dressing.

He strode out shortly after, buckling his sword belt on and bellowed for Gonzales who came dashing up, his shirt-tail flapping behind him.

'Tell the Cañari I want some hot gruel for breakfast pronto. By the saints, this country's weather would make all of them swear.'

Gonzales nodded and scuttled off to deliver the order as Mendoza turned and disappeared behind the shrubs to do his mornings ablutions.

***

It was quite a while before the troop was ready to proceed. The horses had to be fed and watered, then the men themselves. Equipment was checked one more time and Mendoza thought it practical to wait for the mist to clear anyway.

As before. Pedro was ordered to ride with the Cañari alongside De Orlando at the front, with Mendoza in the middle and Gonzales with the prisoners at the rear, following the pack animals.

Satisfied at last that they were ready, Mendoza gave the order to move and the trek began to snake down to the more or less dried up riverbed. It was composed of small stones and gravel, quite flat with the odd boulder dotted here and there and meandered between the sheer red-brown cliffs of the pongo.

It was good terrain for the horses and they made good going during the morning.

As they rode down towards the lower end of the pongo it also became more humid.

The vegetation began to thicken and grow taller. This pleased Mendoza since it meant that fodder for the horses would be easier to find.

Just in time, he thought. Another day in that peculiar, craggy wilderness would have been the end. Also one more thing, because this pongo was wide enough to ride in pairs, the men were in a much better humour, being able to talk with a comrade as they rode.

Mendoza's reverie was ended when De Orlando came galloping back up to him, his face troubled.

'Steady, steady, Alfonzo. What's the rush?'

'Vicente, I have told Pedro to stop. I think there is trouble ahead. The Cañari says that he remembers Uchu saying something about a pucará. You know an Inca fort.'

'Of course I know about the fort. The Princess told me about it. Don't fret about it Alfonzo, there's no need to worry.'

'No, Vicente, that's not it. The Cañari said that Inca warriors have a control post across the river. Nobody, he says, can get past without Inca permission.'

Mendoza's face became a mask and he said in a dangerously quiet voice.

'We will see about that. Mark my words, Alfonzo, we will see about that.'

Spurring his horse to a trot, Mendoza rode to the forward position, followed by a worried De Orlando.

They found Pedro and the Cañari resting under a convenient overhang in the rock face, in the shallows of the river, cooling their mounts' hooves.

'I've a good mind to have you horsewhipped,' snarled Mendoza.

'Why did you not tell me about the Inca warriors before, you ignorant cur?'

Serpienté practically fell off his horse and grovelled on his knees.

'Master, Master, I no remember till I get here and see the cuntur (condor) flying over the pucará (fort). See Master, see,' said Serpienté pointing.

Mendoza turned and saw what he had missed in his rage to get to the Cañari.

The pongo had begun to open out and the river had filled up again somehow. A rope bridge had been strung across with several armed Inca patrolling it.

Circling high overhead were three giant condor birds.

Waiting. Waiting for what?

He could also see a series of terraced fields etched in the side of a steep hill and the semi-dry riverbed he was standing in was joined not far away, by a fast flowing river emerging from a small side pongo.

And overlooking everything was the Inca stone fort.

Mendoza had not got his command for being indecisive and he snapped out an order.

'Pedro, go and tell Gonzales to get the troop to dismount and check all weapons.'

He turned to De Orlando.

'It would appear that we will have to force our way

past this check point, Alfonzo, and seize the fort. Otherwise they will harry us all the way to the Temple of Gold. See to the Falconet will you. I'd like that bridge taken out to stop any possible reinforcements coming from that side of the river.'

De Orlando nodded and rode back to organize the cannon team.

***

Hualpa was bored and his padded tunic itched like mad in the hot sun. The rope bridge swayed as a gust of wind, not even cool enough to be welcome, buffeted the structure.

His bone-tipped spear rested on the footboards of the bridge, his hands clasped high enough to rest his forehead against them.

He stood, leaning on his spear for a while daydreaming, then he decided to walk back across to the command side of the bridge to see if his friend Kunak had left a spare gourd of chica by one of the bridge anchor stones.

'Hualpa. I say, Hualpa.'

A guard standing in the middle whispered to him as he got near. 'What do you think is happening up there?'

Wondering why he was whispering, he looked upriver and gripped his spear tightly in shock.

Where the two rivers met he could just see a group of figures coming down from the upland pongo side, the like he had never seen but by the Great God Inti he had heard of them and the horror they brought to his country.

The Devil Riders, they must be the ones, he thought. *They were riding the beasts from the spirit world.*

'Sound the alarm! Sound the alarm!'

Haulpa screamed as he heard a boom of thunder, though there were no clouds in the sky.

The guard raised his conch shell and had blown three times before the cannon-fired shot, consisting of scores of gravel stone pellets, shredded the bridge and all who were on it.

It was enough. Like an army of ants, the warriors of the fort began to surge down to the river, led by the fort commander easily recognized by his copper feather-festooned helmet and colourful padded tunic.

Mendoza watched in satisfaction through the smoke of the cannon as the rope-bridge jerked and shook with the impact from the shot and split in two.

Those Inca guards still alive screamed in terror as they fell into the water. None could swim and further down river, caiman would deal with them, dead or alive anyway.

At the sound of the cannon and as the cloud of smoke thinned around it, the Inca warriors who had rushed down towards the bridge faltered and stopped as the bridge was cut in two, as they thought by angry spirits.

A howl of fear echoed around the valley. Many of the warriors fell to their knees calling for the Great God Inti to save them. Others turned and ran back to the safety of the fort.

'Now's our chance,' Mendoza shouted and he drew his sword and gave the order for Gonzales to lead the troop across the river where the two rivers joined, calculating that it would not be too deep there.

He was proved right.

Then, as the horses splashed their way to the riverbank, Gonzales spotted a wonderful opportunity.

The terraced strips used to grow food would make it easy for them to climb up to the fort.

They were a ready-made set of giant steps.

'Pedro, Juan, follow me,' he cried as he spurred his horse up onto the first level and rode towards a group of kneeling praying Inca warriors, their weapons by their side.

As more and more made the terrace, Gonzales was seen swinging his sword to and fro like a maniac.

His first kill was the commander in the copper helmet, jabbing him in the throat.

Then slashing and cutting he felled several more of the kneeling warriors before they realized they were being attacked.

To the astonishment of Gonzales, the rest of the Inca warriors stood up and just stared at him and the Conquistadors towering high above them on their horses. Not one bent down to pick up a weapon.

He was unaware that the Inca thought they had been sent by the Gods.

'Spare no one,' Gonzales cried.

'By all the saints in heaven, this is our day. Not one,' he cried again, swinging his sword.'

Level by level the troop moved up the terraces, the horses now nimble enough to cope with the narrow strips, slaughtering every Inca they saw.

Down below, on the far side of the river, Mendoza was in raptures.

'See Alfonzo, they cannot match our fine Toledo steel, eh.'

De Orlando was not so sure that this was all

necessary but when Mendoza ordered the cannon to be trained on the fort, he complied.

Was he not a soldier of Spain?

He helped Miguel set the sight as Anton made ready the shot.

The cannon boomed and a shattering crash came from the fort as a cloud of dust enveloped it.

When it settled a jagged hole could be seen in the wall.

'Bravo Miguel, bravo Anton, magnificent shot.'

Mendoza clapped his hands and then said, 'Ha, can you see them run Alfonzo, can you see?'

De Orlando could see all too clearly.

The warriors who had taken refuge in the fort were now streaming out, running anywhere to escape the spirits' bite and especially the sword-swinging devils, riding on the beasts from the underworld, who were cutting down every screaming Inca within reach.

***

The smell of death was everywhere. Along the ayllu terraces bodies lay sprawled in grotesque shapes, many decapitated.

Inside the perimeter wall of the fort, the mutilated corpses from canon fire were already being eyed by circling condor vultures.

A waft of smoke from the burning huts inside the fort made Mendoza cough and his eye began to smart

He had seen enough. The threat from these Inca was no longer to be feared and he was anxious to be on his way again.

The gold was near. He could feel its presence.

'Come Alfonzo, let's get away from this butchers

yard, the smell is getting annoyingly offensive.'

Then, as he mounted his horse, he yelled across to Gonzales who was searching a body for anything of value.

'I hope you made sure the men got enough food and fodder from the Inca stores before the fires were started?'

Gonzales jerked upright. He had not seen the Capitán coming.

'All done Capitán. Pedro and Juan have just taken the last packhorse down to the river.'

'Good. Good. Make sure everyone is down there soon; we eat first, then press on. See to it.'

'Yes, Capitán, I will.'

'Now Alfonzo, was I right in seeing that lazy cur the Cañari carrying several gourds of chicha a while back?'

'I believe so Vicente and that smoke down by the river is, I think, something cooking.'

Serpienté had made a fire on the far side of the upper pongo riverbed, where the two rivers met. The gravel-like stones were level enough to make a suitable place for a campfire.

From the Inca fort's stores he had made chuñu gruel with cuy (guinea pig) meat and flat bread, the chicha being the finishing touch.

Splashing through the shallow water of the river, the Capitan's dismounted and after removing their saddles, used them as seats by the fire.

A very attentive Serpienté brought over the chicha and scuttled away to take the horses to a temporary holding corral.

'A good afternoon's work, eh, Alfonzo,' Mendoza grinned as he took a long drink.

45

After an early start, it began to get warmer the lower they went and more vegetation began to appear which was a welcome relief from the stark, arid nature of the moonlike landscape that lay behind them.

The pongo eventually widened into a shallow valley with slopes covered with scrub grass and small shrubs, which dropped down to a semi dried-up riverbed.

'It's a good job this is the dry season,' Makhassé said, looking at the gravel-sized stones largely exposed by the shrunken river.

'We can easily walk down it.'

He loosened the A-frame harness and shrugged it off before sitting down on the riverbank, taking off his boots.

'Just a little paddle,' he said, 'Before we make camp and have something to eat.'

Chuck had already offloaded his backpack and sat down with a big groan.

'I'm getting too old for this sort of thing....'

'What?' laughed Esha, taking off her backpack.

'A fit young fella like you.'

Chuck was pleased with the compliment and grinned at her and said, 'Well, I'm more used to carrying things with my heli.....' then he stopped as he recalled the mangled remains of his crashed helicopter.

'Oh, hell, sorry Chuck, I never gave it a thought.' Esha felt awful at reminding him.

'No, it's all right. It was insured... I think.'

'Chuck!'

'Just kidding, Esha, just kidding. No need to get your proverbial's in a twist.'

Makhassé came back and dried his feet and said as he put his boots back on.

'I think we might as well press on as soon as we have rested. I know Chuck is dying for more exercise with the A-frame.'

"Funny guy now are we,' Chuck said laughing as he threw a clump of scrub grass at him.

'Two can play at this game,' Makhassé said, and he bent down and then stopped.

'Hey, look at this.' He held up a 50 centavos coin dated 2015,'

'My God, I bet that was dropped by Chaz,' yelled Chuck.

'Dammit, we must be on the right track.'

'Hold on Chuck,' Esha said quietly, 'After what has happened to us, I think you're right but let's not rush into things, okay.'

'Well.'

Makhassé rubbed the coin between his finger and thumb as though it might disappear at any moment.

'I still think that we should go on as soon as we can, especially after this. And tossing the coin into the air, he passed it to Chuck.

'Here,' he said. 'You keep it and give it to Chaz when we catch up with him.'

'I sure will,' Chuck said with feeling.

'I reckon he needs our help and soon. You're right in what you say.'

Mama Quylur Chaski had just returned from her sortie among the shrubs, looking for more of the herbs and seeds that helped her invocations when speaking to the spirits.

'My inner guide is troubled and I feel that we must try catch up with your friend as soon as we can.' She said with a sense of foreboding.

***

It was late afternoon when Makhassé saw the meeting of the semi dried-up riverbed with a fast flowing river emerging from a smaller pongo on his right.

Then the smell hit him.

He looked across the now widened river and saw a small hill with cultivated terraces rising in tiers from the dangling remains of a rope bridge, up to a stone Inca fort.

The terraces were full of mutilated Inca warriors, their bodies now covered with squabbling vultures, huge beaks jabbing in and out, some hopping from one body to another, with wide-open wings flapping, hoping to find a way in.

It was a nauseating sight. More condors were circling above the fort, waiting for their chance to join the feast with more on the way.

It was too late for Makhassé to warn the others, they had already smelt the odious reek of dead bodies. And both Chuck and Esha puked as soon as they saw the heaving mass of vultures tearing at the bodies.

Mama Quylur Chaski immediately sank to her knees and began a chant for the spirits of the dead to be safe in the world of the afterlife.

Makhassé took a deep breath, these people were after all his ancestors and he made a silent vow to avenge the Conquistadors who had committed this horrendous atrocity.

'We have to go on,' he said in a strangely quiet, yet disturbing way and the deeply shocked group made their way slowly along the riverbank, not noticing the still smouldering remains of a small fire.

46

The fast-flowing river was fortunately shallow enough for the horses to walk through and barely wetted his boots as Mendoza led the troop away from the carnage.

As they followed the river round the back of the hill he was pleased to see that more and more of the riverbed was exposed as the water level suddenly dropped. Before long there was only a narrow trickle along one bank and progress became much easier and quicker down the pongo.

Mendoza wasn't so pleased with the encroachment of the thickening vegetation along the riverbank. He decided to send Pedro and the Cañari ahead, just in case any Inca were around.

Pedro wasn't amused with this new role. In fact he was getting a little tired of being given a job with this little runt who pretended to be a good servant to the Conquistadors. Couldn't the Capitán see that?

Still, he did have his uses. Though he wouldn't go blabbing on about it to Gonzales in particular.

Serpienté for his part was reasonably happy at the moment. He was leading his mount along the riverbed, avoiding the larger rocks and padded in his bare feet through the odd pool without a thought.

Chewing on one of the coca leaves he had grabbed from a handy bush might have encouraged his good mood, though he wished he had some lime to mix it with to make it less bitter.

Then Pedro came up and spoilt his day.

Mount up, he indicated.

Serpienté cringed. An imaginary pain shot through his thighs. *By the Luna spirit, no,* he thought.

A cuff round his ear brought him back to the real world.

'Master, master, I go,' and he hauled himself onto his horse.

'Follow me,' rasped Pedro.

'And keep up.'

The riverbed twisted and turned through a mass of over-hanging branches from which swarms of insects attacked them as though they had not been fed for days.

Pedro's face was red from the slaps that he inflicted on himself. Even Serpienté who normally wasn't bothered by them, began to curse the constant irritating biting, crawling pests. So he slid off his horse before Pedro realized and disappeared into the dense undergrowth.

'Hey, come back,' Pedro yelled at the top of his voice. Then, with a curse of his own, he jumped down off his mount and chased after the Cañari with his sword drawn.

Then he stopped. Serpienté was kneeling by a tall tree. It had large, heart-shaped bright-green leaves with white flowers on long stalks.

As he watched, Pedro saw the Cañari use a small bone knife to cut into the bark of the tree. A dark red sap began to ooze out. Quickly, Serpienté snapped off two of the big leaves and then began to scrape off the sap and save it on one of the leaves. When he decided that he had enough, he rolled up the leaf and then wrapped the other one round it. A short piece of liana tied it firmly together.

Then before Pedro could say anything, Serpienté collected a handful of the still dripping sap and rubbed it over his face and then his body.

Pedro must have made a noise and Serpienté turned and saw him.

'Good, good,' he said, grinning his half toothless smile and made a buzzing sound as he wafted his hands around his head.

'By the saints in heaven, give me some now for God's sake,' Pedro said, as he tried unsuccessfully, not to scratch his face.

A while later, a relaxed Pedro sniggered at the sight of the Cañari, his skin a blotchy mass of dried sap. He knew he looked the same but didn't care. The damn stuff worked. The insects kept well away from him and that was all he wanted as they rode on.

The towering mountains on both sides of the pongo seemed to reach up to heaven Pedro thought idly as they made their way down the winding riverbed, still hemmed in by the lush vegetation and praise be to the saints, with no sign of the accursed Inca.

Then the Cañari called out, in a hoarse whisper to stop.

Pedro jerked up, fully alert and stood up in the stirrups reining in his horse and looked around.

'What is it? Why did you say stop.'

Serpienté shook his head and dropped down to the riverbed and indicated to Pedro to follow him on foot.

Tying the horses to a shrub as quickly as he could, Pedro drew his sword and half bent, followed the Cañari who was creeping slowly towards a sharp bend in the river when he suddenly stopped and turned, his eyes wide in shock.

Pedro couldn't believe what he saw. The half dried-up river had widened out and had become a pool that drained over a precipitous drop.

The trees of the pongo had hidden a huge rift in the valley floor some hundred metres or so below where he was now standing.

He made his way along the side of the pool until he could see over the edge of the waterfall and saw that a rough track zig-zagged down to another pool from which the river renewed its journey down a just visible valley, to a large lake.

Pedro also noticed a ruin on a rocky outcrop not too far from the bottom pool. It looked like an abandoned Tampus. A large semi-circular stonewall with one narrow entrance protected a group of huts, all without roofs.

'By the saints,' Pedro turned to Serpienté with relief. 'We could have been trapped up here. Praise the Lord, we weren't.'

He looked at the Cañari and said quietly, 'Back to the horses. We'll have to wait for the Capitán and the others. Oh, and can you find something to eat. I'm starving.'

Sitting on his saddle, Pedro watched the Cañari disappear into the trees.

Yes, he thought, *he does have his uses.*

***

Mendoza arrived at the pool where that dolt Pedro was sitting. He was in a filthy mood as he removed a bandana that covered most of his face. He was used to the blasted insects of this country or so he thought.

That is, until this stretch of river changed his mind.

Bitten, chewed, crawled on, he must have swallowed an ant's nest by now, he thought.

He coughed up a mouthful of sticky phlegm and spat it out and it landed on a huge hairy spider that had just avoided his mounts front hoof with a big phlut.

He sniggered as it struggled to move its legs, then the rear hoof squashed it flat.

He wiped his face with the sweat-encrusted bandana and dismounted next to Pedro and the Cañari.

They looked a bit strange but as he got closer to them, he saw that it was because they had plastered themselves with a blotchy reddish paste.

He also noticed that no insects were pestering them, even though they surrounded him.

'Whatever it is, give me some,' he demanded, pointing to Pedro's face, before turning round and shouting to Gonzales to see that the horses were looked after first.

Pedro tried to hide his smile at the puffed up face of the Capitán and quickly looked away, as he ordered Serpienté to get the leaf of red sap and help the Capitán put it on.

It worked immediately and Mendoza went over and stood with De Orlando as they looked down to the lower pool, actually glad of the cooling spray from the waterfall blown back by the wind.

He had just drunk the last of a gourd of chicha and as the insects were no longer a problem, he could concentrate on the next problem: Getting his men and horses down to the bottom of the waterfall.

It wasn't as bad as he feared. De Orlando and the Cañari went first, each leading their horse on foot. The rough track was wide enough, though overhung in many places by shrub and tree branches and was rocky in places.

It twisted quite sharply at each bend so care was needed not to catch any overhanging branches. A stumble might mean a fall of tens of metres.

De Orlando was glad to reach the bottom. His sword arm was aching from the amount of hacking he had to do on the way down.

At least, he thought, *he had made it easier for the others following him.*

As he passed the agitated waterfall pool he saw what appeared to be several open spaces among the trees.

They looked like abandoned terraces and would make a suitable assembly point, he thought.

So he ordered the Cañari to meet the Conquistadors and show them a where to camp.

Mendoza was impressed by the way De Orlando had started to organize things and said so.

'Well done Alfonzo, we can rest up here and then......' His eyes sparkled with the look of a man on a mission who was on the cusp of great success.

Most of the troop had just found a place to hobble their horses and were thinking about food as the pack animals came up, when Gonzales let out a shriek to wake the dead.

'Inca, Inca over there.'

Mendoza spun around in shock. On the far side of the old terraces he saw a horde of them, dressed in padded tunics, and with paint-streaked faces. At least five to one against he estimated, armed with bows, bone tipped spears, wooden swords edged with sharp obsidian stones and some with slings which they idly twirled as they stared at their enemy.

Then they started to blow horns and whistles while stamping their feet. Amid them stood Atiq, proud and strong. He raised his spear high and shouted, 'Inti, Inti.'

As one the massed group charged.

'Form a line, form a line,' bellowed Mendoza.

He knew horses were useless in this terrain so he yelled for Gonzales.

'Get the arquebuses behind the line,' he shouted, 'They must fire when I give the order.'

As the sword-wielding Conquistadors rushed forward in a line to meet the attacking Inca, Gonzales was urging Miguel and Anton with the rest of the gun troop to load their weapons faster.

The two sides met with a clash of steel against wooden stone-edged swords and swipes against thrusting spears. The well-trained and experienced Conquistadors, now over their shock, began to cut the Inca down.

Spanish body armour proved too strong to be pierced by the inferior weapons of the Inca and they soon realized that they were being outfought.

'Fire,' screamed Mendoza and as one the sword-wielding Conquistadors dropped to the ground as the arquebuses opened fire. A huge blast of sound and a cloud of black smoke covered everyone in range.

Cries of terror came from the Inca and as the smoke cleared they could be seen fleeing, leaving at least twenty dead behind.

'Make for the Tampus across the river,' Mendoza screamed.

'I want every horse accounted for or else...'

47

As the Inca ran, screaming war cries towards the Conquistadors, Atiq saw that some devil riders had fire-sticks. He gave a quick command to his followers who had made a protective screen around him and they all fell to the ground just as the fire-sticks flashed and roared.

Amid the confusion, cries of the wounded and those fleeing form the wrath of the Gods, Atiq led his small group away through the dark smoke caused by the fire-sticks and skirted the Conquistador line and hidden by thick ferns, came to the side of the of the waterfall pool.

With a start he saw that they were not alone.

A devil rider stood holding a fire-stick over three people lying on the ground, prisoners he guessed. He looked more closely at the prisoners and gasped.

A young Inca woman and boy lay next to a white-faced man dressed in strange clothes and with red hair that stuck out of an Inca noble's helmet.

'Down,' he whispered to his followers.

'Look,' he pointed through a bush. He could hardly speak with the import of what was there in front of him. 'A son of *Viracocha* is a prisoner and we must rescue him.'

A low growl of anger began from the warriors.

'Shssss, be quiet.'

His warning came too late. The fire-stick came round and Atiq had no choice but to throw his spear. His aim was true and it hit the fire-stick just as the fire spirit came out with an ear shattering bang.

The young boy squealed out in pain and rolled in agony across the ground, holding a shoulder before falling into the pool.

Atiq raced over to the metal-clad warrior who was struggling to draw his sword and grabbed his spear from the ground and jabbed it down the throat of his enemy.

'Come,' he said, bowing his head to Chaz. 'You must come now the others have heard the fire-stick's voice.'

Maichu, Maichu, we have to save Maichu,' cried an anxious Princess Inkasisa.

Not understanding the significance of the boy or who she was, Atiq grabbed her by an arm and dragged her away from the pool towards a thicket of ferns.

'We must save the special one,' he cried and turned to one of the warriors. 'Remaq, take the girl quickly. I can hear them coming. Go by the river, we have to get to the qucha (lake) and the Inti Temple.'

Atiq turned to Chaz and bowed again. 'We must hurry they are....'

A shot from a fire-stick splattered against a tree fern trunk not far from them and woke Chaz from the dream-world he thought he was in.

'Friggin' hell, lets go,' he yelled and ran after the princess as the loud report of another fire-stick scattered more screeching birds and chattering monkeys.

Pausing only long enough to order his warriors to throw their spears at the approaching Conquistadors in order to buy a little time, Atiq ran after them before disappearing into the thick undergrowth, not noticing a warrior slumped under a large fern.

'Let them go,' Mendoza's loud voice commanded.

'It could be a trick to split us up. Get up to that old Tampus and God help you if we loose any equipment.'

When the clanking, moaning group of Conquistadors had gone, the surface of the pool rippled and the drawn face of Maichu, etched with pain, emerged from behind a half submerged log. He dragged himself along the edge of the pool until he was practically underneath the waterfall.

Despite the pain in his shoulder and a trickle of blood still oozing out of his wound, he pulled himself out of the water and half crawled behind the falling water into a small cave-like opening which he had seen earlier when he was hiding behind that life saving log. Maichu prayed to Inti that he be out of sight of the devil riders.

48

The Tampus proved to be just what Mendoza wanted.

On high ground, thick perimeter stonewalls and only one entrance. The semi-circular Tampus was also protected from an attack from the back because of a steep cliff face that was impossible to climb.

There had been no casualties and all the horses had been brought up, especially the packhorses.

'Settle the horses in the outer yard,' Mendoza ordered Gonzales. 'And see to it that some of the men get fodder for them. I noticed a lot of scrub grass around here. Those half-wit Inca won't trouble us for a while yet. We certainly gave them something to think about, Gonzales.'

Nodding his head, Gonzales sniggered at the thought of the rotting corpses down below as he went to sort out some men to feed the horses.

Mendoza had another thought.

'Alfonzo,' he called, 'Alfonzo.'

De Orlando appeared from one of the central huts.

The burnt out remains of the thatch roofs once cleared out, would make satisfactory spaces for the men. He had already claimed one for Mendoza and himself.

'Yes, Vicente, what can I do for you?'

'I think it would be wise to set up the Falconet in the doorway, just in case they get the urge to commit suicide - again.'

De Orlando gave his obligatory laugh at one of

Mendoza's so called jokes.

'Of course, Vicente, good idea,' and he turned and called for Miguel and Anton to set up the small cannon.

The last of the flat bread and charqui sticks had been distributed and Mendoza made a mental note to ask the Cañari to find them a functioning Tampu as soon as was feasible.

Hungry Conquistadors were a dangerous breed.

He was leaning against his saddle in the small roofless hut and looked at the gourd of chicha he was holding. He was going to savour it to the very last drop.

The blast from the Falconet firing echoed around the Tampus and a cloud of smoke mixed with dust enveloped the room.

'What the...'

Mendoza sprang to his feet, the chicha gourd flung into a corner, dribbling the last of its contents onto the floor as he rushed to the entrance of the Tampus.

Half deafened by the firing of the cannon, De Orlando turned as someone blundered into him in the narrow entrance and fell onto the hot barrel of the Falconet, burning his hand when he tried to stop himself from hitting it. He began to curse, then stopped just in time when he realized that it was Mendoza.

'De Orlando! I couldn't see you for this blasted smoke,' Mendoza spluttered as his eyes began to water.

Shaking his head to clear it, De Orlando said, 'The Inca are back in force. They had wooden shields and were shaking spears, blowing horns and chanting. I thought they were going to attack.'

Mendoza rubbed his eyes with his bandana and squinted though the thinning smoke. A wall of Inca warriors was beginning to reform.

This was different to their normal behavior, he thought. *They were showing a bit of fighting spirit for once, which was not good news for him or his men.*

'What charge did you use, Alfonzo?'

'Well, I thought a blank would do it. They usually run when we fire the cannon.'

'True, that's true,' replied Mendoza.

'I believe they have a new leader down there. Can you make him out?'

De Orlando stuck his head out of the doorway and got a good look down the open slope of scrub grass, towards the river where the mass of Inca were beginning to form into ranks of spear waving, chanting warriors.

'Yes, right in front of the heathens. He's wearing a bright copper helmet with coloured feathers on top, a red cloak and a padded tunic with some sort of armour on his chest Vicente, and he's holding a big axe. Hold on, two warriors with conch shells have come to the front and are standing next to him.'

Before Mendoza could say anything, the sound of the conch shells echoed round the valley and the chanting got louder.

'They mean to attack and soon,' Mendoza said, 'Miguel, where's Miguel.'

'Here, Capitán,' a voice said in his ear.

'Good, do you have that basket of small stone pebbles ready?'

'Yes, Capitán,'

'Alfonzo. I want you to aim the cannon at the leader.

If he goes, that lot of vermin will scatter like chaff in the wind.'

'Understood, Vicente, I will do my best.'

He saw the look in Mendoza's eyes and swallowed hard.

'I mean that we shall not miss.'

'Good,' Mendoza nodded as he moved to get out of their away.

Anton poured a little of the black powder into the cannon and pushed a wad of cotton in after it. Then Miguel grabbed handfuls of small pebbles from a wicker basket, some broken and jagged and rammed them down the barrel with a wood rod.

'Stand back,' ordered De Orlando, bending down to sight the cannon, using small wooden wedges to align it.

The Inca noble had raised his long handled axe and uttering a cry of Inti, Inti, rushed forward up the hill, followed by the Inca warriors shouting a war chant and waving their spears and other weapons in the air.

'Fire,' De Orlando ordered and Miguel touched the lighted taper to the cannon.

A bright flame shot out of the cannon muzzle and a crack like thunder nearly burst their eardrums. Black smoke covered them and Mendoza joined in the bout of coughing, which everyone around the cannon couldn't avoid.

Eyes streaming, Mendoza rubbed and rubbed until he could see. The Inca noble's body lay on the ground, headless and scores of warriors lay dead or seriously wounded, screaming for the Great Inti to take them to his heart, the rest fleeing.

The Conquistadors, who had suddenly become

apprehensive, began to cheer.

'Well done, Alfonzo, well done,' Mendoza said, grinning with pleasure at the resultant shot, as he patted De Orlando on the back.

'Now, let's take advantage of the situation. As soon as the horses finish feeding, I want to get to the Temple of Gold while those Inca heathens are leaderless. .

49

Atiq urged the son of Viracocha and the young woman to walk faster. He kept glancing back but could see no signs of any Conquistadors. The river was the quickest way to the sacred qucha. Enough of the rocky banks were exposed by its low level to enable them to make travelling, though awkward at times, infinitely better than cutting through the thick undergrowth of its banks.

There had been no signs of anyone pursuing them for some time and when a small pool came into view, Atiq called a halt.

Everyone had a drink and one of the warriors said he would go and look for some fruit or berries to eat.

'Be quick Taqui, we can only stay here for a short time.'

Taqui nodded and disappeared in a moment into the dense bushes, carrying nothing but his obsidian knife.

Chaz looked exhausted, the last day had been a nightmare for him and he looked around at the others in a sort of daze. Things were happening at too fast a rate for him to comprehend and he felt like he was sinking into a depressive state of mind. *Sinking*, he thought. *Jeez, I'm at the bottom of a chuffin' well.*

'You,' the woman had spoken at last, in a loud commanding voice and it broke into Chaz's brooding.

Atiq, jerked around from talking to Remaq.

'Yes you. Do you know who I am? I could have your heart ripped out by the High Priest of the Sacred Inti Temple for the way you have treated me, the royal

Princess Inkasisa.'

Atiq's faced showed a flash of concern and he looked carefully at the woman. He saw that she was younger than he had thought when he rescued the son of Viracocha and he could now see that her dress was of fine woven wool and she wore a gold necklace.

Now her eyes flashed with authority. 'I asked you a question warrior? Don't keep a daughter of the royal Chayna Capac family waiting.'

Falling to his knees, Atiq begged for forgiveness from her. He had been trying to save the son of Viracocha and he bowed to Chaz and then went on. In the heat of battle he had not recognized her.

Inkasisa paused and looked over at Chaz, seeing his pale features and red hair as though for the first time. Now it was her turn to kneel.

'My lord, you have appeared to us like no other I have ever seen. I implore you to be merciful to us.'

Chaz looked on, dumfounded. *What the hell*, he thought, *is going on here? For God's sake think of something.*

He indicated to the princess to get up and stammered a reply.

'I, err,' then he got an inspiration from a TV series he had watched years ago as a kid, *that Doctor thing*. 'Have been sent to err... see if err... you need help against the devil riders.'

'The Gods know that that your sacrifices have been in vain in driving them away. So I have been sent to assist you.'

Jeez, if they don't believe this crap I'm done for.

The Inca warrior, Atiq jumped up, 'Praise be the Great Inti, we are saved.'

Then the next moment he was on his knees again

bowing in front of Chaz.

'Most honoured one; please allow us to escort you and your noble princess to the Great Temple of Inti. I fear that the devils riders are going there as well and we need you to empower the High Priest so that he can cast them out of our land forever.'

Gee, talk about being between the devil and the deep blue sea. I'm in deep shit, thought Chaz. *Still, I'd better stay with this lot rather than be with those bloodthirsty nutters from Spain.*

Taking a deep breath, Chaz looked down at Atiq and then gestured to him to stand. With a furtive look round, he nodded before saying, 'In that case we had better go now and as quickly as we can.'

Princess Inkasisa jumped to her feet with a cry, 'What about Maichu?'

Atiq bowed to her before he spoke. 'The fire-stick's magic struck the prince and he fell into the pool. He has gone to the Great Inti.'

Inkasisa knew he was right and with tears in her eyes, raised her arms and whispered.

'Go my brave brother and ride with the Great Inti.'

Atiq turned to Taqui and said, 'Lead the way and make haste, we have to reach the qucha by nightfall.'

Stopping only to pick up his spear, Taqui with three of the Inca warriors went down the half dried-up riverbed at a fast trot.

Chaz, Princess Inkasisa and Atiq followed them, with the rest of the Inca warriors covering the rear.

50

They had finally reached the bottom of the steep cliff where the waterfall cascaded down like a curtain covered in jewels, sparkling and glinting in the sunlight.

White foam frothed and writhed in countless eddies before settling down into sleepy rocking ripples that barely reached the sides of the pool.

'Ooooh, this is absolutely beautiful.' Esha cooed as she gazed up to the top of the falls. Then as she began to look around the pool she saw it and gave a half choked scream.

'My God, look at that!'

Esha was pointing to a body half hidden by a large fern.

A Conquistador lay there, his dead hands clutching his throat. Blood had seeped through his fingers and formed a large pool by his face, which was now already covered by a mass of ants feasting on an unexpected bonanza.

If that wasn't enough for Esha, as she backed away from the gruesome sight, she nearly tripped over the prone body of one of Atiq's warriors, slain by the Conquistadors.

'Oh God, when will it ever end?' she whispered as she turned away from another horrible sight.

'Well, from what we've seen so far I don't believe in a change of heart with these Spanish butchers. They must have had a reason to hold back from killing more of the Inca warriors,' Makhassé said, as he thankfully dropped the A-frame.

'Come, come over here.'

The urgent voice of Mama Quylur Chaski interrupted them. She was bending over the edge of the pool not far from where the dead Conquistador lay.

'See.'

She pointed to several smears of blood that covered a patch of flattened reeds.

'See,' she said again.

'They point towards the water. Someone injured fell into the water, but there is no body.'

'Gee that's pretty good going. I would never have noticed that in a million years,' said Chuck, approvingly.

Esha was a bit hesitant. 'What if they....?'

She looked around, holding her backpack as though she was getting ready to run.

'I mean...'

'Mama, Mama.'

A childlike voice could just be heard above the roar of the waterfall.

'What the....'

Chuck wasn't alone in his shock at hearing a voice from nowhere.

No one could be seen, yet the voice was certainly near.

'Mama,' the voice called again.

'MAICHU! MAICHU! By the Great Inti, it's Maichu,' cried Mama Quylur Chaski.

'There. There in the waterfall.'

'What. How in God's name could he be in there?' shouted Chuck.

'He'd drown for sure.'

Makhassé wasted no time. He tore off his boots and

jacket and dived into the pool and swam over to the foaming cauldron of falling water, then disappeared.

Opening his eyes, Makhassé found himself behind the cascading curtain. He was able to stand, waist deep, on a rocky shelf that rose a metre or so above the water and saw in the gloomy light, a cave-like formation in which lay a boy, clasping a bleeding shoulder with one hand.

Thank goodness it was the dry season, he thought. *Otherwise, this place would have been flooded.*

The noise of the waterfall was loud but he could just hear Esha shouting. So he turned and saw her dim figure through the torrent of falling water and shouted that he was okay and had found the boy.

She waved back.

So Makhassé turned back to the boy who had now struggled to sit up.

His Inca face was drawn in pain and he looked exhausted so Makhassé scrambled up to him and said that he was a friend of Mama Quylur Chaski.

Maichu nodded weakly before falling back with a whimper of pain.

Grabbing his water bottle, Makhassé eased off the top and gave the boy a drink.

Maichu drank greedily and Makhassé was forced to take it away, saying that drinking too much water was not a good idea when wounded.

The wound. Makhassé had neglected to inspect it. *By the Great Inti he was a fool. The boy could be bleeding to death.*

He saw that the boy had been shot, probably with a musket type gun. He ripped the top of the boy's tunic wide open and saw that the lead ball had penetrated the shoulder and exited through the upper muscle, fortunately missing the bone but leaving a nasty gash from which a trickle of blood still oozed.

Makhassé untied his bandana, which was round his neck and wet it before cleaning the wound as best he could. He then used it to bandage it as a temporary dressing.

'Can you stand?' asked Makhassé.

Maichu grimaced and shook his head.

'This will hurt but I'm going to lift you up,' Makhassé said as he bent down and trying to be as gentle as he could, picked up Maichu.

Makhassé felt the boy stiffen in pain but he made no sound.

He will make a good warrior some day, he thought.

***

Mama Quylur Chaski was like a mother hen. Once Makhassé had laid Maichu down on a bed of fern leaves she had already prepared, she began to light a fire in a small pit she had made whilst waiting for her prince to be brought back from the waterfall cave.

A small bronze bowl filled with water was hung from a forked stick over the flames and while the water was beginning to boil she went to a nearby bush and scraped off some of the bark, which she put into the bowl of water.

After a brief stir, she hurried over to the dead Conquistador, which Chuck had covered with some cut branches from a tree fern as a mark of respect. He had already done the same for the poor Inca warrior.

Mama Quylur Chaski bent down and picked up several large ants that were scurrying to and fro from the dead body.

Returning to the fire, she gave the bowl of bark infused in boiling water and now reeking with a nasty smell, another stir, before picking off the heads of the ants she had collected earlier.

Chuck and Esha, sitting on their backpacks, watched fascinated at what Mama Quylur Chaski was doing.

Makhassé was too busy changing out of his wet clothes and putting them out to dry on a nearby bush to notice what was going on.

Satisfied that the potion was ready, Mama Quylur Chaski drained the bowl and then emptied the mushy bark onto a broad leaf.

Squatting next to Maichu who was in a sort of coma, she removed the bandana from the wounded shoulder. Maichu groaned but remained still.

It looked ugly, the skin blackened and all puffed up around the gouged out flesh, then blood began to fill the hollow gap now exposed to view.

Dipping into her bag, Mama Quylur Chaski took out a wad of kapok and swabbed the wound dry. Then taking a handful of still warm bark pulp gently filled the wound with it.

Maichu groaned again, louder but did not wake.

Mama Quylur Chaski paused and raised her arms into the air and uttered an incantation to the spirits that Maichu would get strong again.

Satisfied that she had done enough, Mama Quylur Chaski pinched the wound closed with her fingers and holding it tight with one hand, picked up one of the ant heads she had collected earlier with the other and squeezed the big jaws together, making a crude clamp.

Only three more ant heads were needed to complete the operation.

Then she used a large leaf to cover the wound and tied it securely with a length of liana vine.

Then Esha broke the silence.

'Of course, the Pepper tree.'

She nudged Chuck.

'The bark is a kind of antibiotic. How wonderful that she knew that!'

'Err, excuse me,' Makhassé interrupted. 'I wonder if you know that the Inca have been using these preparations for centuries, way before the Europeans knew about them. Even brain surgery has been a common means of treatment too. I could go on,' said Makhassé, smiling.

Esha felt her face go red with embarrassment.

'I didn't mean... I....'

'Don't worry about it, Esha. You wont be the last to think that. We don't advertise our medical knowledge. So many people think that we are the stereotype backward, ill-educated people of long ago.'

Chuck picked up a blade of grass and chewed on it for a while and then said, 'Anyway, that sure as hell impressed me. Yes siree, it surely did.'

While Maichu lay recovering from his treatment, they took the opportunity to catch up with the basics of daily life. Once their ablutions were over, a meal of sorts was eaten and then a welcome rest, despite the proximity of the corpses.

Mama Quylur Chaski had thought it better not to move Maichu just yet.

When he groaned and tried to sit up a while later, she gave him a drink of water and a coca leaf with a little lime powder to chew.

It wasn't long before Maichu responded to the coca

stimulant. It eased the pain of his wound though it made him a little light-headed, so that when he saw Mama Quylur Chaski talking to the others, he hardly noticed their strange clothes and gear.

It took him a while to tell the story of what had happened when the devil riders took him and his sister prisoners. He found it difficult to concentrate and keep on the same subject, often switching from monsters to underground worlds and noisy, smoke-making spirits.

Eventually he fell into a deep slumber and Mama Quylur Chaski covered him with her punchu and in silent agreement, they all moved far enough away not to disturb him whilst they discussed what to do next.

They had learned one important fact. Some Inca warriors had rescued Chaz and the Princess from the Conquistadors, much to Mama Quylur Chaski's relief.

'They must be taking them to the Great Inti Temple in the qucha.'

'She means a lake,' explained Makhassé.'

'Yeah, and that's where the Conquistadors are going, right,' Chuck added.

'In that case, I suggest that we stay here the night and hope that Maichu is fit enough to travel in the morning,' Esha said, meaningfully.

Chuck nodded in agreement and said, 'Well, I for one could use a break. My dogs are killing me.'

The others just looked at him; his choice of words no longer fazed them as they might have done, a day or so before.

Makhassé stood up and stretched and as he rubbed his back said, 'Let's make a fire then,' he being his usual practical self. Then with a grin, added.

'Come on Chuck, let's take your dogs for a walk and get some firewood.'

51

The course of the river began to follow a natural depression around the steep, wooded slopes of a high volcano from which could be seen wisps of smoke drifting like clouds across the sky.

Atiq stopped and pointed to the sky. 'Apu is waking, we must hurry.'

Chaz joined the others in looking up and thought that he heard a rumble of thunder as he did so.

That's all we need. Rain, he thought.

The sound made Atiq jump. 'Apu is not just waking, he is angry.'

The other warriors waved their spears in the air and chanted for the Great Inti's help.

'What's going on,' Chaz asked the Princess. 'Why are they all looking scared?'

She stared back at him in amazement.

'Surely you know my Lord. Apu is going to send down a message in a stream of fire. If it is not for you, it will consume you for being unfaithful to him. We must hurry. I feel that it is not for us.'

Chaz looked at her, thinking fast.

Jeez, this is a bloody volcano getting ready to erupt.

He looked around, this time more carefully. This part of the river was different, he saw. The upper sides of the banks were quite smooth relative to what they had already passed. Then it clicked.

Oh, my God. This river channel is in the trough of an ancient lava flow and it's getting ready to blow again.

Taking a deep breath, Chaz decided to bluff it out.

'Atiq is right; we must hurry before A... Apu speaks. We must reach the Island of the Sun. It will be safe there,' he added, fingers crossed.

He had overheard the Princess and her brother whispering about a temple of the Great Inti and how they were to get to the island. It made sense now.

With a quick word, Atiq silenced the warriors and the group set off again, though this time with more speed.

The pongo began to widen as it dropped down to the edge of the lake, the sides gradually becoming less steep and more open. The river took advantage of the extra space to widen itself and it became a wide shallow beach upon which small waves lapped over the rocky bed.

Chaz was surprised to see that the edge of the lake was covered with a mass of tall reeds, not only growing there but further out into the lake as well.

He got a further shock when the warriors, instead of squatting down for a rest, split up.

Those that still had their spears stabbed them into the riverbank and drawing their obsidian knives began to cut reed stems. Two went away along the lakeside.

In an amazingly short time, the warriors had cut down scores of thin stems of what Chaz thought were giant bulrushes. Most were at least four or five metres long. The ones chosen were last year's growth he was told later, because they would float better.

'Enough,' commanded Atiq.

Then turning to Taqui, he added. 'Take four warriors and make enough strands of thin-plaited split green stems and tie the cut reeds together.'

Atiq squatted as he watched them while at the same

time keeping an eye on the Princess who was squatting next to him. He was pleased to see Remaq and the other warrior return sometime later with several large fish.

'The Gods are with us today Remaq. A good catch,' he called out.

Remaq waved in acknowledgement.

'Make a fire and we will eat soon. The Princess will, I'm sure, help me gather some fruit to go with them.'

Atiq gave Princess Inkasisa a hard look.

He was in a difficult position. The High Priests of the Temple of Inti would be very pleased to receive his gift of a royal princess but she must not be forewarned of her situation. However, without the royal guards, she was helpless.

Still, he thought, *a bit of grovelling will not be wasted.*

'Most honoured one.'

Atiq got to his feet and bowed to Inkasisa.

'Please assist me in collecting some fruit for the industrious warriors.'

Inkasisa nodded and stood up, thinking that the sooner they were fed and the boat made, the sooner they would reach the Temple of Inti. This pompous warrior would regret his lack of respect to her.

Then Atiq remembered the 'Special One.'

He looked over at Chaz who was still absorbed at the activity of the warriors. Atiq didn't want to leave him here unsupervised; every warrior was working as fast as possible and none could be spared to keep an eye on him.

'Please, most honoured one.'

Atiq bowed to Chaz, who suddenly felt his face go red with embarrassment at being addressed like this.

'Come and join our search for some fruit.'

Chaz knew he had no real choice in the matter and so just nodded in agreement.

Atiq led them towards the nearest trees lining the riverbank and up a side gully made by a small stream.

The undergrowth was fairly sparse at this point and they walked through easily for a while before Atiq stopped and pointed to a tall shrub.

'Chirimuya,' he said, and started to pick several hand-sized knobbly fruits, which he passed over to Inkasisa.

Chaz gave a start. *Jeez,* he thought, *it's that bloody poisonous fruit Makhassé gave me. It tasted good though.*

Atiq paused a moment and with a nod of his head, passed another armful of the ugly looking fruits to Chaz who cradled them in his arms.

Once Atiq had his armful they returned to the beach where a fire had been started and several gutted fish, stuck on sticks over it, were being cooked.

Atiq ordered the warriors to join them around the fire and have some of the now ready to eat fish and fruit.

Chaz made damn sure that every black seed was found before he dared eat his share of the ugly looking but delicious fruit.

After a short rest, Atiq sent the warriors back to finish the half built reed boats.

***

Chaz was impressed as the warriors dragged the boats to the waters edge and gently launched them.

Three long fat bundles of cut reeds, each tightly bound into sausage shapes and then tied together, the middle one slightly lower to form the 'deck', floated easily in the placid waters of the lake. The front (bow) had been cut and tied in such a way as to make a smooth curve that would enable the boat to plough through the water easily.

Atiq wasted no time.

He ordered five warriors to man one boat, Remaq in charge and indicated to the Princess and Chaz that they get behind Taqui already at the bow of the second one.

His split bamboo paddle jabbed into the shallow water and muddy bottom holding the boat steady as they and Atiq boarded.

The last warrior pushed hard and the reed boat flexed and rocked as it moved into deeper water and he lunged into the back of it, taking a bamboo paddle from Atiq as he did so.

It was cramped for all of them. Chaz had his knees in his face but he had realized that in the time available to him, Atiq had built the biggest craft he could.

Squinting into the sun, Chaz could just make out the mountain-tops of the island of the Sun God.

It must be about a mile offshore, he thought, *but why was he being brought here, to the island?*

Princess Inkasisa was uncomfortable but was prepared to suffer a little longer.

This Inca warrior, Atiq, she was thinking, *was going to regret his insolence once she had the ear of the High Priest of the Inti Temple.*

A now relaxed Atiq, pleased to be safe from the Devil Riders but unaware of the Princess's thoughts, was having some more of his own.

The Festival of the Sun was due in the next day or so, depending on the signs that only the Temple Priest could divine and he was bringing them a special gift. He looked at the Princess squatting in front of him and smiled.

52

Mendoza looked at the remains of cut and shredded reeds scattered about the lakeside and cursed as he turned to De Orlando who stood beside him.

Behind them, the troop led by Gonzales had already dismounted and were leading their mounts up a slope towards a grassy area, which appeared to offer a good place to make camp.

'The heathen swine have got away Alfonzo,' he said, looking at the lowering sun and kicking at a mound of discarded reeds.

'What are our chances of making enough reed boats ourselves, Alfonzo?'

De Orlando, paused for a moment, then gave an honest answer.

'With the men we have, Vicente none at all.'

Mendoza scowled and swore as he kicked the reeds again.

'Vicente,' De Orlando said hurriedly. 'There may be a way.'

With a twisted smile, Mendoza looked up and said harshly, 'Make my day, Alfonzo. How?'

'Last year I was involved in a set to with the Inca at Pichachu, a fort protected by a wide river and those damn sheer mountains at the rear. The only way was to cross the river.'

'And....,' Mendoza was already getting impatient.

'Well, some of our Cañari guides told our commander that rafts made from bamboo could carry us across the river. So we did and took the fort.'

'By all the saints in heaven, Alfonzo.' Mendoza's face had a grin as large as a slice of melon.

'That's it. Get that cur Serpienté over here and tell Gonzales to assemble the men at once, at once do you hear.'

De Orlando nodded. He had feared the worse when he had said they wouldn't be able to make the reed boats but now....

'Pedro. Pedro,' he called loudly to the nearest group of men. 'Go and tell Pedro I want him. Oh, and tell Gonzales that the Capitán orders him to line up the troop.'

The half finished camp quickly emptied, some rashly grumbling aloud at being dragged from what they thought was going to be an easy time.

Pedro approached De Orlando wondering what all the fuss was about. *The Inca they had been following had gone, so what the rush.*

'For Gods sake where's the Cañari?' whispered De Orlando.

'Oh, he went to the lake to catch a bird or something... I think.'

'Well go and find the little runt. The Capitán wants to talk to him. So get the hell out of here and find him quickly or else...'

Pedro turned pale. He knew the wrath of the Capitán of old and he scurried away as fast as he could.

Fortunately for him he met Serpienté on his way back from the lake, holding a struggling water bird.

'Drop that and come with me.'

The Cañari stood and looked at Pedro as though he had gone mad. A piece of meat like this was a treasure.

'No, I keep....'

A blow from the tall conquistador knocked Serpienté flat to the ground and the bird suddenly found that it was free to fly away.

'Get to your feet and come with me,' growled Pedro. 'Or I'll carry you by your ears.'

A sullen looking Cañari stood before the Capitán and had the shock of his life when the Capitán smiled at him.

'Ah. Serpienté. My little friend, I want you to find some bamboo trees for me.'

The smile disappeared.

'Now, at once and when you find them, I want you to tell my men which ones to cut down suitable for making rafts.'

Serpienté realized that this was something the master wanted urgently and he had to comply or else.... He knew about the or else, fire ants or something equally nasty.

Swallowing hard, he managed to nod and say that he understood.

Mendoza straightened up.

'Gonzales,' he shouted, 'Make sure that each man has his hatchet and they are to follow the Cañari and cut down any tree he tells them to and bring them back here. Oh and bring back some of that hanging creeper, it can be used for tying them together.'

***

The pile of cut mature bamboo (bamboo is not a tree) grew rapidly by the lakeside. A constant line of conquistadors snaked down from the place where Serpienté had led them to a bamboo grove. It was of a sufficient size for him to select enough of the older drier stems (which floated better), for them to cut down with their sharp steel bladed hatchets.

Mendoza had a quick word with the Cañari about the size and carrying capacity of rafts, made more difficult because the runt couldn't count, well at least not to the satisfaction of the Capitán.

He had decided that four rafts would do. Of course the horses would have to stay. Lopez with a broken arm and Sanchez, who had belly rot and fit for nothing for the next few days would see to their needs.

There was good news in that Gonzales had found that three of the men had sailed in ships before becoming conquistadors. This had solved the problem of who was going to tie the lengths of bamboo together along with the Cañari, well enough to withstand the journey to the island.

Mendoza had the three brought to him and with a reluctant Pedro as a sort of go-between for the Cañari, who after all, had the experience of raft making - if not to the size he wanted.

Once Serpienté had grasped the largest number of men each raft would carry was eight, he took the three ex seamen to the pile of bamboo poles and told them to lay out four hands (twenty), of equal length of about – he took seven paces and then looked at all of them.

Pedro broke the silence. 'Well, that seems to be it. Go and get some of the men to bring the right size poles over here and set them out.'

He looked around. The lake edge was barely a good gob-spit away. 'This place is as good as any, I would say. Though I'm not a raft expert.' he said.

The three designated experts nodded and with sighs of resignation went to get some labourers.

De Orlando who had been watching came over and said to Pedro, 'To save time, get the Cañari to sort out that pile of creepers and start to cut it into workable lengths. You'd better give him a hand as well. You don't know what the little runt will do on his own,'

Pedro groaned mentally. *God, why is it always me. The bastard Capitán will want me to sleep with him next.*

He kept his mouth shut and just nodded and walked over to where the Cañari was trying his best not to be buried under a pile of creepers. Then the whole lot erupted and a small green snake flew over Pedro's head as a stream of curses came out the mass of vegetation.

The bamboo carriers laughed like a lot of demented squirrel monkeys.

The four rafts were finished in remarkably quick time. Split into two teams, the ex-seamen and Serpienté soon got into a rhythm once Serpienté had shown them how to weave the liana creeper in and out of the bamboo poles, knotting it every other one.

Across the middle section, four short transverse thicker bamboo poles were tied firmly to the bottom of the raft. They were the 'seats' for the occupants. A platform of cut reeds placed in front of the seats was to be used to put the larger weapons on. The arquebus guns were to be wrapped in canvas to keep them dry, along with a small keg of gunpowder, also wrapped in canvas.

In the case of the fourth raft, the Falconet cannon carrier, the forward area was strengthened with several cross pieces of bamboo large enough to fit the cannon and two kegs of gunpowder, as well as several sacks of small pebbles and the other bits and pieces required by the cannon team. On reflection, it was decided to make this raft slightly bigger than the others.

Once the basic rafts had been finished, one of the ex- seamen went over to De Orlando and said that he thought that there was one more thing to be done.

In order to launch the rafts, he said, they have to be pushed or carried to the water depending on how big and heavy they were.

Their rafts though big, were not too heavy but to make it easier, he had seen boats launched with poles placed underneath them and then the craft was easily rolled over the round poles.

De Orlando spotted the logic right away. *What a simple idea* he thought. *A good way to move heavy cannon as well, something to remember. It might come in handy.*

'Well done err, Ramon, isn't it. I believe you have saved us a lot of work and time. See to it will you.'

Ramon nodded, pleased that he had done the right thing and went and told the others that they hadn't quite finished yet.

***

Mendoza was very pleased with the afternoons work but kept that thought to himself. He then decided that loath though he was for any kind of delay, the men needed to eat and rest.

So he told Gonzales to tell the men that the rest of the day was free for them once the horses had been seen too. Then they could do what they liked as long as they were fit for duty the next morning.

Once the news spread, the mood changed. Banter and laughter could be heard all over the camp. Fires were lit and the smell of cooking pervaded everywhere, though what they had saved or found to cook always amazed Mendoza.

Serpienté was not so lucky; he had to find something to eat for both Capitáns before he could feed himself.

53

Chaz was pleasantly surprised with the reed boat's progress. It floated high above the water and he guessed that the makeshift bamboo paddle was good enough to propel the craft quite easily. He wasn't to know that these 'paddles,' had been used on the lake for hundreds, if not more, years.

They reached the Island of the Sun without any mishaps and it would be a while before the actual sunset, so Chaz was able to have a good look at their destination.

Tree covered hills dominated the skyline. He was sure that he saw a flash of light on the highest one. Then they began to approach a sheer cliff wall that stretched away, both to the right and left of a jetty that had been made from large rocks covered by a layer of small stones.

Several reed boats of different sizes had been hauled onto a small-pebbled area that nestled at the foot of the cliff.

At first he thought there was no way off the 'beach', then Chaz gave a gasp of surprise. He saw a huge cleft in the cliff face, in which the steepest steps he had ever seen had been laid with stone slabs. They seemed to go straight up forever.

The trees and shrubs growing on each side of them made a sort of triumphal arch, though a somewhat gloomy one.

'Move, honoured one, we have to ascend quickly before our Holy Inti goes to rest for the night.'

Chaz jerked round and saw Atiq standing on the jetty alongside the Princess. The other reed boat was on the other side of it and the Inca warriors were sorting out what little gear they had so as to be ready for the big climb.

He grunted with pain as he tried to get up. His legs had locked up with cramp and trying to pretend that they were just a little stiff, he fell flat on his face at the feet of Atiq who moved quickly to grab an arm and helped him to his feet with a look of concern.

'I'm okay, err I mean, I'm alright thank you.'

Chaz gave a limp smile. *My bloody leg muscles must be playing up again*, he thought.

Atiq glanced around and saw that his warriors were ready, so he indicated to the Princess that she go first, then Chaz.

A few minutes later Chaz was breathing hard.

Breathing, he thought. *Jeez I'm going to have a frigging heart attack*.

He stopped, wheezing like a busted foghorn, hands on knees. He was, in actual fact, at around four thousand metres and the air was naturally a lot thinner than he was used to.

Of course everyone else stopped and looked at the *Special One* in amazement.

Atiq climbed up the three steps to Chaz and said, 'My warriors are dismayed by your lack of vigour, most honoured one. May I offer you one of my coca leaves as a gift to one so holy.'

Chaz turned and looked at Atiq through smarting eyes and sensed that it would be important to accept. He nodded and took the proffered leaf and lime.

He had a sudden flash of inspiration, 'I have just

retuned to *Pachamama* (Mother Earth) and have not fully adjusted to it.'

Atiq and the other warriors nodded in relief that their Special One would get better.

The short rest and the immediate effect of the coca leaf gave Chaz the boost he needed and the group set off again.

Atiq now decided to send Remaq ahead to warn the High Priest that they were coming.

Not too soon for Chaz, the steps ended and changed to a rough track that wound its way through the upper part of the cleft, towards the top of the hill.

The gradient eased and opened out into a large plateau on which a cluster of thatched buildings, dominated by a much larger one, had been built.

The trees by the track obscured the view of the site at first and Chas was gob-smacked by the sight of the temple which had sheets of beaten gold covering the walls, dazzling all who saw it reflected in the sunlight.

A stonewall surrounded the site. The entrance, he saw, was dominated by a huge trapezium shaped gateway made from massive blocks of marble.

Atiq led them through into a stone paved area. The cluster of huts were to their left, so he turned towards the Temple of Inti shining in all its glory, as the suns rays were reflected back with such brightness that Chaz wasn't the only one to lift up a hand to protect his eyes.

Several temple servants, who lived and worked there, stopped and stared at them curiously before returning to their duties.

As Atiq continued to lead them towards the Holy Temple, which was end on to them, a large door opened and several gaudily robed priests appeared with a bowed Remaq amongst them.

'Welcome to the Temple of the Great Inti,' said one.

'Before you enter, lay down your weapons. The Great Inti is the God of peace.'

The Inca warriors holding spears followed Atiq's example and placed them on the ground by the temple door, alongside their obsidian edged wooden swords and four bows.

'Follow us and greet the humble voice of the Great Inti,' the priest added and nodding to his companions led the way into the temple.

Remaq stood to one side, head still bowed, as Atiq ushered the Princess and Chaz through the doorway.

Chaz squinted.

The temple was in semi-darkness. Apart from the doorway they had come through and another one at the far end of the room, the only light came from a series of narrow openings along one wall, high up to where the thatch roof began.

A line of wood pillars, built on stone pedestals of about waist height, was spaced down the center of the temple, supporting the thatched roof.

The twinkle of reflected light from several niches built into the sidewalls aroused his curiosity and he peered more closely at the nearest one.

Wow, he thought, as he saw a gold animal placed in it. The next one had several gold fruit and then a gold bird sparkled in another one.

My God, every niche had some sort of gold offering in it. No wonder the Conquistadors were coming here.

The priests in front stopped.

They had reached the end of the temple, not far

from the other doorway, which opened out into a small plaza like arena contained by a circular wall, apart from a small gap directly opposite the door.

Along the wall to the left of where Chaz and the others stood was a solid block of white marble about the size of large table. A channel had been chiselled in its surface from the centre to a hole in the wall.

Funny, thought Chaz as he saw it. *Is it an altar?*

Then he noticed the figure on the far side of the stone table sitting on a stone plinth.

Small, he was dressed in a richly embroidered gold tunic, a feathered cape draped around his shoulders. A gold disc embossed with a face with ray lines radiating from it, hung from his neck. (A smaller copy of the large one hung on the wall behind him) A gold band around his head held three large bird feathers. Gold sandals covered his feet.

The High Priest, *he must be,* thought Chaz, was holding a long golden staff, which he tapped twice on the paved floor.

It was then Chaz noticed his elongated head more clearly in the gloom. It was sticking up through the gold band like a squashed balloon. It was twice as big as his but so narrow.

Ugh, he thought.

The poor sod, having to walk around like that.

A sound behind him made Chaz turn and he saw that three young maidens, (mamakunas – priestesses), dressed in fine white full length tunics, yellow blossoms pinned to their long hair, had come out from a side chamber in response to the signal from the High Priest.

They were each holding a shallow reed basket and in

turn placed a gourd of chicha, a gold goblet and a smaller gourd and then a folded white tunic onto the marble table before moving to one side.

The High Priest stood, leaning his staff against the wall and motioned for them to face the altar and as Atiq, the Princess and the warriors shuffled around, Chaz followed suit.

Arms outstretched, the High Priest began to chant a prayer to the Great Inti.

All the Inca immediately held their arms straight out in front of themselves and uttered cries of; *Inti is Great. Inti is Good. Inti will save us.*

Then picking up the gourd, the High Priest uncorked it and poured the contents into the chiselled groove. The amber coloured liquid flowed down the channel and disappeared into the hole in the temple wall.

Then with arms outstretched again, he called out in a surprisingly strong voice.

'Great Almighty Inti accept our offering and give us protection from the Devil Riders who are pillaging our land.'

Chaz sniffed the air, *Hells bells,* he thought. *That's flaming chicha. What's going on?*

The High Priest beckoned the Princess. She daren't refuse and so took the few steps towards him.

At a wave of his hand two priestesses came forward and without any warning disrobed her.

She was completely naked, apart from the golden necklace round her neck. If being seen in her nudity embarrassed her, it was not apparent to the others.

One of the priestesses went to the altar and picked up the folded tunic and she handed it to the Princess who quickly dressed herself.

By now the High Priest had filled the gold goblet from the small gourd and handed it to the Princess.

As she took hold of it she smelt the odour of the liquid and her eyes opened wide in shock.

'Drink,' commanded the High Priest.

With a look of resignation she drank from the goblet, then gave a shudder and dropped it on the stone paved floor with a loud clatter.

Everyone looked at her as she clasped her mouth and choked and then slowly collapsed to the floor.

The High Priest was unmoved.

'Take her away and prepare her for the morning sunrise. The Great Inti is most pleased with today's offerings.'

The three priestesses managed between them to lift the Princess up and staggered with her limp form to the side chamber.

'See to the guests,' ordered the High Priest to the group of attendant priests. 'And make sure they are ready for the service too.'

'Follow me,' one of the priests murmured quietly to Atiq. 'A guest hut is ready for you.'

In a daze, Chaz followed Atiq, with the rest of the Inca warriors and as they left the Temple of the Sun, asked him what that had it been all about.

Atiq gave Chaz a look that said. *You mean you don't know.*

Then he remembered. *The most Honoured One was still recovering from.... Yes that must be it,* he thought.

'The Princess is to be offered to the Great Inti tomorrow,' he said. 'The drink of chicha, coca and some other herbs will make it easier for her to participate. Even though I know she would be willing to do so with her full faculties.'

'What! Are you saying she's been drugged?'

'It is for her own best interest that she be in the dream world,' answered Atiq as they reached the guest hut.

It would be a bit of a squash with all the other warriors but Chaz had enough trying to get his head round what he had just witnessed.

54

Shivering in the early morning chill, Mendoza nevertheless felt a surge of excitement.

The first rays of sunlight had illuminated the hilltops of the Inca island and he imagined himself surrounded by piles of gold objects not knowing which one to pick up first

'Master, Master I bring food.'

'Dolt, don't sneak up on me like that again,' snarled Mendoza, annoyed that he had been daydreaming unaware of the Cañari's presence.

Clutching the Inca punchu more closely to his shoulders, *at least the heathens knew how to make a warm cape,* he thought, he sat on a convenient rock and grabbed the bowl of hot maize porridge from Serpienté.

'Any of that flatbread crud?'

Serpienté nodded vigorously.

'Well next time bring it straight away. Get me some, pronto.'

Serpienté trotted away thinking he had got off lightly and then froze when the Capitán called out. 'Stop!'

A dribble of porridge had run down his beard when he had shouted out and he wiped it away with his cuff.

'Tell Gonzales that I want the rafts ready as soon as the men have finished eating and that they can have as much gold as they can carry for themselves.'

Serpienté nodded again and ran back to the camp as fast as he could.

Mendoza smiled to himself when he heard a loud

cheer coming from there.

***

'Pull, pull,' Gonzales screamed at the two unfortunate men standing waist deep in the lake straining like mad on the twisted vine rope attached to the first raft.

Ramon had supervised the laying of the bamboo poles in front of the raft and it was just a matter of getting some momentum going.

Four more men pushed from the back and then with a sudden rush that left the four at the back lying face down on the ground, the raft rolled over the poles into the water.

'I say Alfonzo, that went well.' Mendoza was all smiles as the two men in the lake pulled the raft round and waded back to the shore, towing it as though they had been doing it al their lives.

A sarcastic cheer came from the rest of the troop who and been lounging around watching the poor sods doing the work as the team started to launch the next raft.

That soon changed when Gonzales turned and screamed at them to get their kit and weapons or else...

'I think he means us as well Alfonzo, don't you?'

De Orlando nodded. *The Capitán was in good humour but for how long*, he thought.

***

The four rafts were ready. Gonzales had command of the first one, with seven men. Four of them had been delegated to paddle (two each side).

Weapons were laid out on the reed platform and tied

down with twisted vines - just in case of any mishaps.

Ramon commanded the next one with seven more men, with a similar set up to Gonzales.

The largest raft, made to carry the Falconet, was under the command of De Orlando, who was not too keen with the idea of going into battle over water in what he thought was a precarious raft. Fortunately Mendoza was unaware of his reservations. And he did have Miguel to keep an eye on the cannon.

He felt even better after Ramon had suggested that the cannon, because of its weight should be positioned in the middle of the raft with the two heavy kegs of gunpowder in front of it. The weight of 'crew' at the back would, he said make the raft more stable too.

Mendoza in the last raft took one last look around and saw the two invalids left to look after the horses, sitting on a rock watching the proceedings.

'If one horse is injured or not fit to ride when I get back, you will both be flayed and left for the ants,' he shouted as loud as he could and smiled as they jumped off the rock and scampered towards the horse corral.

'Now then Gonzales, what are you waiting for? Let's go.'

'You heard the Capitán. Paddle,' snarled Gonzales.

Four split bamboo stems splashed in the water and with each stroke the raft began to slowly pick up speed and by using only one pair of paddles at a time, turned towards the Island of the Sun.

The others watched with interest as Gonzales guided the raft away from the lakeshore. It floated perfectly.

'By all the saints, Serpienté, they work,' Mendoza grinned and patted him on his back. He'd been doubtful from the beginning but also knew that he had no choice but allow the runt his head and he had been justified.

'How about a gold armlet for you? No, two. What about a gold necklace?' Mendoza babbled on.

Serpienté, squatting next to Pedro just nodded.

All I want is to see you eat gold until you choke to death, he thought.

Mendoza stopped rambling and looked around. All the troopers were silent, looking at him in amazement.

'Well, what are you waiting for. Paddle, paddle and catch up with Gonzales.'

'Alfonzo! Come on, we haven't all day.'

'Ramon! Get on with it man.'

Splash.

Twelve paddles hit the water and the three rafts began to slowly follow Gonzales, who by now had got a good rhythm going and was already pulling away from the others.

55

Mama Quylur Chaski was up first. A quick look at Maichu showed that he was still asleep and his breathing was normal.

She gave a big sigh of relief and a short prayer of thanks to the Great Inti before heading for the trees.

Makhassé saw her go and knew then that Maichu must be okay and sat up to put his boots on before going over to the smoldering remains of last nights fire. He had thought it best to let it die down naturally; the smoke might deter some flying beasties.

Chuck and Esha were still snug under their mossie nets and he smiled at how well they had coped so far with what was a pretty precarious situation. Then he thought of Chaz and the smile faded as he offered up a silent prayer for his safety and wellbeing.

Shrugging away any thoughts of failure, he raked over the ashes with a small stick and found several glowing embers warm enough to ignite with a good blow. A handful of dried grass was enough to start a fire to which he gradually added twigs and then, larger pieces of wood.

A long supple branch supported by a small-forked one both stuck into the ground, held his small kettle over the flames. He knew the benefits of a hot drink at altitude to ward of the morning chill.

Both Chuck and Esha woke at the noise of his fire making and after their morning walk, asked if they could help with making the breakfast.

'No need, thanks,' replied Makhassé.

'I think some maize porridge and fruit to go with a hot drink should do. Am I right?'

'Yes siree.' Chuck answered.

'That's just the ticket for me.'

'Same here,' Esha called over from Maichu's bed where she had just taken some water.

Maichu by now was wide-awake too and had been quietly watching them and he gladly took Esha's water bottle and had a long drink before nodding his thanks to her.

Mama Quylur Chaski came back and seeing that Maichu was sitting up and looking much better, went over and helped Makhassé dish out the porridge and fruit.

After they had finished their breakfast, Maichu said that he was fit enough to travel and wanted to find his sister as soon as possible.

The urgency in his voice convinced that he would not take no for an answer, so it was agreed to start as soon as they had cleared the campsite.

Despite his wound Maichu set the pace, though he did have to make frequent stops. The loss of blood had weakened him more than he realized but he would not give in.

Makhassé happened to be in the lead, (Chuck having lost the toss and so was trailing at the back, lugging the A-frame) and as the riverbed went round the next bend the valley dipped down towards the lake, which was now in view for the first time.

What little water there was rushed down one side of the smooth-sided bank, splashing over small stones and skirting round the larger rocks.

'Hold it.'

Makhassé suddenly called out.

'I think we need to talk about what we do next.'

The others came up and crowded round him, Chuck puffing and blowing last of all.

Esha looked around and pointed to a small depression away to their left in the riverbank that had no trees and an inviting patch of scrub grass.

'What about over there,' she said. 'I could do with a sit down anyway.'

Maichu looked at her, puzzled.

Makhassé explained, 'She means having a rest, Maichu.'

'Oh, right.'

'Come, come.' Mama Quylur Chaski had wandered over and climbed up to the patch of grass and was waving at them.

'What has she found so interesting,' Chuck muttered as he led the others to see what the fuss was all about.

The patch of grass was growing on the lip of a deep hole, which could only be seen when you were right on top of it.

Makhassé looked at it with mounting excitement. 'I don't believe it,' he said, as he bent down and examined the inside of the hole.

'Ooooh, what is it Makhassé? Inca treasure or...'

'No, nothing like that, Esha,' he said smiling.

'It's an empty lava tube. We're on the side of a volcano. Look at the sides of this river. They're far too smooth for a normal riverbank. This river is making use of an old lava flow too.'

'Well, that's all very interesting, Makhassé but where does that get us?' Chuck asked.

Makhassé stood and pointed towards the lake.

'Can you see any horses Chuck?'

'What! Horses down there, come on... Oh heck, yeah. I can see a corral with lots of horses. That means..., oh..., oh..., the Conquistadors.'

'Yes, I'm afraid so.'

'Inkasisa! Inkasisa!'

Maichu cried out aloud and stared down at the lake.

Mama Quylur Chaski rushed over and clutched him tightly, trying to comfort him.

He had, for a moment, become a young boy again.

'We're too late,' Chuck said, 'Look out into the lake. Can you see some rafts? It can only be them. I reckon they have just left.'

Makhassé looked serious and said quietly, 'We have to get over to the Island of the Sun and we can't do it with those.'

He pointed to the backpacks, then to Chuck and Esha.

'Take only what you can put in your pockets. Things of value, your passport, any important papers, photos, letters. We will not be coming back here again ever.'

'What, why?' Esha and Chuck asked together.

'We can't leave twenty first century stuff around in this time frame to be found. All sorts could happen, don't ask me what. I just have this feeling. Besides, how the hell are we to get them to the island? I'll go and check for Chaz's things.'

Mama Quylur Chaski and Maichu looked on, not understanding anything that had just been said.

They became more perplexed when they saw the backpacks (which were items of wonder to them though Mama Quylur Chaski had no problem of accepting the abnormal, as she was after all a Shaman), were unceremoniously dumped down what seemed to be a bottomless pit.

After Makhassé had finished stuffing the few items from Chaz's backpack that he thought would be of value to him in one of his pockets, he sat down next to Esha, who was looking very pensive.

'What now?' asked Chuck, knees tucked under his chin, arms clutched tight around them.

'We're up here and they're on the lake and we can't do a thing to stop them.'

'Maybe I can help.'

Mama Quylur Chaski squatting next to Maichu looked at them and went on.

'Not stop them but make it difficult for them to reach the Holy Island soon. We have right on our side and I'm sure the Gods will help us.'

Getting to her feet, she went over to where she had left her bag.

'Makhassé, would you make a small fire for me while I prepare myself.'

Nodding, Makhassé scouted around and found several pieces of dead wood and proceeded to make a small fire pit some distance from the others.

A handful of dried grass made good tinder and using his lighter he set it alight. Adding bits of wood he soon had the fire burning nicely.

Mama Quylur Chaski rummaged for a while, then picked out of her bag a small length of bamboo with a stopper tightly tied with a piece of liana vine.

Then she pulled out her headband with the coloured feathers attached to it and put it on.

Grunting with the effort, the old shaman bent down

again and took out with a gentle tinkle, her two chacapa nut bracelets and placed them on each wrist, before lifting out a small gourd plugged with kapok fibre.

Satisfied that she had what she needed, Mama Quylur Chaski squatted down in front of the fire and began to chant in a low voice.

Eyes closed, she began to sway in time to her incantation, her head bobbing up and down in sympathy. Then her arms suddenly went rigid and rose up to the sky, her wrists twisting and shaking, making the bracelets rattle.

Suddenly a bright beam of light shot out from them into the fire, which became incandescent, so bright that the onlookers had to turn away.

The chant stopped as Mama Quylur Chaski picked up the gourd and removing the kapok, shook a handful of white powder over the fire. With tremendous hissing noise, a cloud began to form above the fire, which seemed to shrink in size and loosen its intense glare.

Without haste, Mama Quylur Chaski picked up the small stick of bamboo and pulled off the stopper and shook a grey-green powder made from the seeds of the Vilca tree onto the back of her hand. Dropping the stick, she bent her head and sniffed the powder up her nose.

With a load screech Mama Quylur Chaski jerked upright and fell backwards to the ground, her arms and legs twitching, eyes turning up so only the whites could be seen.

Then sitting up, arms raised to the sky, she called out in a hoarse voice.

'I see you Oh Mighty Kon. We, your pitiful subjects, beseech your help to right a wrong that we, your everlasting servants, will always remember in our prayers. The Devil Riders are on their way to the Holy Temple of the Inti. You must help us.........'

Mama Quylur Chaski's voice died away.

The fire was out. The last plume of smoke drifted away and then Mama Quylur Chaska stirred, shook her head and tried to get up.

'Well I'll be....'

Chuck was nearly speechless at what he had just seen.

Makhassé just acted.

He went over and lifted Mama Quylur Chaska up to a sitting position and said, 'Mama, are you all right and was that actually the Deity Kon you were speaking to?'

Licking her dry lips, she nodded and whispered, 'Can you see anything, anything on the lake?'

Not fully understanding what she meant, Makhassé was about to speak, when Esha interrupted.

'My God! Look! Look at the lake.'

They all turned and saw that a dark mass of clouds had suddenly appeared over the very spot where the Conquistador rafts had been, and a flurry of white capped waves were being whipped up by what appeared to be very strong winds.

Mama Quylur Chaski smiled and said, 'I will just rest for a while.'

And with that she lay back in Makhassé's arms.

He looked over at Chuck and Esha.

'That my friends, is how you get the Deity Kon, the God of Wind and Rain, to come to your aid.'

Then looking at Maichu in particular, Makhassé added, 'We'll let Mama Quylur Chaski rest for awhile but we must press on. Unfortunately, we have no way of knowing that the Conquistadors are destroyed. So we had better rest too, okay.'

It did help and they had nearly reached the lake when Esha said in a loud whisper.

'Stop, I thought I heard a horse neigh.'

Maichu moved past her, wondering what she meant and climbed up the riverbank and had a look.

He saw a grassy area rising up from the river; a large number of Devils were grazing and keeping guard were two men, one with an arm in a sling. He was sitting on a rock. The other was crouched down behind a bush, his breeches round his ankles.

*

The one sitting on the rock suddenly jumped up and shouted out.

'Antonio get over here quick. I can see some Incas.'

Caught with his breeches down, Antonio gave a grunt of disgust as he jumped up and tried to run and pull them up at the same time.

'Hurry, hurry,' Rodrigo called as he struggled to hang his sword belt over his head and shoulders with his good hand.

'Get your sword and grab two horses and bring them over here, I'll have to mount one standing on this rock. We can't stay here if you value your life.'

Antonio needed no urging.

Inca practices on prisoners were well known. Unfortunately for him, his belly problem agreed and he felt a warm trickle inside his breeches.

Oh ...., he thought and made a desperate lunge for the nearest horse.

'Come on Antonio,' Rodrigo called, and then eagerly grabbed the simple halter from him so as to pull the horse closer to the rock.

Antonio turned and managed to seize hold of another horse before they spooked and ran off. By the time he had mounted it, Rodrigo had already spurred his mount and was disappearing through the trees.

'Come back you selfish bastardo,' Antonio yelled as he furiously followed his so-called friend, wishing he had stirrups so he could take the weight off his squelchy breeches.

*

'Two men on Devils, they go,' Maichu said, as he slid back down the riverbank.

'In that case, let's get down to the lake as quickly as possible. There's no point in staying around here,' Makhassé said.

They found the lakeside strewn with bamboo poles of varying sizes, piles of cut reeds and liana vines.

'Well, I think we have found their boatyard. Yes siree this is it,' said Chuck knowingly.

'Can it, Chuck, this is serious,' Esha muttered as she looked out over the lake.

'What can we do now?'

Makhassé looked at them and let out a big sigh. 'There is only one thing we can do, build our own raft.'

'What!' exclaimed Chuck. 'How....'

Makhassé smiled.

'We have are own experts right here,' he said, looking at Mama Quylur Chaski and Maichu. 'And we have all the material we need lying at our feet.'

'Well I'll be darned.' Chuck grinned.

'Say the word, I'm ready to learn how to build a bamboo raft.'

56

It was still dark when Chaz was roused from his sleep by the quiet chatter of the Inca warriors, as they made ready for the first day of the Sun God festival.

A small torch of woven straw stuck in a clay holder by side of the oven, gave just enough smokey light to see across the hut.

Atiq came over to Chaz as he sat up on the llama skin that had been his bed for the night and offered him a small gourd of water.

Chaz drank gratefully and passed it back saying, 'What happens now?'

'We go to the mesa; the sacred altar and make an offering to the Great Inti. If he is pleased we will have a bounteous harvest. Now you must put this on.'

Atiq held out a multi-couloured cloak.

'And don't wear your hat.'

Chaz took the cloak with a frown of indecision and with a sense of foreboding put it on, using the gold stickpin that Atiq passed to him to fasten it below his chin.

He ruffled his red hair, now quite long and straggly, wishing he could comb it.

'We must hurry. It is nearly time for the great Inti to wake. Oh, at the back of the hut there is a suitable place for ... you know what.'

Chaz nodded before making for the door.

Across the paved area in another hut, two priestesses were helping to dress Princess Inkasisa by the light of a similar torch.

They had given her another drink of chicha and coca, (though not as strong as the one given to her the day before) as soon as she awoke. It had made her woozy and light-headed and completely malleable to any suggestion.

They had already brushed and braided her hair and wrapped the finely woven anaku, a full-length piece of material around her, fastening it with three gold stickpins (tupus).

Then they gently tied a wide colourful *chumpia* belt round her waist and a brightly embroidered mantle or shawl, fixed with another gold stickpin, around the shoulders.

All this time Inkasisa sat placidly on a stone plinth carved with images of the Great Inti. She did not even flinch when a gold headband with a large green emerald on the front, was forced down because it was too tight though a tear fell down her cheek, indicating that it must have hurt her.

With great reverence, the two priestesses then placed on her head a plumed yellow feather fan, which arched over a feather-covered cap.

Bending down, a priestess fitted a pair of gold studded sandals to Inkasisa's feet.

Standing back they were admiring the Princess, now dressed in the temple's finest clothes when a tap on the reed door told them that the Festival of the Sun was about to start.

***

The circular Mesa – plaza, still in darkness but with that tinge of predawn when the stars begin to dim, was crowded with Temple servants and attendants, all dressed in their finest colourful tunics and with yellow painted faces.

They were standing on either side of the gateway overlooking the sacred pool and faced the main doors of the Temple of the Great Inti. Many were holding musical instruments.

In the centre of the Mesa was the sacrificial table, a large stone slab, supported on four small plinths, with two small gourds placed in the middle next to a coloured braided headband, which had two large feathers attached to be worn at the front. Woollen tassels hung on each side to cover the ears. Arranged in a row at the back were several gold objects, a pair of human figurines, a bird and a llama.

Three small stone pedestal seats were arranged in front of it.

Several priestesses had been going around the crowd dispensing drinks of chicha and by now there was a sense of excitement spreading through them.

Inside the gloomy Temple, barely lit by starlight, the High Priest could just be seen and he was standing by the marble altar, gold staff in hand, in his gold headband with its two feathers (covered in gold dust) and his tunic of embroidered patterns, protected by a gold coloured cloak.

Two lines of priests in their best tunics, all with faces painted yellow, stood facing each other with their backs to the Temple walls.

Atiq and his warriors, in borrowed tunics but now with hurriedly painted yellow faces, stood with Chaz in his newly acquired cloak, just inside the door furthest away from the temple altar.

The reed door behind Chaz rattled and he quickly

moved aside as a priestess, dressed all in white but with a yellow painted face came in holding a woven reed basket, full of flower petals. Every few paces she threw a handful of them onto the floor.

Then to the complete surprise of Chaz, a litter, carried by four priests, edged past him.

He gave a strangled gasp as he thought he recognized the figure of Princess Inkasisa sitting on it. The litter moved on down the centre of the Temple and as it did, the rest of the priestesses came in to follow the Princess to the Mesa.

The priests then moved to join in the procession two by two until it was time for Atiq to nudge Chaz. He was next.

The timing was perfect.

As the litter passed the High Priest at the entrance of the Mesa, the first rays of the sun rose over the distant horizon and illuminated the giant gold disc fixed above the doorway.

An embossed human face with rays radiating all around it to the edge of the disc became visible as a brilliant shining replica of the sun itself.

A shout, a roar, came from the assembled throng.

Inti. Inti. Inti.

Then the beat of drums began, flutes trilled and whistles blew as the litter stopped by the sacrificial table and was rested on the ground.

Princess Inkasisa was helped to one of the pedestals. She was totally unaware of the proceedings going on around her and sat unmoving.

The rest of the priestesses and priests formed ranks behind her as Chaz came out into the awakening day, blinking in the brightening dawn.

He was on one of the pedestals before he knew what was happening and so just sat there, bemused and half deafened by the enthusiastic cries and musical cacophony made by the religious fervor of the Inca faithful.

The sudden entrance of the High Priest stilled the noise in an instant.

He paused and raised his gold staff into the air and cried out in a loud voice.

'The Great Inti has risen again. Praise Be to the Great Inti.'
Inti. Inti. Inti.

The servants of Inti responded fervently.

Hands held high the high priest silenced the throng of worshippers.

'We have a gift,' he announced.

'We needed the help of the Great Inti in these troubled times and when I called upon the Great Inti he listened to me and sent an aqilia (Virgin of the Sun). She is a chosen one whose destiny is linked with us. We cannot refuse this gift from the Great Inti. I shall prepare her for the great journey that she alone can travel.'

The High Priest turned and pointed his gold staff at Princess Inkasisa and screamed.

'She is the one'
Inti. Inti. Inti.

The assembled faithful stamped their feet and chanted again but louder.

Inti. Inti. Inti.

With the chant still ringing around the Mesa, the High Priest went to the sacrificial table and picked up one of the gourds.

He went back and offered it to Princess Inkasisa who, still in a dazed stupor, took it and drank.

Immediately, the four priests who had carried her on

the litter, came forward and as one helped her to her feet. The others went to the table and collected the gold offerings.

Then, with the Princess in the middle, they all walked through the now silent worshipers, to the gate in the wall that led to the sacred pool below.

At once a group of priestesses went round offering drinks of chicha and the mood became festive again as the drums began to bang out a short rhythmic beat which encouraged a sort of dance with lots of arm waving.

One priest took the lead as a narrow stone paved path led to a platform that ended abruptly on the edge of a sheer drop, which fell about ten metres down to a large pool, fed by a small waterfall. There appeared to be only one outlet for the water and this seemed to be the entrance to a cave on the far side of the pool.

The priest ignored the platform and turned left where a series of stone steps had been cut into the rock face. Forming a single file, now with two priests in front of Princess Inkasisa and two behind, they slowly climbed down to the level of the pool.

Having reached level ground, a rough stone track wound its way to the other side of the pool and then dipped sharply before making a zig-zag path down the steep side of the rocky hill. Somehow the Princess kept her footing. Some kind of instinct of self-survival must have been retained in her inner consciousness. The drugs had removed all sense of awareness from her.

Eventually the track reached the lake and a small, beach like cove at the bottom of a cliff. A reed boat, big enough for all of them had been tied to a convenient rock.

The Princess was helped into the boat and she squatted meekly in the middle. Once the four priests had boarded, they passed around a gourd of chicha, which had been left with a basket of food, before each taking a paddle and once the vine rope was freed, set off into the lake.

The volcano Apuchujo lay straight ahead, the plume of steam and ash, a good marker to follow.

***

Chaz couldn't believe what he had just seen. Right before his very eyes, he had seen a Princess kidnapped by priests for Gods sake. Then reality sunk in.

He slumped forward, shoulders hunched, hands on knees feeling wretched.

The sodding beat of the drums and those whistles were getting on his nerves. Who the hell thought of bringing those to a festival, they belong on a football pitch. Jeez, I'm really losing it, big time.

Chaz bit his lower lip, trying to get some life back into his system. He tasted blood.

Oh bloody hell, that's all I need. Isn't that what that frigging table over there's for. Sacrifices.

Then he became aware of cheering and chants as the High Priest thanked the Great God Viracocha for sending his messenger to them. Especially one with the features of the Great God's son, white faced, bearded and with red hair.

Chaz looked around, Atiq was pointing to the sacred table.

No, oh no. He can't mean me, he thought.

Then he saw the High priest picking up that stupid looking hat.

It wasn't a hat, it was that braided headband with two

frigging feathers sticking up.

The high priest gestured for Chaz to stand.

With the greatest reluctance he did and felt a right pratt as the headband with two chuffin' earmuffs, would you believe, was placed on his head.

The High Priest wanted to play down a potential rival to his position, so he quickly went back to the sacred table and picked up the other gourd, inwardly thanking the other Deities that he often gave offerings to, for the idea of bringing another drugged drink.

Chaz was fidgeting with the headband when the High Priest came back with the gourd. The tassels were tickling his ears.

Turning to the crowd of worshipers. The High priest raised the gourd to the sky and a great roar echoed around the Mesa.

Viracocha! Viracocha! Viracocha!

With disarming smile, the High priest offered the gourd to Chaz who unsuspectingly, drank from it.

It tasted funny, not the familiar chicha. Then he felt his chest tighten. He couldn't breathe properly and he saw three wobbly High Priests in front of him – all with big smiles.

Then they were gone.

Chaz collapsed to the ground with cries of anxiety from the faithful as the High Priest, trying his best to look concerned, beckoned some of the priests to take the crumpled form of the Holy Messenger away.

Then, hands raised, the High Priest assured them that the Holy Messenger was only fatigued from his long journey and would speak to them when The Great Inti appeared the next day.

With more cries of Inti, Inti, Inti, ringing in his ears,

the High Priest left the Mesa, feeling quite satisfied the way things had gone.

57

Chuck was a willing learner and his practical skills linked with his pilot training were a tremendous asset. With time being of the essence, they had none to waste.

Mama Quylur Chaski's lack of physical strength was more than outweighed by her advice in the construction of the bamboo raft using only the liana vines as ropes, which she and Maichu braided together at a record rate.

There were enough cut bamboo poles lying around for a decent sized raft and Makhassé with Chuck were getting more proficient with every minute.

They made speedy progress.

Esha made two simple reed baskets to carry enough fruit for the trip which, she with Maichu's local knowledge soon filled.

Just in case of an emergency, at Makhassé's suggestion, they also chopped down four medium sized lengths of green bamboo (suitably plugged), as extra water supplies.

When the raft was getting towards the finishing stage, Mama Quylur Chaski made a fire and using the last of her maize flour, made some stick flatbreads.

These, along with some fruit, might be their last meal for some time.

The way Chuck devoured his share you might think he was having a gourmet meal.

Even then Makhassé kept looking up at the sky. The sun had by now risen quite a bit.

'We must leave. Now.' he said, with a touch of anxiety in his voice.

58

Mendoza was at peace with the world as he surveyed his little flotilla; they were making good progress he thought.

They had left the lakeshore far behind and as he glanced back, he saw that the trees were now quite small and the place where they had built the rafts indistinguishable against the hilly background.

He gave a friendly wave to Alfonzo, lagging behind in the more heavily laden raft.

'A change from the horses Alfonzo,' he called in a friendly tone.

Alfonso waved back and answered in a loud voice, 'Very much so Vicente but I miss my saddle. This hunk of wood of a seat has made my backside go numb already.'

Mendoza smiled. The little runt the Cañari, had given him the punchu, nicely wrapped up, as a cushion to sit on.

Then Gonzales in the first raft, called out in an anxious voice.

'Capitán. Capitán. Look. Look at the sky.'

Idly, Mendoza looked up. *Gonzales is always worrying about something,* he thought.

Then he jerked upright. A massive black cloud had materialized out of nowhere and was bearing down on the group of rafts.

Within moments of seeing it, strong gusts of wind began to buffet them and the lake began to form waves, which rocked the rafts alarmingly.

'Hold tight,' screamed Mendoza, as the raft lurched clumsily up an even bigger wave. Then for a completely unknown reason, not having any idea of boating, he ordered the men to keep paddling.

He bellowed the order to the other rafts just before the wind became too loud for him too be heard by them.

The howl of the wind and the sudden downpour of heavy rain made it impossible for them to see and any speech to be heard. In fact nobody, including Mendoza, had the time to talk.

The paddlers were straining every sinew to keep the raft moving, with just enough control to stop it from capsizing. Everybody else just held tight and prayed like mad to be saved.

The fury of the wind began to push the rafts off course and before long they were way past the Island of the Sun.

Lashed by the wind, buried every few minutes by deluges of water from huge waves, the rafts somehow survived and as suddenly as it started the storm stopped.

The bobbing eased and as one the crew of each raft stood and stretched, some removed a shirt and wrung it out. Most of them, including Mendoza and De Orlando used their soaking bandanas to wipe vomit from their clothing. Not one of them had ever experienced anything like this before.

Unbelievably, the rafts had kept together during the storm and Mendoza called out in a croaky voice.

'Is every one accounted for?'

Gonzales called back, 'We lost Juan, he lost his grip on his paddle and when he tried to grab it, he lost his balance and fell into the water. He was swept away in an instant.'

"What about injuries?'

Once he knew that they were none, he asked Ramon, the ex-seamen where they were. As far as he could see they were in the middle of a vast lake dotted about with several islands.

Ramon looked up at the now bright sun and turned and pointed to an island.

'That is the one, Capitán.'

Mendoza had to believe Ramon; he knew he had no other option. 'Every one have some fruit, then we go back, as fast as we can paddle.'

He glared at each raft and eyes fell as he caught them. No one was brave enough to contradict him, he knew. He thanked the saints that he had listened to the Cañari runt, who had suggested bringing some juicy lulo fruits along.

59

Chuck found the split piece of hollow bamboo awkward to use. He had whittled away the top part with his pocketknife to make it more comfortable for his hand to grasp. The sharp edges were smoothed and he had made a couple of notches lower down so that his other hand wouldn't slip.

He was sitting at the front of the raft on the right and he raised the paddle up out of the water, dropping it in again with a splash as he pulled it back alongside him.

His arms were now aching like mad. He glanced back and saw that Makhassé was paddling as though he was on a picnic.

Easy for some, he thought. *Thank God they were nearly there.*

The raft was just big enough for them. Maichu, feeling a lot better now, squatted besides Chuck with Esha and Mama Quylur Chaski in the middle. Makhassé knelt at the back, on a pad of woven reeds and grass, on the opposite side to Chuck.

Makhassé took control of the landing. He saw two reed boats tied up at a small rocky jetty, which was built at the bottom of a long sheer cliff face, in a tiny stony cove.

'Chuck, can you hop onto the end of the jetty and hold us with that vine rope attached to the front of the raft, until we're are all off. I can't see a better way of landing.'

'What if I try and hold onto a rock while Chuck gets

across, will that help, Makhassé?' Esha asked.

'Good idea Esha, I'll keep paddling and try to keep as near as I can.'

Chuck agreed but when he stood he felt as though his legs were on fire, they were so stiff.

'Give me a minute will you, I can hardly move.'

He bent down and rubbed his calf muscles vigorously, then said, 'Okay, I'm ready.'

He took hold of the braided vine rope and jumped past Esha onto the jetty. He then wrapped the end round his wrist and held the raft as the others joined him. Of course Mama Quylur Chaski refused all offers of help and made her own way off.

Chuck had just secured the raft to a rock when he saw the steps.

'My Gawd, will you just look at them there steps. Talk about a stairway to heaven.'

Mama Quylur Chaski ignored the comment, didn't understand it anyway and after a quick word with Maichu to see if he was all right, took off and started the climb leaning on her staff, up to the Temple of the Sun God on her own.

Of course she had to slow up and even with the help of a coca leaf, stops for a rest became more frequent and so the others eventually caught up with her about half way up.

They all sat or squatted and had drinks of water as their heart rates slowed and breathing became less ragged.

Chuck, lying back against a convenient tree trunk, feet comfortably stretched out, looked over the lake. He suddenly sat up.

'What the hell, I think we're in big, big trouble folks.

Just lookee down there.'

Coming into view were four rafts, one carrying a small cannon.

Esha stifled a scream by jamming a fist into her mouth. Then whispered, 'It's the Conquistadors, isn't it? They're going to kill us, aren't they?'

Makhassé stood up to get a better view. 'It will take them a while to get to the jetty. Maybe there is just enough time for us to warn everyone up at the temple.'

Mama Quylur Chaski looked at Makhassé and said, ''Take Maichu with you and let them know that the Devil Riders are here. He can explain what has happened better than you to the High Priest.'

Makhassé nodded and looked at Maichu who had already got to his feet, a fierce expression on his face.

'We go,' he said and turning round started to climb the steps as fast as he could.

'Wait, Maichu,' Makhassé called out and then with a shrug, followed him.

Esha gently got hold of Mama Quylur Chaski's arm and said quietly, 'Let's go but maybe not so fast.'

Mama Quylur Chaski smiled and picked up her khapchos bag and staff and they began to climb the steep steps.

Chuck scrambled to his feet and moving as best as his aching muscles would allow, tried to catch up with them, casting furtive glances behind him as he did so.

So far, no one was in sight. *That's got to be a good sign*, he thought. *Yes siree, it must be.*

60

The rafts closed in on the jetty. Mendoza called across to De Orlando.

'I want you and the cannon to land first, Alfonzo. Get the men to haul it up those steps and find a suitable firing position near the Temple.'

De Orlando blanched at the thought of hauling the Falconet up the steepest steps he'd ever seen.

'We'll do our best, Vicente,' then regretted what he had said instantly.

'Don't fail me Alfonso, don't fail me.'

The response was swift, as he feared it would be.

The jetty was full of craft already tied up, some reed boats and strangely, another bamboo raft very similar to their own.

De Orlando looked over at the stony cove and noticed the there was plenty room for his raft to land and unload the cannon.

In fact it was better than the jetty, since no lifting off the raft was required.

Four men led by Miguel, using braided vine ropes managed to haul the cannon, attached to a two wheel wooden frame, off the raft and onto the stony cove.

Anton his assistant was left in charge of the gunpowder kegs and the basket of stone shot until they came back down for them.

It was an almighty struggle, two men pulling and two pushing. Without the wheeled frame it would probably have been impossible to haul the heavy cannon up the steep steps.

Every ten or so steps, the wheels were wedged to stop them rolling backwards and they took a rest.

Mendoza was furious at the delay but held his tongue as he and the rest of the troop sat and waited for the news that De Orlando had reached the top.

It happened so quickly.

De Orlando had moved ahead to see if there was a suitable site to place the cannon, when one of the men pulling it, suddenly screamed out loud and let go of his rope. The snake that he had unfortunately trodden on had bitten him.

The weight of the cannon was too much for three men, especially on such a steep slope. It rolled backwards over one of the 'pushers' and crushed his foot. His screams of agony echoed with the other around the cleft and several troopers crowded at the bottom of the steps to see what was going on.

The cannon barrel had become detached from the wheeled frame and came bouncing and clattering down the steps at such a speed that the crowd at the bottom didn't know what hit them.

The iron barrel weighing nearly as much as any man, smashed into them with such force that five were knocked into the lake, so severely injured that they died immediately or were drowned. The barrel then hit a rock with such force that it broke in two.

The tumbling wheel frame minus one wheel just missed the remaining troopers and ended up in the lake.

De Orlando, hearing the screams rushed back and found Miguel trying to bind the foot of the injured man with his bandana. Further down the steps where he had rolled, was the trooper, writhing in pain from the snakebite. Already his face was sweating and bloated and his breathing so difficult that he couldn't speak.

As De Orlando climbed down to see if he could help, the trooper suddenly vomited, gave a strangled cry and died.

The other trooper, terrified of snakes, had fled back down the steps, ostensibly to see what had happened to the cannon.

Miguel and De Orlando half carried the crippled trooper down to the cove and met a crazed Mendoza.

'The cannon! The cannon! Can it be repaired? Tell me, can it be repaired?'

He had rushed up to Miguel as soon as he saw him at the bottom of the steps.

Miguel who had just left the injured trooper with one of his friends turned to his Capitán.

'Without a forge, it is impossible.'

Mendoza took a deep breath and was about to speak when De Orlando came across.

'A word Vicente, perhaps we could go over to the raft.'

Swallowing hard, Mendoza managed to keep his rage under control, just, and followed De Orlando.

''What is it Alfonzo? Make it quick. I've got to sort out this mess.'

'We've just lost six men, seven with the storm and one seriously injured. Then there is the loss of the cannon, a most unfortunate accident. (He wasn't absolutely sure of that and so hurried on). The men are upset at losing so many of their comrades and since we don't know how many Inca are in the temple, I think this calls for a re-evaluation of the situation.'

'Oh you do, do you. Since when have you been in command, Alfonzo? Tell me.'

Mendoza nostrils flared and he seemed to be about to explode.

'Vicente, Vicente. What a thing to say. I have followed you to the letter in everything you have asked me, isn't that it true, Vincente.'

"Well, maybe but we go on, Alfonzo. We are so near. So near to a fabulous treasure, I can feel it. Breathe it. Can't you smell it in the air, Alfonzo?' Mendoza's eyes blazed with an inner fervor that sent a shiver down De Orlando's spine.

'Make sure that the long guns are loaded Alfonzo, as soon as you can. They will lead the attack. See to it at once.'

De Orlando nodded and shouted for Gonzales.

The troopers were called together and told to put on all armour and see to their weapons. The four arquebus carriers were told to get enough black powder and shot from Anton for a short engagement.

'The Capitán has said,' Gonzales added before they broke away to get ready. 'That after one or two shots the Inca will run and hide and there will be enough gold for everyone. Take as much as you can carry.'

A loud cheer came with that announcement which disturbed De Orlando so much, that he went and had a quiet word with Miguel and Ramon. He now realized that his troop had been won over by Mendoza and would do his bidding no matter what happened.

As soon as they were ready, Gonzales was ordered by Mendoza to lead on, with the four long guns to the fore. He would be in the middle with the Cañari runt. He would be useful if they captured any Inca on the way up to the Temple and De Orlando was to follow at the rear.

With a rattle and jingle of equipment, Gonzales set off up the steep steps, a murmur of excitement rippling through the line of troopers waiting their turn.

As the last trooper disappeared up the steps, soon to be hidden from sight by the swathe of overhanging branches growing down the sides of the cleft, De Orlando, Miguel and Ramon, helping the injured trooper, emerged from the far side of the jetty,

'Quick Ramon, free one of the reed boats. We haven't much time before Mendoza finds out that we are not with him and make damn sure you have the paddles.'

Ramon smiled and rushed to one of the bigger reed boats and untied the line. Then he helped each of them into it before casting off, just as Anton came rushing up from guarding the black powder kegs.

'I thought you lot were up to something,' he said, as he leapt onto the boat, which rocked alarmingly.

'Take this and keep quiet,' De Orlando said, passing a paddle, glad that another one of his men had decided to chance his luck with him rather than probably die rich in this hellhole.

Then, with the energy of desperate men, they began to paddle hard and left the Island of the Sun with hardly a glance at the sudden blaze of light reflecting from the gold clad Inti Temple walls, perched precariously on the cliff top, high above them.

61

They had reached the top of the steps and stopped at the beginning of a short track. The walled enclosure of the Temple of the Sun was visible through a gap in the trees. It was strangely quiet.

The normal hustle and bustle of a Temple was missing and Maichu was at first confused.

Then he smelt the odour of spilt chicha and remembered.

The feast of the Great Inti.

Makhassé nodded when Maichu whispered it to him and with a finger to his lips, pointed to the imposing gateway.

Maichu crouched down and crept along the track until he could see a paved area with several huts arranged neatly in rows.

Then he saw the Temple. The gold covered walls were gleaming and shining so brightly in the sunshine. Seeing no one around, he waved to Makhassé, indicating that the way was clear,

The problem was which hut to approach first.

They were all quiet, their reed doors closed. Then one opened and Maichu gasped as he recognized the warrior who had come out, carrying a gourd bowl.

Atiq held the foul smelling gourd as far away from himself as he could and went to the corner of the hut and emptied the contents into a small pit before returning to the hut.

The wind carried the nauseating smell of vomit to where Maichu and Makhassé were hiding.

'That's the warrior that saved me when the fire-stick struck me at the pool,' whispered Maichu.

'In that case he is our friend,' Makhassé whispered back. 'We have to go and speak to him....'

'He must know where my sister, Princess Inkasisa is,' interrupted Maichu.

'We must go and ask him.'

'Steady, steady, we can't...'

Too late, Maichu was already up and running towards the hut.

'Maichu! Come back.' Makhassé called out. Unfortunately, it was too loud.

The reed door was flung open and the warrior stood there holding a spear.

'My sister! My sister. Princess Inkasisa. Where is she? What have you done to her?'

Atiq froze in the act of throwing his weapon. This boy, how could it be? He had left him for dead at that pool. What spirit was this coming towards him and then he saw Makhassé in his outlandish clothes and his resolve faltered. His spear wavered from one apparition to the other as a weak voice came from the inside of the hut just loud enough for him to hear.

'Atiq, Atiq, that's my friend, Makhassé.'

Slowly, Atiq lowered his spear.

Totally confused he went back inside the hut.

Maichu hurried after him with Makhassé following on, trying to make some kind of sense of the situation.

In the gloomy interior a smell of vomit mixed with the stale odour of chicha, notwithstanding the distinctive body tang of the slumbering warriors who were sprawled about the hut in an alcoholic stupor.

Chaz lay on an animal skin by the stove.

Another gourd bowl, the receptacle of the last bout of sickness that had been the cause of hours of bellyache for him, was by his side.

Makhassé knew that Chaz was the first priority and so gently took hold of Maichu's arm and whispered, 'I know you want answers about your sister but I need to see to him first, understand?'

Maichu wasn't too happy but nodded his head.

Atiq stood by the door, still not sure what he should do but with his warriors unfit he decided to wait and see what would happen.

Makhassé went over to Chaz and felt his forehead. It was hot. Before he could think about what to do next, a commotion at the door made him turn and look.

Mama Quylur Chaski brushed aside Atiq's spear with her staff and entered the hut followed by Chuck. Esha stood outside, not sure what to do.

Atiq was having palpitations, more strangers from nowhere but one was a holy one, he was sure. So if she was their guardian he was free to stay back out of the way.

Not caring about the consternation she was causing, Mama Quylur Chaski went straight over to where Chaz was lying.

Sniffing loudly, she brushed Makhassé aside and squatted down by Chaz. Gently lifting an eyelid she peered at him and prodded his stomach.

'Ouch, that bloody hurt,' he whispered.

Ignoring him for the moment, Mama Quylur Chaski looked at the oven, which still had a few embers emitting tendrils of smoke. Bending down, she blew on them a few times before a flame flickered and she had a small fire going.

A small ollas cooking pot, conveniently half full of water had been left on the oven itself. It was already hot. So, giving it even more time to heat up, she delved into her bag and pulled out a twisted leaf, which when opened contained a yellow spice powder. A handy wooden cup was filled with some hot water and the yellow powder was then mixed in.

Chaz had been watching all this with groggy interest and when asked to drink the mixture, he thought it was better than nothing and so drank it.

At first he felt nothing but the hot liquid going down his throat. Then, like a miracle, his rumbling stomach and the stabbing pain eased and then went away.

He handed back the cup and smiled.

'I don't believe...' he stopped talking and fell back onto the animal skin, out cold.

'He will wake later,' Mama Quylur Chaski said quietly.

'Now where is Princess Inkasisa?' she demanded.

Atiq saw the old woman looking at him in such a way that it sent a stab of fear through him.

He glanced over at the Special One and saw a remarkable improvement and knew that she must have given him some kind of magic potion.

He dropped his spear and knelt down before her. Then, with arms outstretched, cried out.

'Mama, the High Priest has sent her to the Sacred Mountain of Apuchujo. He anointed her as the Virgin of the Gods and with the Great Inti's blessing ordered her to be dressed by the priestesses in the finest ceremonial robes.'

Mama Quylur Chaski face became a mask.

'You,' she pointed her staff at Atiq.

'Wake your warriors and bring the High Priest to me.'

Trying hard not to show his real feelings, Atiq stood and went over to kick the nearest warrior awake. He was thinking that the Princess had picked on the wrong man to be ordered about like a dog. And as for the High Priest, he will pay for being blinded by his own delusions of grandeur.

The sudden sound of a fire-stick echoed round the Mesa and Atiq stopped in astonishment and with amazing reactions dived to the floor and grabbed his spear. Then with the agility of a squirrel monkey, darted across to Remaq and jabbed him in the ribs with the butt of his spear.

'Hey....!' Remaq cried out, trying to get up.

'Quiet,' whispered Atiq putting a hand over Remaq's mouth.

'The Devil Riders are here, wake the others.'

The hut door suddenly burst open and a hysterical Esha rushed in.

'They're here. It must be them. What can we do?'

Mama Quylur Chaski went over to her and held her tight, trying to comfort her as Chuck slammed the door shut.

Maichu, wide-eyed with alarm crept into a corner and crouched down as low as he could.

Remaq, eyes wide-open in shock at the sight of strangers, shook his head and began to crawl from one warrior to the next, shaking and saying that the Devil Riders were near.

Faster than Atiq had hoped, the warriors had their weapons ready, though more than one was not in a fit condition to use them effectively.

Thrusting his spear to one of them holding a bow with obviously unsteady hands, Atiq snatched the bow and a handful of arrows from him and rushed towards the door.

'Wait,' Makhassé said, trying to keep his voice low.

Atiq ignored him and opened the reed-woven door and was about to step outside the hut when the firestick spoke again. More by luck than judgement, Atiq dropped to the left side of the doorway as a load of shot smashed into the right side of it.

'Get back inside now if you value your life.'

Quivering in fear, Atiq turned and dived back inside as Chuck hurriedly closed the flimsy door.

'I think we are in a mighty critical situation, yes siree,' Chuck said, as he crouched down besides Atiq, checking that he was not injured.

He then sat down, back against one of the walls and looked around the single room.

It might have been worse, he thought. *Good solid stonewalls up to the thatched roof. Uh uh, the thatched roof – not so good.*

The chinks of light that squeezed through gaps in the thatch were just sufficient for him to make out the warriors, now huddled in a whispering group around Atiq who was trying his best to rally them for what they thought was to be a one sided battle.

Chuck heard the word magic several times and firestick even more. Atiq was going to need help if they were to be won round.

He looked over to the oven side of the hut and saw the dim shapes of Mama Quylur Chaski and Esha kneeling by Chaz who had been woken up by the gunshot. He didn't look too bad from where he was sitting and then Makhassé suddenly joined him out of the gloom.

'We can't stay here.' he whispered. 'A couple of those armoured maniacs wielding their swords in here and we're dead meat.'

'They don't have to come in,' Chuck replied quietly.

'A burning torch on the roof and they would cut us down as we tried to escape the flames through the one doorway.'

Before Makhassé could say anything more, Chuck went on. 'I wondered why the hell I brought this along. You wont believe how many times I thought of throwing it away during the last few days.'

A rustle in the semi-darkness made Makhassé curious as Chuck fiddled with one of his many pockets in his flying jacket, before bringing out his flare pistol.

62

Gonzales knew he must be near the top of the cleft because his leg muscles were seizing up. He saw the gateway to the temple through the overhanging foliage, as he edged his way along the track.

The arquebus carriers were some way behind as he sank to his knees, panting heavily. Sweat ran down his face, attracting one of those damn biting flies and he slapped it hard, trying unsuccessfully to kill it. He swore to himself and eased his metal breastplate in order to get at an infernal itch that never seemed to go away.

The climb up those steps had been hideous. He pitied the poor sods carrying the cumbersome arquebuses in their armour.

He noticed that it was eerily quiet as he slowly rose upright and after a few deep breaths, went stiffly on towards the gateway set in the boundary wall of the temple site.

He stopped just before it, making sure that he couldn't be seen crouching down behind a large bush. He gave a gasp of surprise as he saw the blinding reflection from the gold covered walls of the Temple.

Then he grinned to himself. Now he could make his fortune and to hell with the likes of the Capitáns.

The rattle and clink of one of the troopers made him turn round. It was Andrés. He was gasping from the effort of the climb and with a big sigh of relief sank down next to Gonzales. Sweat dripped down his face, his beard wringing wet. He wrenched his steel helm off his head and rubbed his hands through his soaked hair.

'By all the saints, I'm going to join the galleon fleet. I'm too old for this.'

'Before you make up your mind Andrés, look over there.'

Gonzales pointed towards the Temple.

'My God, it's true,' cried Andrés, eyes wide open in shock when he saw the golden walls in all their shining glory.

Just then a priest appeared from the far side of the Temple and he was coming their way.

'Stop him Andrés, before he gives the alarm,' Gonzales whispered hoarsely.

He had nearly wet himself with the thought of what the Capitán would do to him if that happened.

All thoughts of tiredness disappeared as Andrés picked up his weapon. With practiced ease he opened the pan and deftly poured a few grains of black powder into it from his powder horn and stood to take aim. Bracing his feet, he saw that the Inca was nearly at the gate when he pulled the trigger.

The boom of the shot echoed all around and a dense cloud of black smoke enveloped Andrés and Gonzales, making them retch.

When it cleared the Inca lay sprawled across the stone slabs, blood seeping from his chest.

'What's haaappp... happening?'

Carlos had come up with the other two Troopers, gasping and wheezing from their climb.

'Never mind that, get your weapons ready,' Gonzales snapped.

This could get out of hand in no time, he thought.

'Hurry. Carlos, you cover the nearest hut while these

two dolts get themselves sorted out and Andrés is reloading.'

Keeping to one side of the gateway Carlos glad that they had been told to load earlier, grabbed his powder horn, pulled out the stopper with his teeth and sprinkled some black powder onto the open pan above the trigger and then closed it as soon as he returned the horn back in his belt.

He was just in time. The door in the hut opened and as a figure appeared on the threshold, Carlos fired.

'Mierde.'

The shot had gone wide, splattered against the side of the stone doorway.

When the smoke of the discharge had thinned enough to see, the figure had dodged back inside the hut.

63

Makhassé paused for a moment, then turned to the group of Inca warriors who were still whispering but to him sounded like they were not going to be much use against the Conquistadors. Not in the state of mind they seemed to be in now.

A scuffle near the stove made Makhassé look over and in the gloom saw that Chaz had sat up and was trying to stand but Esha was holding him down despite his protests.

'Esha. Esha, let him go.'

'Just let Chaz see how he feels when he's back on his feet. Okay.'

'Well if you think so.'

'I do and it's important that he is fit so give him a hand and check that he is well enough to travel.'

'Hey, I'm right here you know and I'm not a complete idiot. That stuff Mama gave me is a miracle cure. I feel one hundred percent okay. So lay off, right.'

Chaz sounded a bit peeved and shrugging Esha away, got up by himself.

'See!'

'Okay, Okay.' Makhassé replied in a friendly tone.

'I was only trying to help.'

'Apology accepted,' Chaz answered in his more natural voice.

'Now can someone tell me what the hell's going on. Oh, anyone got a drink I'm as dry as an empty well.'

Esha, now more composed after what at first she had thought was a rebuke, smiled at Chaz and said, 'Sit down and have some of this,' as she offered him her water bottle.

'Now pin your ears back and listen.'

Esha then proceeded to bring Chaz up to date.

"My God, I can't remember even half of that,' he said. 'What are we going to do?'

Makhassé had beckoned Mama Quylur Chaski over when Esha began to update Chaz and whispered something to her.

Mama Quylur Chaski thought for a moment and nodded before going across the room and began to feel for something in her bag.

Sensing something was up, Chuck stopped fiddling with his flare gun and whispered to Makhassé.

'Okay. Give. What are you and Mama over there hatching?'

'Well Chuck,' began Makhassé.

'I don't give much for our chances once the rest of the Conquistadors get up here. It's obvious to me that there are only a few of them. Otherwise we would be....,'

He cut a finger across his throat.

'So I thought it was time to ask for Mama Quylur Chaski's help. She is going to call on the Spirit Gods to save us from the Devil Riders.'

Chuck swallowed and licked his lips. This was becoming surreal and he looked down at his flare pistol and squeezed it hard. Yes, it was there in his hand and the damn grip hurt his fingers. So it wasn't a dream.

Mama Quylur Chaski had by now moved over to the stove and was stuffing a handful of flower blooms into a cooking pot, the one that she had put the yellow spice in. It was still bubbling away and immediately a pungent stink filled the room.

Feeling a bit better, Maichu watched with interest as Mama Quylur Chaski prepared her concoction.

"Bloody hell, what's in that?' Chaz said anxiously.

'I hope it isn't meant for me.'

With a cursory glance at him, Mama Quylur Chaski picked up a twig and stirred the concoction before taking two small fruits from her bag, along with an obsidian knife.

Beside the oven were several different-sized clay bowls and she picked the largest one and squatting in front of it, proceeded to put sliced pieces of fruit into it.

Amongst the clutter around the oven were several pebbles and choosing one, Mama Quylur Chaski gently squeezed the sliced fruit into a mushy mess. Then she asked Esha who like everyone there, including the warriors now captivated by what Mama Quylur Chaski was doing, to pass her a large gourd full of water.

Pouring enough water to half fill the bowl, Mama Quylur Chaski began to stir the mixture.

In moments the water turned blood red and a rich sweet smell, similar to the *wanqor* plant was a welcome relief as it masked the other nasty odour that was still lingering in the room.

This caused a sudden gasp from the warriors. They at least, had some idea of what was happening.

Moving the large bowl to one side Mama Quylur Chaski, wrapping the ends of her shawl over her hands, carefully took the bubbling, stinking pot of petals from the oven and placed in on the floor to cool.

With a slight groan, Mama Quylur Chaski stood up and rubbed her back, which had begun to ache from all of her stooping and stirring.

'Atiq, come over here and help me,' she said, as she pulled a wad of kapok from her bag and split it into two pieces before giving one to him.

'You know what to do?'

Atiq nodded and called Remaq over to him as Mama Quylur Chaski beckoned one of the other warriors to join her.

They both knelt down and pulled their tunics off their shoulders exposing their bare chests and waited as Atiq and Mama Quylur Chaski dipped the kapok into the bowl of red dye.

First the faces, then the chests were daubed until they were covered down to the waist.

A strange thing happened during the application of the dye.

As it began to dry it turned black and both warriors stiffened in their posture and with hands clenched, muscles on the upper body swelled and rippled.

With a nod from Mama Quylur Chaski, they rose to their feet and walked back to the other end of the room with the stance and boldness of a warrior about to strike a killer blow.

By the time all the warriors, including Atiq had been daubed, the hot brew of 'petal' stew had cooled.

So Mama Quylur Chaski, using a small wooden cup, gave each warrior a drink of the foul smelling brew.

At first it seemed to have no effect.

The warriors had just begun to act about like they usually do when not involved in any training: A bit of pushing, lewd comments to each other.

Then some of them began to foam at the mouth. Others suddenly began to jerk about, arms and legs twisting uncontrollably.

Then the faces took on a crazed look, eyes wild and some shouting that there were sprits outside waiting to take them to the Sun God.

Esha had rushed behind Chuck and Makhassé thinking she was about to be attacked while Chaz by the oven, pressed himself back against the wall muttering to himself.

'Frigging hell, Frigging hell, this is worse than a Saturday night at Club Xoyoo.'

Maichu crouched next to him wondered what sort of prayer that was.

Mama Quylur Chaski squatted patiently by the stove as the warriors went quiet, one by one, until the last twitch and jerk had finished.

From inside her shawl, she brought out a small bamboo tube and getting to her feet and deftly stepping over the odd pool of vomit, went over to the recumbent form of Atiq, bent down and taking out the stopper, shook a red powder over Atiq's nose and mouth.

He sneezed violently and sat up, looking wildly around only relaxing when he saw Mama Quylur Chaski.

'They are ready,' was all she said.

Makhassé looked at Chuck and Esha.

'That, my friends, was what a drink of 'maiqu' does to you. I wouldn't recommend it.'

Before either Chuck or Esha could ask, he went on.

'They have now become what you might call zombies, their minds have been, what shall I say, made subject to manipulation. They will do anything they are told to do.'

'My God,' exclaimed Esha, 'How horrid, the poor things.'

'Before you get too attached to their welfare,' added Makhassé, 'Why don't you think about your own position? The Conquistadors are about to attack us and they are the only ones around to save us.'

'What's all the black stuff for?' Chuck interrupted, his heart rate now settling down to a steady sixty-three beats.

'The black dye gives them the stealth and strength of the panther. That they believe truly. They will fight more bravely with it on,' said Makhassé quietly.

64

Mendoza was livid. He strode over to Gonzales who was crouched down by the side of the gateway with Andrés and Carlos.

'Capitán.'

Gonzales jumped up in alarm. He had to think of something and quick.

'Capitán, the huts are full of Inca warriors and we managed to kill one,' he said pointed to the body lying on the other side of the gateway.

'What! Inca warriors here?'

Mendoza looked at the body and struck Gonzales across the face.

'Warriors! Warriors! Does that look like a warrior to you, dolt.'

Gonzales cringed, 'I.... I...'

Mendoza was no longer listening; he had just seen a flash of light.

A passing cloud that had been obscuring the sun finally drifted on and a sunbeam struck the gold clad walls of the temple with dazzling effect.

'By all the saints in heaven, God be praised. Did you see that Gonzales? Did you see that?'

Gonzales swallowed and tried to speak. He knew that he had just escaped from something unpleasant by the skin of his teeth.

Mendoza misunderstood the lack of a response. He thought that Gonzales was as awestruck by the sight of the gold clad walls of the Temple, as he was.

He grinned like a madman at Gonzales, who

shuddered at the sight.

'Once all the troopers are here, that rabble of Inca warriors will disappear like a gourd of chicha down my throat. Then we take as much gold as we can carry.'

'Gonzales, Gonzales where the hell are you?' Mendoza squinted as the sun shone more brightly into his eyes.

'Get your arquebus men ready to fire on my command.'

Then he turned and looked down the track.

'Pedro, come over here and listen. Take five troopers and that cur, the Cañari, with you as soon as the guns fire. Grab as many priests as you can and get them to tell you where the rest of the gold is hidden. Don't take no for an answer, understand.'

Pedro, at the front of the rest of the troopers, had been watching like the rest with some apprehension at the Capitán's behaviour.

He nodded, thinking that maybe he was now in the wrong place. Still orders were orders and he went to sort out the men and that pain in the arse, Serpienté.

Angrily flicking at the feasting flies of this accursed country from his sweating face. Mendoza drew his sword and said excitedly, as drool dribbled from his lips, 'Gonzales, now is the time. A fortune awaits every man who stands by me and for the King of Spain. Spare only those young enough to carry the gold.'

Excitement and greed is contagious and Gonzales grinned and cried out to the arquebus troopers.

'Follow me,' as he rushed to the gateway, sword in hand and tripped over the dead priest's body.

Carlos, just behind him, managed to jump over Gonzales' sprawling, cursing figure and as he tried to regain his balance saw the hut door open.

Skidding to a halt, Carlos lifted his cumbersome weapon to take aim and saw a figure dressed in unusual clothes that somehow reminded him of someone but before he could recollect whom, the figure fired a strange weapon.

A ball of fire shot towards him and hit his midriff where he hung his black powder horn. It exploded and black smoke enveloped him as his entrails hung down to the ground.

Someone screamed in pain. Carlos' last thought was that it was him as he slumped to the ground.

Mendoza froze as he stared at Carlos' body. Then his training clicked in.

'Pedro, stay here with your group and support Gonzales. Once the dolt has gathered his wits, attack the hut and leave no one alive.'

Having given the order, Mendoza called to Serpienté. 'You come with me,' he snarled.

Then with pent up frustration he ordered the remaining group of five troopers to follow him inside the Temple mesa.

Careful to avoid the two bleeding bodies, Mendoza led the way towards the Temple door that faced the huts. He had decided that there might be some smaller golden objects inside. The big panels on the walls could wait.

As soon as Mendoza and his party of armed men had entered the temple, four troopers raced away from Gonzales before he could stop them, over to the gold clad walls and started to hack at the nearest glittering panel with swords and then with their hatchets.

The panels were of thin sheets of beaten gold and

had to be prised off. Seeing the success that some were having, Gonzales raced over with Pedro at his heels.

The rest of the troop not wishing to miss out, clanked after them and the clash of metal hitting metal rang around the mesa as a line of troopers attacked the golden wall, each one steadily adding more sheets of gold to their own pile.

65

Chuck thought it was time for another look to see what was happening down by the gateway and was glad that he had. He eased the reed door open just far enough for him to see that several armed men, some holding those long musket-type guns, were about to enter the Temple grounds.

Taking a deep breath, Chuck stepped through the door and aimed at the first Conquistador with his flare pistol. To his amazement, the leader, who was only holding a sword, tripped over a body lying across the gateway entrance just as Chuck pulled the trigger.

The second one, carrying a long gun, jumping to avoid his fallen comrade, saw him and tried to bring his weapon up to his shoulder, as the flare pistol fired.

Chuck watched mesmerized as the flare, emitting a trail of smoke, struck the Conquistador in the belly and somehow caused an explosion.

He didn't wait to see the results of his shot. He dived back inside the hut, slamming the damn flimsy door behind him.

Makhassé jerked around when Chuck burst back in through the door but when he saw that he was okay, looked back at the warriors.

They were at least aware of their surroundings but ignored Chuck's hasty entrance.

Squatting in a group, they were now strangely quiet. Atiq who had been partially brought back to normality by one of Mama Quylur Chaski's concoctions, was looking agitated and was fidgeting with his fingers.

The others seemed calm enough.

Chaz and Esha were sitting by the oven wall whispering to each other but both looked pale and tense.

Chuck sat back against the wall wiping the flare pistol with a piece of cloth, looking a bit confused, as Maichu watched, fascinated by the strange shiny object.

Mama Quylur Chaski suddenly clapped her hands and all the warriors looked at her in a dazed fashion.

'Atiq has something to say to you. You will obey him and do everything he tells you.'

The warriors nodded dumbly and looked at Atiq.

Atiq stood and shook his head, the voices still whispering and commanding. His voice spoke.

'The Devil Riders are outside. You will pick up your weapons and attack them until they are all dead. If you drop or lose your weapon, use your hands. Warriors of the Great Inti go and do his will.'

As one, the warriors stood and silently began to pick up their spears and wooden swords edged with obsidian shards. Atiq with his bow and arrows then led them to the door where Mama Quylur Chaska was standing, holding a small bowl of white ashes she had earlier mixed into a paste

Deftly, she went to each warrior and marked his face with two vivid white slashes, then stood aside and watched them walk out in silence, slightly stooped with weapons ready

Across the open space to the temple, the only activity to be seen was the frantic hacking by the troopers each trying to get as many sheets of gold for themselves as they could.

There was no movement from any of the other huts.

The blast from the fire-sticks was enough to keep everyone cowering out of sight.

The banging made by the troopers, inadvertently covered the approach of the warriors as they closed in.

66

The temple was in semi-darkness and as Mendoza went in, he paused to let his eyes adjust to the gloom. He saw that narrow openings set high along one wall were the only light source.

It was enough for him to see that the thatched roof was supported by a series of pillars positioned down the middle of the temple.

Gripping his sword more tightly, he moved forward and then stopped with a strangled gasp. In a niche of the nearest wall a golden bird twinkled and gleamed as dust motes wafted around it, momentarily blocking the shafts of light before it resumed its sparkling splendor.

'I want it. I want that one,' Mendoza cried passionately.

'You. Luis isn't it. Get it for me now.'

He nearly screamed with excitement.

The trooper picked up the golden bird, a hawk with flashing quartz eyes and nearly stumbled, it was that heavy.

'Guard it with your life,' Mendoza said with a wild grin. 'You can pick your own later.'

He was about to say more, when the sounds of banging from outside the Temple walls stopped him and he turned to send someone outside to see what it was.

'In the name of the Great Inti, how dare you enter the sacred walls of his house without preparing yourselves for...' the voice trailed away.

The High Priest, in his splendid embroidered gold

tunic, feathered cape around his shoulders, gold disc embossed with a face with sunray lines hanging from his neck, stared in the gloom of the Temple, leaning on his staff. He suddenly realized these people were not Inca.

With a hoarse cry of alarm he turned to flee, his bald domed head covered in sweat, knowing that help would not be forthcoming because all the priests and servants would still be recovering from the festive Inti celebrations of the night before.

Mendoza, eyes only on the gold disc, pointed at the priest and shouted, 'Seize him.'

In a panic, the High Priest dropped his golden staff and ran back towards the sacred offering table and the outer mesa. The doors were shut and as he fumbled to open them, a trooper ran up and struck him on the head with the hilt of his sword, knocking him to the floor.

'Bind him,' ordered Mendoza as he bent down and wrenched the gold disc from the High priest's neck.

Two troopers stooped and roughly pulled the semi-conscious High Priest upright and dragged him to one of the side rooms.

Immediately one of them rushed out again shouting, 'Capitán! Capitán!'

'What now?' Mendoza didn't want to be disturbed. He was examining the gold disc.

'Chicha, chicha, lot's of it Capitán.'

Mendoza smiled, 'Good man, Good man. You can't drink gold. Bring some to me.'

He looked around. 'Now where the hell is that Cañari runt, 'I'll skin....'

'Master. Master I come.' Serpienté rushed up and

grovelled in front of Mendoza.

'Open the doors runt. I want to see what's outside.'

Serpienté slid a wooden bolt back and pulled open the double doors.

Sunlight flooded in and everyone covered their eyes for a moment.

Taking his hand from his brow, Mendoza saw the small circular plaza-like area, with the sacrificial table in the middle and three stone pedestals in front of it.

'My, look what the Gods have provided us,' said Mendoza sarcastically, walking over to one of the stone pedestals and sitting down.

He was slightly mollified when Serpienté brought him a gourd of chicha.

Taking a sip of it, Mendoza idly looked around the area and then he spluttered and coughed so much that his eyes watered. He had just seen the giant gold sun disc with an embossed human face that was positioned above the Temple doors.

He jumped up and ran back to see it more clearly. By all the saints in heaven, that alone will make me famous. He thought.

'Serpienté, bring me some more chicha. Now we really do have something to celebrate. Oh and have one yourself.'

If looks could kill, Serpienté's glance at the Capitán would have felled a giant panther as he went for more gourds of chicha. *I bet he won't taste my spit when he gets his drink* and he sniggered at the thought.

The small chamber that acted as the chicha store was half empty because of the Inti festival and as Serpienté went to the back wall he thought he heard the sound of fighting. The troopers might have caught some of the priests. No matter, he gave a shrug. They were only Inca and he was a Cañari.

So picking as many gourds as he could carry, he started back to the small mesa, only stopping by the slumped form of the High Priest, hands bound and out to the world. Sneering at the sight, Serpienté tried to kick him but loosing his balance, gave a curse instead.

Mendoza was sitting on the stone plinth, gazing up at the giant gold sun disc, mumbling to himself.

'Ah! The runt. Give me some of those and go and see what Gonzales's doing. He should be here by now.'

Serpienté carefully placed his armful of chicha gourds on the stone slabs of the mesa and handed over two of them.

67

Pedro was sweating so much from hacking at the gold sheets that the Inca had somehow wedged tightly into the gaps between the stones.

Dropping his hatchet, he pulled at the leather fastenings that held his front and back armour plates together and threw them down to the ground next to his metal helm, gauntlets and sword.

He glanced around and saw that most of the others had done the same, some earlier than he, by the number of gold sheets they had hacked off.

By the saints, he thought.
Why didn't I think of doing this before?

Then with renewed vigour, he raised his hatchet to strike the wall as an arrow pierced his side and then heart. He never knew what had hit him as he tumbled to the ground, dead.

Gonzales sort of sensed that something had happened and turned towards Pedro as his comrade collapsed.

Before he could call out a warning, he himself was hit in the thigh by an arrow and fell with a scream, clutching his leg.

As he lay squirming with pain, he saw a group of black figures, armed with spears and swords, running towards the temple.

The only sound that Gonzales heard was a muted cry of Int, Inti, before a spear was rammed down his throat.

The rest of the troopers were overwhelmed before

they knew they were being attacked.

Having removed their front and back armour plates, with no helmet and swords on the ground, their only defensive weapons were hatchets.

The Inca wooden swords, edged with obsidian shards, proved lethal to the near defenceless troopers.

They were hacked or stabbed to death, several with missing limbs before they were put out of their agony.

Blood tarnished sheets of gold lay strewn about unnoticed by the victors, who gazed about indifferently at the bodies in mute silence as though they had suddenly appeared out of nowhere.

Atiq clapped his hands and the group of blackened warriors turned towards him, blank faced, eyes dulled.

'You have done well and the Great Inti is pleased. You have not yet finished. There are more Devil Riders. You are to follow me. Strike when I tell you.'

There was no response, just a deadened acceptance as they formed into a line ready to enter the Temple.

68

Serpienté cursed as he entered the Temple and casually walked through to the far end. He had decided that helping the devil riders to get rid of the Inca from his homeland was not as easy as he had expected.

The magic weapons and the metal body shells they wore were so superior but he was treated like a dog. He had reached the stage of thinking maybe the Inca weren't as bad as his people thought. From what he had seen so far, these devil riders only thought of themselves. He was being used and he didn't like that and he now wanted out.

Pushing the reed door open, he stopped and he gave a gasp of horror. Devil rider bodies, mostly mutilated, lay sprawled amid piles of sheets of gold that had been ripped off the Temple walls.

Quickly retreating back inside, Serpienté hoped that the group of strange looking Inca warriors listening to their leader, hadn't seen him.

As fast as he could, he rushed through the Temple and ran out into the small mesa.

'Master! Master!' he called out urgently. He now knew that his own life was in danger. He was in deep trouble. The Inca would not spare him, a Cañari.

Mendoza spilt some chicha down his chin as he lowered the gourd.

'What now runt?'

He had been admiring some of the gold objects that had been brought to him from more of the niches in the temple. Animals, fruit, even replica food items, all laid out on the sacrificial table.

He was drunk. On his third gourd of chicha, he looked blearily at Serpienté.

What was all the fuss about, he thought. *The Inca must have run away. Apart from the High Priest and that one shot, there's none about now.*

'Where the hell is De Orlando, go and tell himmm... or Gonzales. Yes, that's it, go and tell Gonzales.'

'Gonzales, he dead.'

'What are you talking about? Runt,'

Serpienté lost his head and flew into a rage. Master or not, the constant ridicule, name-calling and being treated worse than a dog had finally got to him.

Ignoring the group of troopers who were more concerned with the chicha they were drinking to notice what he was doing, Serpienté reached into his loincloth and pulled out a small bamboo tube that had been hidden there.

With all the pent up loathing that had been eating into his brain for so long, he rushed up to Mendoza, who had divested himself of his body armour and helmet and blew down his tiny blowpipe.

The dart, tipped with ourare pierced Mendoza in the neck.

Dropping the gourd, Mendoza jumped up and shouted, 'Why you...' then he just slumped to the ground, unmoving not speaking.

'Hey.'

One of the troopers shouted out.

Serpienté had already started to run towards the small gate that led to the sacred pool, though he was not to know that. It seemed the best way to escape.

He had just passed through the gate and had run

onto a small platform, a dead end. There was only a big pool far below. He paused.

A long arrow hit him in the back with such force that it knocked him off the platform and he fell screaming into the pool. The fear of water was more terrifying than being hit by the arrow.

When the all the waves and ripples caused by the falling Cañari had subsided, the surface of the pool returned to its previous tranquility.

No body broke the surface to disturb it again.

Atiq came through the double doors of the Temple carrying his bow, arrow notched ready to fire again.

The five troopers were trying desperately to rouse their Capitán and had no idea that a group of Inca warriors were about to attack them.

Luis saw them first. 'Inca,' he cried. It was the last words he uttered as an arrow pierced his throat and he fell, fatally wounded.

The other troopers tried to draw their swords but too much chicha had slowed their reactions and the warriors with the determination of mindless zealots, unaware of any injury to themselves, clubbed, slashed and speared until all the troopers were slain.

'Spare the leader,' Atiq shouted as the robotic warriors turned towards Mendoza, still slumped on the ground.

'Lay down your weapons and go and stand by the Temple doors.'

As the warriors meekly obeyed and lined up next to the temple, Atiq called out, 'Remaq and Taqui you two wait here. Then pick up this man and put him on the sacrificial table.

Mendoza was helpless and terrified. He could hardly

move a muscle or speak and only see through his half closed eyes, what was in front on him. His breathing was becoming ragged and the fear of what they were going to do to him was intense.

69

Mama Quylur Chaski looked at them and said, 'It is time. We need to go to the sacred sacrificial table.'

Makhassé got to his feet and looked at them.

'I guess that this is going to be very difficult for you. I have the spirit gods to give me strength. I hope you have something similar to draw on.'

'Hey steady on, Makhassé, you sound as though we are going to our doom,' said Chuck uneasily.

'What,' exclaimed Chaz.

'Have I missed something while I was out for the count?'

'I think that what Makhassé means is that things are going to get a bit hairy.'

'I don't understand that word Esha but I get your meaning. Yes it's more than possible that it might get dangerous for us,' said Makhassé.

'Well in that case, what have we to lose but our...... You can put you own ending,' Chaz said with more than a bit of bravo.

Mama Quylur Chaski hurried to the door and went outside followed by Maichu and Esha who suddenly screamed, 'Oh my God, there's bodies everywhere.'

Chuck came out next and nearly retched. He could see the body of the Trooper he'd shot with the flare pistol. He looked again and his breakfast shot out and covered his boots with a stinking mess.

He held his hands o his face and cried out. 'I didn't mean to kill him, no siree and he sank to his knees, shoulders shaking. 'I didn't mean to....'

Makhassé came out and bent down and taking Chuck by the arms lifted him up and hugged him.

'Chuck. Chuck. You saved our lives. Without your action all of us and I mean all of us would be dead. I know that doesn't help you now but it will, over time.'

Chuck took a deep breath and said, 'Okay, I know you are right but……. err, just let me clean my boots man.'

Esha came over and patted his arm and went to Chaz who was looking ghastly. Too many horrendous things had happened in such short time and he was beginning to wilt under the pressure.

'Let's walk on a bit and let Chuck follow when he's ready, okay.'

Chaz nodded and they tried to catch up with the others.

Mama Quylur Chaski led them through a small door that let them into the small circular arena not far from the big Temple doors.

They saw Atiq standing next to the High Priest who looked forlorn and uncomfortable on his knees, clad in a simple cotton tunic, hands still bound.

The warriors Remaq and Taqui were in attendance, glassy-eyed and each holding a Devil Riders sword. The rest were lined up by the sacrificial table on which lay Mendoza, stripped naked but otherwise unharmed and still totally immobile.

'Just lookee at that,' Chuck said. He had followed them in and was as shocked as Esha and Chaz at what they saw.

Mama Quylur Chaski wasted no time. Pointing to the High Priest, she said to Atiq, 'Bring him to the sacred table.'

Atiq smiled to himself and quickly obeyed.

Standing awkwardly, with muscle cramps in his legs from kneeling so long, the High Priest looked at Mama Quylur Chaski and knew that he was dealing with a Shaman and he felt a stab of anxiety.

'The Princess, why did you send her as a sacrifice to the Great Inti?'

The High Priest suddenly knew how he could shift the blame. 'Your most Honoured One, it was not me that brought the Princess for sacrifice, it is he,' and lifting his bound hands pointed to Atiq who suddenly began to shiver with fear

A young voice shouted out. It was Maichu. 'Yes it was him – Atiq.'

Mama Quylur Chaski's face became a mask of hate.

She pointed at Remaq and Taqui and said, 'Seize Atiq.'

Atiq looked at her in horror, all his conniving and planning undone by the devious, crafty High Priest. He looked at his bow, propped up against the Temple wall.

Too late, Remaq had stepped forward, his new deadly metal sword aimed at his throat.

'Kneel Atiq,' commanded Mama Quylur Chaska. She had seen his glance at the bow.

Having no choice, Atiq knelt.

'Now on your face, arms out-stretched.'

Atiq complied.

'Taqui, stand on Atiq's arm.'

'Remaq,' Mama Quylur Chaski's voice was barely audible. 'Cut that hand off,' pointing down.

'Nooo, Aghhhhhhhhh.' Atiq screamed as the sword severed his hand from his arm.

Mama Quylur Chaski nodded, 'Now throw this

'..........,' she rubbed her eyes as tears began to flow. 'Into the sacred pool.'

Through the excruciating pain of his wound, Atiq grasped what had been said.

'No, no, please Mama ......' Atiq begged.

'Take him,' she ordered.

The screams faded as Atiq was dragged away, then silence.

Chaz and the others were in shock at what they had just witnessed. They were speechless.

Then as Remaq and Taqui returned, Mama Quylur Chaski spoke to the High priest.

'Atiq did wrong but it was you who sent the Princess to the Great Inti. Now you shall go the Great Inti before your time too.'

She wiped her eyes again, her face fixed with hatred, as she pointed to the High Priest.

'Bring him,' she ordered Remaq and Taqui. 'We go to the sacred pool.'

'No. No. By the Great Inti.....'

Remaq using the hilt of his sword hit the High priest's head to silence him.

Esha grasped hold of Chaz and Chuck as they silently watched Mama Quylur Chaski followed by Maichu, lead the High Priest onto the platform overlooking the sacred pool and saw Taqui rip off the High Priest's tunic, leaving him naked, hands still bound.

Still dazed by the knock on his head, the High Priest watched as Mama Quylur Chaski pulled out an obsidian knife and began to make small cuts on his arms and chest. He hardly felt the warm trickle of blood run down his body.

She then passed the knife to Maichu who with the determination of the righteous, made several cuts himself before returning the knife.

The High Priest suddenly realized what they were doing.

'No, no you can't,' he pleaded desperately.

He, more than anyone, knew what lay in depths of the pool below. After all, had he not had sent many sacrificial victims down there to meet the Great Inti before now.

'He is ready,' Mama Quylur Chaski said, as she casually wiped her knife clean on the hem of her shawl.

Remaq with no apparent awareness of what he was doing, pushed the High Priest in the back, who loosing his balance, tumbled over the edge of the platform and fell down into the sacred pool with a great splash.

As the waters settled and the High priest reappeared, his bound arms flailing about, a sudden flurry of foam erupted around him. Scores of piranha fish thrashed about his body.

He screamed for help as the pool turned red. Then the screams became a gurgle and the waters still.

70

Chuck pulled at Makhassé's arm. They could hear the screams and he whispered, 'This is going too far. It's murder. Murder, no matter where you look.'

Makhassé paused before speaking. It was difficult, he knew, to explain that they were not in the twenty first century when only a few days ago they were. The paradox had to be faced. They were not only in a different time but in a place where the norms they were used to didn't apply. Mama Quylur Chaski's magical skills were a case in point.

'Chuck, what we have just seen is more than difficult for you to cope with. Actually it is the same for all of us. I just happen to have an affinity with the people of this time. After all they are my ancestors and I can relate to their beliefs such as spirits that live all around us. What you call murder is this culture's way of rectifying wrongs. We can't interfere. Do you see, at least not deliberately.'

Shaking his head, Chuck gave a big sigh. 'Well, I suppose when you put it like that it sort of makes sense.'

Chaz, who like Esha had been listening said, 'I guess that we have to somehow get back to our time but how the hell are we going to do that?'

'Hang on Chaz,' Esha interrupted, 'Mama Quylur Chaski's back.'

In fact, Mama Quylur Chaski with a somewhat subdued Maichu, Remaq and Taqui, walked straight to the sacred sacrificial table and stopped by the group of warriors who had been told to wait there.

She spoke to two of them who put down their weapons and came over to the Temple doors and with that strange, stiff posture of the possessed, went inside.

'What's going on,' whispered Chaz.

Makhassé was himself bemused by what was happening and he shook his head.

Not long after, the two warriors returned, each staggering under the weight of several panels of beaten gold that the troopers had taken off the Temple walls.

'Well lookee at that,' said Chuck with a low whistle.

'What on earth do they need those for?' Esha asked to no one in particular.

With evident relief, the two warriors dropped the gold panels with a loud clatter.

Mama Quylur Chaski called the warriors together and spoke to them for some time. Then they split up.

Two came back to the Temple and disappeared inside.

Several went to the sacred sacrificial table and lifted up Mendoza, still naked, off the table and placed him on his feet.

He was still paralyzed and so with arms rigid by his sides, mouth closed, he looked like a statue. A warrior stood on each side to make sure he didn't fall.

Anyone able to observe Mendoza's face would have seen that his half open eyes were flicking to and fro in frantic, desperate efforts to communicate with someone.

The two warriors returned from the Temple carrying coils of vine ropes.

At once the warriors began to place the gold panels around Mendoza. They were thin and flexible and so were quickly molded to his figure. Then they were made secure with the vine rope.

When Mendoza was completely encased with the gold panels. Mama Quylur Chaski pulled a tiny gold disc with the image of the Great Inti embossed on it.

With great reverence, she prised open Mendoza's mouth and slid the gold disc in, then pushed the jaw shut.

Backing away from the gold clad figure, Mama Quylur Chaski give the signal for four warriors to pick up and carry, the now very heavy Mendoza, to the sacred pool platform.

It was an effort, a big effort but they managed to reach the platform with no mishap.

By now Mendoza was more or less hysterical, totally unable for the first time to order and get an instant response, unable to speak or breathe properly.

His eyes flashed impotently, he was totally helpless and he knew it. For the first time he really felt afraid. He tried for the umpteenth time to flex his muscles, nothing happened.

'Now,' Mama Quylur Chaski commanded.

Maichu, with a little help from Remaq, pushed hard and Mendoza, now the man of gold, fell. As he twisted and tumbled down to the pool, just for an instant the sun blinded him - The Great Inti.

With hardly a splash, the gold clad figure sank to the bottom of the sacred pool where it was so dark even untarnished gold did not shine.

71

A crowd of priests and attendants followed by a group of hesitant priestesses assembled in front of the huts, carefully avoiding the dead troopers.

They were strangely silent. None wanted to enter the Temple of the Great Inti. They stood and stared, wondering what would happen next.

In the circular arena Mama Quylur Chaski had come back from the sacred pool with Maichu and the two warriors.

After telling Maichu to wait by the sacrificial table and ordering the warriors to go inside the Temple until she said otherwise, she approached Makhassé and the others.

'The spirits are getting restless,' Mama Quylur Chaski said, looking at them with sad eyes.

'I have lost my Princess and the Temple of the Great Inti is in disarray. A new High Priest must be appointed before sunset but the spirits say that until the cosmic disharmony is repaired it cannot be done.'

Makhassé got to his feet. They had been sitting against the Temple wall after he and Chuck had moved the bodies of the five troopers to a space behind some bushes along the mesa wall.

'Mama Quylur Chaski.'

He held his hands together as a mark of respect.

'Am I right in thinking that we have caused the cosmic disharmony?'

She nodded her head.

Makhassé paused for a moment and looked at her

hoping for some sort of inspiration.

'In that case how can we help to balance the cosmic harmony?'

'The only way is for you to move to your own Kaypacha and you must do it today.'

Makhassé looked at the others and said, 'We know that we are here by accident but how can we go back to our Kaypacha?'

'I can help but we must do it now.'

Chuck leaned over to Chaz and whispered, 'That's the best thing I've heard in days.'

Mama Quylur Chaski gave Chuck a look that made him blush, something he hadn't done in years. Then went on to call Maichu.

He waved and started to walk over to them as Makhassé sat down again.

'You must wait here while I prepare and do not interfere no matter what you see or hear. Most importantly, when I say go, you must go down to the sacred pool immediately or you will be doomed to wander the cosmic Kaypacha forever. I can only help you so far and you must not eat anything from now on.'

Chaz immediately thought of the MacD's in La Paz. *Now that's the place to be.*

Mama Quylur Chaski was looking at Chaz, a sort of reticent but at the same time respectful look.

'Come when I signal I need your help, Special One.'

Chaz felt his stomach turn.

Jeez. She's at it now, he thought. I'm going to get my bloody hair dyed black if we get back.

Mama Quylur Chaski wasn't finished. 'Maichu, get me some firewood.'

Then as he started to go, she beckoned him and whispered something to him. He looked startled but nodded. Then she added. 'You will need this,' and handed him her obsidian knife.

As Mama Quylur Chaski walked slowly to the sacrificial table, Maichu scurried off to some bushes to find some wood.

There was enough dry wood around and he hurried to the sacred table and left it near one of the stone pedestals before rushing to the Temple and disappearing inside.

Esha nudged Chaz who, still perplexed about being required for some sort of ceremony, jumped.

'Sorry, what did you say?'

'I said,' she whispered, 'Why has Maichu gone into the Temple?'

'How the hell.... sorry Esha, I've got something on my mind,' apologized Chaz. 'I haven't the foggiest idea.'

A plume of smoke suddenly began to rise from the side of the sacrificial table and Mama Quylur Chaski left the small fire burning steadily and arranged an assortment of items taken from her khapchos bag on the sacred table.

Satisfied that she had everything she wanted, Mama Quylur Chaski squatted in front of the fire, waiting for the return of Maichu.

The door of the Temple opened. Maichu had used his shoulder as both hands were cupped together. They were covered in blood, some still dripping between his fingers.

'What the....' Chuck was the first to notice him.

'Do you see what I'm seeing?'

'My God,' Esha gagged.

'It's some kind of animal and he must have skinned it to have bloody hands like that.'

Makhassé gave a groan. 'I don't believe it,' he whispered. 'Maichu has the heart of one of the troopers.'

'What!' cried Chaz.

'That kid has just cut open a dead body and taken the heart out. You're kidding me, aren't you?'

'Sorry Chaz but I'm not. The Inca's did make human sacrifices, though not many involved cutting out the heart. Usually the victim was a child and they were drugged and left to die high up a mountain.'

'You mean they were left to freeze to death,' Esha said incredulously.

'My God, what a system.'

'Hold on. Hold on.' Makhassé held up his hands. 'Remember what I said about the Inca culture of hundreds of years ago.'

'Yeah, but we're here now,' Chaz said.

Everyone suddenly turned and looked over at the fire and Mama Quylur Chaski.

She had stood up when Maichu came back and hurriedly went to the sacred table and picked up the top part of a jaguar's skull, the brain cavity.

'Put the heart in here,' she said, holding out the upside down skull.

Maichu was glad to oblige. This was something he had never done before and he didn't want to do it again any time soon.

As Mama Quylur Chaski put the skull onto the sacred table, Maichu bent down to wipe his bloody hands on a tuft of grass growing between two stone slabs. Then he returned the blood-stained knife.

'Go and wait with the others. You can tell the Special One he can come to me now.'

Maichu nodded and went back to give the message.

Chaz wasn't really surprised to get the message and with a shrug of resignation walked over to Mama Quylur Chaski. Wondering what the hell she wanted him for.

Mama Quylur Chaski had wiped her knife on the hem of her shawl and when Chaz came up, she solemnly grasped one of his hands.

'You are the Special One and I need some of your life's energy.' Mama Quylur Chaski pulled his arm and he naturally followed.

The jaguar skull containing the heart of Gonzales was on the edge of the sacred table and Mama Quylur Chaski held Chaz's hand over it. Before he realized what she was doing. The knife was jabbed into his thumb, and several drops of his blood fell onto the heart before he could react.

He snatched his hand away. 'What the hell are you doing?'

'Oh Special One. Thank you for the gift of your eternal energy. Now you may go back to your friends.'

Mama Quylur Chaski had already dismissed him and so he walked back sucking a stinging thumb.

The fire was now burning brightly so Mama Quylur Chaski went to the table and picked up her headband with the coloured bird feathers attached. Then she placed the chacapa nut bracelets on each wrist.

She opened a short bamboo stick containing the grey powder of the wachuma cactus and sprinkling some on the back of her hand, sniffed hard. Before the drug could take effect, Mama Quylur Chaski picked up a small gourd and pulling off the stopper, threw the contents of powdered a*yaska* onto the fire.

The flames flickered and then grew brighter and brighter until they were consumed in a billowing, swirling amber coloured smoke.

Mama Quylur Chaski placed the jaguar skull and heart in front of the fire and then started to dance around it, shaking her bracelets which began to rattle and tinkle before a series of yellow and red lights shone, ray-like around her body.

With a loud scream, Mama Quylur Chaski began to writhe and twist. Her face contorted as she began to chant the name Copacati, Copacati. Over and over.

Then, the glowing figure of yellow and red paused and picked up the jaguar skull and threw it and the heart into the flames, whilst shrieking, 'Copacati, you must kuti. Send Qualuoch to your everlasting servants.'

The smoke turned white and from it, a voice, the voice of a woman said, 'I, Copacati hear you Mama Quylur Chaski. Do not delay. Do not delayyyy.....'

Then the smoke disappeared.

Mama Quylur Chaski stumbled to the ground and then weakly gained her feet and called out, 'Makhassé, Makhassé go, go now. May the Great Inti protect you.'

They were her last words as she collapsed by the fire.

Maichu rushed over, frightened by her still, quiet form, shouting, 'Mama, Mama.'

Makhassé jumped up at Mama Quylur Chaski's words. 'We have to and go quickly,' he said anxiously, 'We haven't a moment to lose.'

'Hang on .....' Chaz tried to speak.

'For God's sake get on your feet and MOVE.' Makhassé actually screamed the word, and his urgency got through.

Esha, white-faced stood and looked wildly around.

'Where do we go?' she stuttered.

'The damned sacred pool,' Makhassé shouted again. 'Move, Chuck. Move.'

Chaz grabbed Chuck and said, 'It looks as though the shits hit the fan Yank. Lets get the frigging hell out of here. I'm off even if you're not.'

'Hey, wait for me you lot of bastards,' Chuck yelled after them as they rushed through the gate that led to the sacred pool.

'Yes sirree, they sure are a lot of selfish bas...'

He slowed, breathing hard, then he got his second wind and caught up with them as they reached the steep steps leading down to the pool.

The ground levelled off at the bottom and everyone paused to get their breath back and at the same time have a good look at it.

A sheer rock face rose up to the platform that jutted out slightly over it. The rough track they were standing on went round one side of it before dropping out of sight.

Chuck was leaning forward, hands on his knees and with his heart rate nearly back to normal, stood upright and asked the question that Chaz and Esha had also been thinking about on the way down to the pool.

'Well Makhassé, what was that all about? You know, up there.'

Makhassé sat on one of the steps and then gave a grim smile.

'Mama Quylur Chaski was in a bit of a quandary. She

wanted to help the priests of the Temple but realized that we were the problem why she couldn't.'

He went on.

'You all know how we got here, through some kind of time-shift. It would appear that our presence in this period and place is distorting or will distort the energy flow of the different realities between them and of course the many unseen spiritual forces that reside here. We have just experienced one such force, the Copacati or Lake Goddess.'

Makhassé saw the puzzled looks on their faces, Chuck's in particular.

'Mama Quylur Chaski called upon the Lake Goddess to help us return to or own place – time.'

'Yeah, but how,' interrupted Chuck.

'You heard Mama Quylur Chaski ask the Lake Goddess to send Qualuoch, to kuti. That means roughly set or put right.'

'Okay, okay,' Chaz now interrupted. 'What or who is Qualuoch?'

'Now this comes to the hard part,' Makhassé said. 'This Qualuoch is a kind of ghost ship....'

'Say that again,' Esha was now getting more than a bit confused.

'A damn ghost ship?'

'Well,' Makhassé hesitated for a moment. 'When I say ship, I believe that many people think that it is actually sentient.'

'Oh my Gawd, come off it Makhassé,' Chuck groaned. 'You don't expect us to believe that do you?'

Makhassé looked over at the pool. He thought he had heard something. His eyes widened and he swallowed before he croaked out, 'Why not see for yourself Chuck?'

The others turned and looked at the pool and gasped in amazement.

'Well, just lookee at that, yes siree I take my hat off to you Makhassé. How the hell did you darn well time that?'

Coming out of the cave on the opposite side of the pool was the most unusual craft any of them had ever seen.

It was about seven or eight metres long, shaped like a reed boat but with a less distinct prow.

As it got nearer they couldn't make out what it was made of. Half natural materials and half what? It lay low in the water, the deck, or the upper part, was broken by a large bulge set before a stubby mast, which held a tiny triangular sail.

The boat silently approached the side of the pool and two transparent apertures or holes suddenly appeared. Just like a pair of giant eyes.

Then, as the boat stopped parallel to the side of the pool, the 'bulge' semi-retracted to reveal a lower-deck room or cabin.

Makhassé spoke, jerking everyone back to reality. 'I think we had better get on board as fast as we can. Remember what Mama Quylur Chaski said about not waiting.'

Chaz need no urging. He was across the gap in no time, saying that the deck was not slippery but seemed to be a bit flexible but nothing to worry about.

The 'bulge' was indeed the entrance to a sort of cabin. A short ramp led to a neat room with benches on each wall but nothing else. It slid shut the moment they were inside.

'A bit spartan,' Esha said, sitting down on a bench, which seemed to soften as she did so. 'Wow it's really comfy. Try one.'

Chuck had just sat down when the boat began to move. The two eye-windows showed the cave entrance and without a sound it began to sink as it got closer in.

'Jeez, it's a sub as well,' exclaimed Chaz, as water began to rise over the eye-windows.

It got darker of course as the craft sank deeper and before long they couldn't see a thing.

'I hope it's got lights,' said Esha.

Then, 'That's better, I can see now.'

Through the eye–windows it was as bright as day.

The day though was in a different time.

'Hey, I think I recognize that beach.' Makhassé said with a great big grin.

'See that pointy top mountain. Well that overlooks the town of Copacabana and just behind us is the Isle of the Sun and I can see cars on the road above the beach.'

The boat nosed its way slowly through a crowd of pleasure craft, swimmers and jet skis to the beach without drawing much attention. It fitted in remarkably well, with its ultra 'mod' design.

They disembarked as fast as they could, which was just as well, because the boat backed away from the beach almost at once.

'Well lookee at that,' exclaimed Chuck, 'I could have sworn that the darn thing winked at me.'

'Maybe, maybe not,' Makhassé said quietly. 'At least we got back safely. Anyway I'm ready for something to eat.'

That galvanized Chaz, 'Jeez, it must be ages since we

last ate. Come on, I'm starving.'

'There must be a beach cafe or something,' Esha said, looking around.

The first cabin-kiosk was a newsstand.

Chaz was just about to walk by it when he read the billboard poster and stopped in amazement.

Another Ice Maiden discovered on Mount Apuchujo. Experts think the mummified remains are of a princess, because a yellow-feathered fan-cap and a gold headband with a huge green emerald were found with the body.

'I don't believe it. Just look at that headline. It's got to be Princess Inkasisa.'

*

Footnote:

Exclusive- LPN-MEDIA

The authorities have dismissed claims that a skeleton was found encased in sheets of gold, in a pool on the Isle of the Sun in Lake Titicaca, as a hoax.

They have also dismissed the claim that the Isle of the Sun is the site of the fabled El Dorado gold hoard.

***

The Author

Watercolour painting by
Rita Clements Lee

http://ritaclementslee-artist.co.uk/

The Author

Watercolour painting

Rita Clements Lee

ritaclementslee-artist.co.uk